DAYBREAK

Also by Viktor Arnar Ingolfsson
The Flatey Enigma
House of Evidence

DAYBREAK

VIKTOR ARNAR INGOLFSSON

Translated by Björg Árnadóttir and Andrew Cauthery

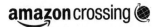
amazon crossing

Daybreak was first published in 2005 by Forlagid as *Afturelding*. Translated from Icelandic by Björg Árnadóttir and Andrew Cauthery. Published in English by AmazonCrossing in 2013.

Published by AmazonCrossing
PO Box 400818
Las Vegas, NV 89140

ISBN-13: 9781611091014
ISBN-10: 1611091012
Library of Congress Control Number: 2012922276

My father, Ingólfur Viktorsson, radio operator from Flatey in Breidafjord, died during the creation of this story. This book is dedicated to his memory.

DAYBREAK

Only one who has woken in the early hours of an autumn morning, risen from his bed, dressed, ventured out into the darkness, and experienced dawn in the cold, clear sky can truly comprehend the sublime glory of returning day; only one who has, all alone, sensed the night slowly surrender to the first pallor in the east and felt the pleasure of the rising sun bringing the promise of warmth upon his shoulders. These are the sensations owned by the goose hunter as he sits motionless, waiting for his prey, listening to the deep silence as a new day breaks.

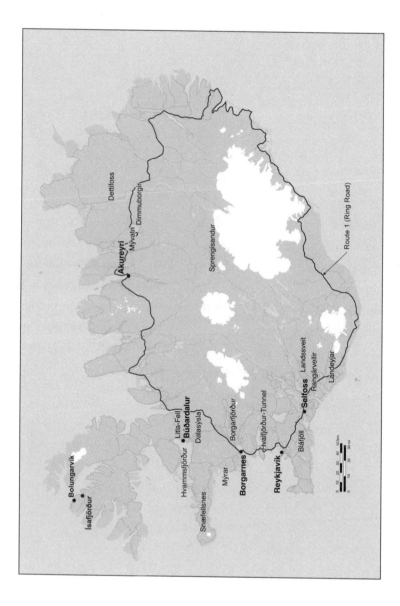

CHAPTER 1

06:10

In a remote spot in the western district of Dalasýsla sat a lone hunter. Sheltering behind a tumbledown stone wall—remnant of a long since ruined hut—he gazed across the waters of Hvammsfjördur toward Fellsströnd, where the first rays of the sun, breaking through clouds in the east, lit the very tips of the mountains. The slopes below, the lowlands, and the fjord still lay in deep shadow.

The man was in his forties—in good shape with sharp features. He wore high-quality camouflage gear and a thick cap, and the exposed parts of his face were painted in the same mottled earth colors as his clothing. On his comfortable camping stool, he could wait here in shelter and shade unnoticed. Leaning against the wall in front of him was his shotgun in its green-and-brown shoulder bag.

A black dog lay in the grass next to the man, its head on its paws, eyes closed—perfectly still but for the occasional flick of its ears and twitch of its snout. Now and again the man leaned toward the dog and stroked its back gently. They were waiting for the morning flight of the greylag geese.

Below the ruin was a small cultivated hayfield with a fenced-in potato patch beside it where fourteen geese could be seen among the plants, eight of them grazing, four resting, and two on guard, their long necks erect. In the dim light, only an experienced eye would spot that these were artificial birds, decoys. The man had arranged them in a tight group so there was plenty of space for another gaggle to settle on the patch in the face of the wind. The range was just right—about thirty meters.

There was a faint rustle as two field mice scurried along the wall, and across the hunter's arm resting on it, before disappearing into their hole. Silence returned. The man inhaled the earthy scent of vegetation half decayed by the onset of fall. Here, against this wall, sheep had sought shelter during summer, when the midday sun's heat was too much for man or beast. Now, however, it was near freezing, and the man felt chilly despite his warm clothes. He crossed his arms and waited for the new day as he looked out over the fjord, its waters still cloaked in semidarkness.

The dog opened its eyes and sniffed at the air a second before the man detected the first sounds of the geese beginning their morning flight. It was a while longer still before he sighted them in the west. Flocks winged their way across the fells without moving in his direction, but he was not worried; his geese would show up this morning as they had always done before. Fall after fall the same families of geese returned to this patch to feed and gather strength before the migration south over the Atlantic Ocean. This was reliable stock that had not suffered from overhunting, and the force of habit was strong. He shot a few geese each week, and still the flock returned to the potato patch again and again.

The dog pricked up its ears and lifted its snout, every muscle tense and yet completely motionless. The man took his shotgun carefully out of its bag and loaded it. A newish, five-shot, pump-action 12 gauge, with magnum cartridges. A sturdy and easy-to-handle weapon.

Another flock of geese now appeared, heading closer than the earlier ones. The man counted nine birds. If they came within range, he would be able to bag his prey with the three shells loaded in the gun. That would be enough, and he could head back to the car for his morning coffee and a much-needed cigarette.

The geese circled wide over the potato beds, seeming to assess the situation. The decoys told them this was safe ground, and, circling more closely, they warily approached.

The man stopped thinking about coffee and took careful aim. The geese descended farther and made for the patch, flying into the wind. Suddenly, with about a hundred meters to go, they took fright and, with much honking, gained height again; before long the whole flock had disappeared north.

The hunter cautiously stuck his head out from his hiding place and tried to determine what might have caused this disturbance. He could see no movement anywhere. The dog also got to its feet, raised its snout into the air, sniffed, and softly growled.

"Good boy, Kolur," the man said, as he continued to scan the surroundings. About thirty meters from the ruin, just by the edge of the hayfield, was a shallow ditch overgrown with tall, yellowed grass. On the hillside just above, over to one side, were some large boulders that had been carried there by a landslide long ago. The lowland was still in the shadow of the mountains, so visibility was poor.

Suddenly, there was a loud bang as a shot hit one of the decoys in the potato patch, knocking it over.

"Hello, who's there?" the man called out. He paused for an answer and then shouted louder, "Who's there? This is private property."

Hearing no reply, he shouted again, "Trespassers are banned from hunting here."

There was utter silence, apart from the dog's quiet growling.

"Kolur!" the man snapped at the dog, silencing it.

"Hello?" the man called again, but still there was no answer.

He peered out from his sheltered spot, seeing no sign of the other gunman. Then another shot rang out, throwing up a mass of grass and earth as it hit the ground a few meters in front of him. Swiftly ducking down, he considered the situation in disbelief. Somebody was firing heavy bird shot at him. Who the hell was playing a game like that?

"Hello," he yelled at the top of his voice. "Stop shooting!"

He tore off his cap and hung it over the muzzle of his gun. Hesitantly, he lifted the gun above the wall and waved. There was another shot, and some pellets hit the cap and the barrel of the gun. By now the dog had had enough and launched forward, barking and running toward the gunman.

"Kolur!" the man cried, but a shot rang out and the dog yelped once and fell silent.

"Kolur!" the man yelled, peering over the wall. The dog lay in a pool of blood, halfway between the ruin and the edge of the ditch. The man knelt down again. He was petrified and took shelter by curling up below the wall. What the hell was going on? The dog had been his best friend for seven years, but uppermost in his mind now was fear for his own life. He was caught in something that was way beyond his control. There was someone out there in the dawning light who meant to do him harm.

He thought of phoning for help but realized he had left his cell phone in the car. Anyway, there was no reception here. Then he remembered that he always carried three emergency flares in his ammunition belt; they were very old, but they might still work.

He unloaded his gun, replaced the shells with the flares, and fired once, straight into the air. The flare exploded high above his head and shone brightly for a few moments, though the lightening sky reduced its impact. He quickly fired twice more—three shots in sequence being a recognized distress signal. Then he reloaded with magnum shells, first removing the pin that normally limited the capacity of the magazine so that he could get two extra shells in; now he had five shells loaded—one in the chamber and four in the magazine. Normal hunting laws did not apply here; he might have to defend his life.

Another shot rang out, this time from an altogether different direction—behind and to one side of him—and he felt the pellets hail down on his back. Instinctively he jumped over the wall to find cover again. The range was long enough that the shot did not penetrate his parka, but it hit him with uncomfortable force nonetheless; it was as if someone had thrashed his back violently with a cat-o'-nine-tails.

He knew he had to do something to escape this ambush. Frantically, he reviewed his options. He could try to get away by running across the potato patch and down the hay field, but that left him without cover. Perhaps it would be better to shoot back and see how the other guy reacted. He steadied his gun on the wall and fired blind toward his invisible assailant, who immediately responded with two more shots. The man couldn't tell where these landed. Again he poked his gun over the wall and fired. Stillness followed.

In silence he waited. Then he heard a shot ring out from one side and felt the pellets clattering against his parka again, and something hit his cheek. He threw himself facedown and lay still. The pain in his cheek was sharp, but it quickly subsided. He wiped his cheek with his gloved hand and saw that the wound seemed to be bleeding quite a lot. It stung somewhat, but it wasn't too bad. Besides, he had other things on his mind. Two more shots rang out, hitting the ground in front of him. Either there were two gunmen, or one who moved position very quickly.

He discharged his remaining three shells in the direction from which he thought the last shots had come and then tried to hide behind the ruined wall while he reloaded. Three shots rang out, the pellets lashing his parka like hailstones in a wild storm, but the range was still far enough for his clothing to protect him.

Adrenaline was pumping through his body now, and he wasn't really scared anymore. He was angry, determined not to let his adversary control this game to its finish.

Three more shots were fired, and the sharp impact where the pellets hit his less-well-protected calves was painful. The gunman must be moving closer, and that would mean a swift end to things if he didn't act.

Suddenly he had an idea. The shots had come in threes. His assailant likely had a gun that took only three shells at a time; each time he had to reload, it would take a few seconds. Maybe this was his chance. He fired two shots, reloaded immediately, and fired once more. Again three shots reverberated around him. The other guy must now be reloading. It was worth the risk; he jumped up and sprinted toward the ditch, firing off one shot as he made for the tuft of withered grass. He was only a few steps from his goal when he heard a loud bang and felt a blow to the front of his left thigh just above the knee. With his next stride he felt as if he were stepping into a deep hole. He landed flat on his front, dropping his gun. With difficulty he lifted his head and looked behind him. A ways off lay a solitary leg. He felt down his left thigh in disbelief, finding where it ended in an open wound, the artery pumping tepid blood into his hand. He became aware that someone was crouching down next to him, picking up the gun he had lost. He tried to look up. He was helpless.

"Who are you?" he asked. "Wh…wh…why?"

He heard no reply, nor did he hear the shot fired into his head.

You ask why. I don't know if it's possible to answer or explain it. This action is so completely beyond all understanding. To take a life, a human life. To feel the nearness of a person and engage with him to the death. Then he exists no more. All that is left is a pile of meat, bones, and blood. Memories, emotions, skill, and a lifetime's experience are gone. It is an overwhelming thought…

You ask why. What do you want to hear? A detailed analysis of the animalistic qualities still buried in man's DNA? The qualities that enabled him to survive an evolutionary period stretching over millions of years and become what he is, or thinks that he is…

You ask why. Will that change anything? It is done and cannot be undone. What is that urge that drives the hunter a far distance into the predawn cold to bag a few geese he will hardly bother to eat? Or the urge that prompts some people to go fishing and then release their catch in the hope that the fish will either live and breed or be caught again?

My nature is to kill. I hunt men and I never let go.

10:20

"I fell."

There were three of them in the reception area of the emergency room at the National University Hospital in Reykjavik—a petite young woman with red hair wearing the uniform of a student nurse; a detective; and a boy lying on a gurney, who answered all the questions being directed at him with two words: "I fell."

Livid swellings almost completely hid his eyes, both lips were split, and his bleeding gums were missing their upper front teeth. Two fingers on his left hand were obviously broken, and there were ugly burn marks on the back of his right hand.

"Who did this to you?" the detective asked for the tenth time, gazing out the window, his dark-brown almond eyes dulled with boredom.

"I fell."

Patrolmen had discovered the kid lying on a traffic island earlier that morning, summoned an ambulance for him, and called in the detective division.

"Do you owe anybody money?" the detective asked.

"I fell," the boy groaned.

The student nurse surreptitiously checked out the policeman. He was of Asian origin, short with jet-black hair. She put his age at just under forty. He looked fit—slim and muscular—but apart from that he seemed rather ordinary; he didn't look anything like the cops on TV.

"I'm in pain," the kid said to her. "Give me more morphine."

"I can't increase the dose without the doctor's permission," she said firmly, continuing to eye the policeman, who was busy adjusting a digital camera. His sleek hair was still damp after his morning shower, and she caught a masculine scent, maybe some kind of aftershave. He was wearing a well-pressed gray suit, a dark-blue shirt, and a neatly knotted black tie. He had evidently just started his morning shift.

Actually, not too bad-looking, she thought, although perhaps a bit old. The ID pinned to his jacket pocket read BIRKIR LI HINRIKSSON.

The patient seized her arm with his unbroken hand and said menacingly, "More morphine."

The policeman grabbed the hand and carefully loosened its grip. The girl rubbed her arm.

"I'm in pain," the boy said.

"I'm not surprised," Birkir said, "and they'll do this again if you don't tell us who these people are."

He aimed the camera and took some photos of the kid's injuries.

The nurse watched Birkir. "Where are you from?" she asked.

"Iceland," he replied.

"Yeah. But I mean, originally?"

He glanced at her testily and was about to give a sharp answer, but her innocent expression made him change his mind. "I'm sorry," he said. "My parents were from Vietnam."

The nurse smiled. "Have you been there?" she asked.

"I was born in Vietnam, but I haven't been there since I was very young."

"Do you want to go there?"

Birkir shook his head.

Another woman, considerably older, entered the room— a doctor, her ID indicated. After greeting them brusquely, she looked at the patient, who whispered, "Morphine."

"We'll see about that, but first we must deal with this mess," she said. She clipped an X-ray of his hand to the backlit glass on the wall and peered at the broken bones.

Birkir leaned over the kid. "They'll end up killing you," he said.

"Not on purpose, because then they'll have to write off the debt. By mistake. They'll hit you too hard in the wrong place. That's all it takes."

The boy thought about this for a bit and said, "I fell."

Another detective entered the room. He was tall—nearly six foot five—and fat, with a red face marked by a heavy double chin that almost hid his thick neck. He had large blue eyes and close-trimmed strawberry-blond hair around a shiny pink bald spot.

"Any news?" he asked, biting into a half-eaten sandwich.

Birkir looked at his colleague and shook his head.

"Can I please ask you to eat outside?" said the doctor.

The newcomer wrapped the food in a plastic bag and shoved it into his jacket pocket. The nurse watched with disapproval as he wiped his greasy hands on his pants. His ID read GUNNAR MARÍUSON.

"Did you manage to find a witness?" Birkir asked.

"No, but we stopped a car that was cruising the neighborhood. There were three guys, and one of them was wearing steel-capped shoes. Said they'd just left a party."

He licked a finger. "Sharp dressers when they go visiting, these kids. We took them in for questioning and sent their shoes to forensics. Looked like there might be blood on them. Maybe high command will feel generous enough to book a DNA test, and then we can compare it with this kid." Gunnar nodded toward the patient, who groaned quietly.

The nurse had wiped blood from the boy's face and thrown the tissues into a garbage can. Birkir bent down, fished one of them out, and slipped it into a plastic bag.

"That gives us something to compare with," he said.

A cell phone rang, and Gunnar dug his phone out of his pocket.

"Gunnar speaking," he said in a loud voice.

"Cell phones should be turned off in here," the doctor said irritably, but the detective seemed not to hear her. He just grinned broadly, revealing a prominent gap between his large front teeth.

"Yes, let's hear it," he said.

His smile quickly disappeared and he covered his free ear with his other hand to better hear the voice on the other end.

When the call ended, the nurse heard the large detective say quietly to his colleague, "We've got to put this on hold and drive up to the Dalasýsla district immediately. To Búdardalur. Someone's been killed with a shotgun."

12:40

"Left here," Gunnar said. He grabbed the handle above the door with his right hand to brace himself for the turn and pressed his cell phone to his ear with his left. They were about to reach the intersection at Dalsmynni in Borgarfjördur; the sign ahead indicated that a left turn would lead them to Route 60. Birkir was, as usual, driving—quickly but safely—while Gunnar alternated between talking on the phone and eating the dried fish he had bought at the gas station in Borgarnes, where they had stopped to fill up. In between activities, he felt obliged to give Birkir directions.

"I know," Birkir said, braking sharply before taking a tire-screeching left-hand turn. "And I know how to get to Búdardalur," he added, accelerating out of the turn and onto a straightaway. They raced up an ascent and then onward into the valley. Driving conditions were good; it was bright and dry, if somewhat chilly, and traffic was light. They were in an unmarked squad car, but they had stuck a blue priority light on the roof before leaving. Although Birkir was mostly thinking about the investigation that awaited them, he was enjoying the trip; he rarely got the chance to drive fast over such a distance.

Gunnar put his phone away and checked his safety belt for the fifth time. Then he divided the rest of the dried fish in two.

"Want some?" he asked.

"No, thanks," Birkir replied, and Gunnar stuffed both bits into his mouth at once. The two of them had very little in common, including their eating habits. Gunnar was continually hungry and always snacking, whereas Birkir ate three regular meals a day and nothing in between.

They drove over the Brattabrekka pass and on through the dales of Middalir. A succession of isolated small farms flashed by on the right; on the left, a rocky stream and the mountain above it flanked the road. Eventually the valley widened on both sides.

Gunnar's efforts to get information about the case as they drove had produced few results. They had the name and address of the victim—the sheriff of Búdardalur had provided that when he'd called in for assistance. Forensic specialists had already driven west ahead of them; no doubt they had arrived and were starting their work. Two teams back in Reykjavik, where the victim came from, were looking into his personal history, informing his relatives, and so on. The whole operation was under the command of Magnús Magnússon, the detective superintendent in charge of the Violent Crime Unit at Reykjavik's police headquarters. Birkir and Gunnar knew that everyone was waiting for them to arrive at the scene and begin their investigation.

It was almost two o'clock when they neared Búdardalur, and Gunnar called the sheriff's office for directions to the location, an area next to a remote farm named Litla-Fell. They soon found the turnoff and drove slowly a couple of kilometers along a bumpy dirt road.

As they rounded a sharp bluff, the farm buildings came into view, five hundred meters or so farther into the valley. The farmhouse itself stood on a beautiful ledge halfway up a hillside clad in low birch scrub that swept gently up to the foot of the mountain behind. At the bottom of the slope were the outbuildings—a jumble of shacks with corrugated iron roofs and turf-and-stone walls. A large pile of manure sprawled in front of one of the shacks, and outside another was a small, dilapidated corral made from rotten bits of wood. The three lambs inside it nuzzled at the enclosure.

The farmhouse was a steep-roofed, single-story building clad in corrugated iron, which at some point had been painted green and white. Next to the house was a tarred timber storehouse. In the farmyard stood two old tractors and some rusty hay-making machinery.

Birkir stopped the car and considered the farm. It was as if time had stopped here decades ago and failed to start again, he thought.

"Valley of time…house of silence," Birkir murmured, not caring whether Gunnar understood this observation. His partner was used to hearing him utter weird phrases and knew that a reply was not expected. Sometimes Birkir spouted bits of poetry; at other times it was just his own abstract thoughts that came and went. They were never written down.

"The field's a bit farther in, I think," Gunnar said, pointing to a rough track that led off the road. Birkir drove on. Four horses by the side of the track looked up and followed their progress for a moment, then resumed their leisurely grazing. They seemed to be used to people passing this way.

After a few hundred meters they came across an abandoned vehicle, a Nissan Patrol that had been parked next to the track, at the edge of the hay field. They stopped there for a minute to assess the situation.

Two more vehicles were parked about a kilometer west of the farm buildings, next to some neglected meadows—a police patrol car and an unmarked van they knew belonged to the detective division's forensic team. Tall grass growing between the wheel tracks brushed the underside of the car as they continued on toward the other vehicles.

As they arrived, two men got out of the patrol car and walked toward them. One was a uniformed officer with a beard; the other, striding ahead of him, was a slim man in his sixties wearing a gray suit.

"You do speak Icelandic, don't you?" he asked, scrutinizing Birkir.

"Yes, I speak Icelandic," Birkir replied wearily, adding, "Admittedly, I occasionally misuse the dative case in the second- and third-person plural, but apart from that my Icelandic is quite passable."

The man looked at Birkir suspiciously, seeming not to know what to make of this. Then, having studied the ID badges the pair wore, he introduced himself. "My name is Hákon Einarsson. I am the district sheriff."

The uniformed cop standing behind the sheriff gave a quick salute and said loudly, "Good afternoon."

"Thank you for coming," the sheriff said. "Your colleagues have started their investigation." He pointed toward two white-clad forensic officers crouching over a bump a hundred meters away.

"What happened?" Gunnar asked.

The sheriff replied, "It's a goose hunter. He's been shot; he must have died instantly."

"Accidental shooting?"

"No, definitely not. At least two shots fired at him. Maybe more."

"What was his name again?" Gunnar looked at his notebook.

The sheriff replied, "His name is Ólafur Jónsson. A lawyer from Reykjavik."

"Who found him?"

"Gudjón, who lives on the farm here at Litla-Fell, found him this morning."

"Do you have any more information?"

"More?" The sheriff thought about this and looked at his feet, uneasy. "Well, there is one thing I think…" He hesitated, unsure of himself. Finally he straightened up and said firmly, "I think you should know that the deceased was the legal owner of this land. He bought it at a court-ordered auction just over two years ago. There was a verbal agreement that the former owner might continue to live here on the farm. Ólafur rescinded that agreement this summer, but old Gudjón has utterly refused to leave the farm and is still residing here, along with his livestock."

The sheriff nodded in the direction of a few sheep lying in the field nearby, chewing their cud. "He's got nearly a hundred sheep," he added, scanning the valley as if he were counting. "Ólafur's legal representative has made a formal request to my office to evict Gudjón from the farm. That matter is being dealt with according to the appropriate procedures, but it was, as I say, indeed the former owner and current occupant of the farm who discovered the body this morning."

"So was there actual hostility between them?" Gunnar asked.

"Yes, well, I think you could say that they were not on the best of terms."

"So do you think Gudjón could have done this?"

The sheriff was flustered. "I hope not," he said, "but the old man is, apparently, extremely eccentric and hot tempered. I am told that when he was a young man he was known for getting into fights. I have been dreading having to deal with this cursed eviction all fall."

"You said that Ólafur had a legal representative acting on his behalf," said Birkir. "Why didn't he deal with this matter himself?"

The sheriff gave a slight shrug. "My understanding is that he was always busy with bigger cases. He had a lot of foreign dealings, apparently."

"Have you spoken to Gudjón today?" Gunnar asked.

"Not really," the sheriff said. "He called us this morning to report the incident and then met us here at the farm to show us the location. We decided not to pursue further questions since we knew you were on your way. We don't have much experience with cases like this in our district, as I'm sure you know."

Gunnar turned to Birkir. "Let's go take a look." He nodded toward the crime scene. "We can talk to Gudjón afterward."

They walked along the edge of a ditch toward where the forensic officers were working. They quickly spotted a dead dog, but did not make out the body of the lawyer until they were almost upon it—his camouflage gear blended in with the ground beneath his corpse.

Gunnar said, "Did you know that color-blind people can't see camouflage?"

"Oh, is that a fact?" Birkir replied.

"Yeah. Color-blind soldiers see their opponents just as plainly whether they're wearing camouflage or not. That's why they're often drafted to the front line."

"Do you think that the killer was color-blind, then?"

"No, not really," Gunnar answered. "It was just something that popped into my head."

"I see," said Birkir.

The blood that had collected into a big pool beneath the body was now dark brown and mixed with the earth. The body was missing its left leg, which lay close by. The head was in terrible condition, evidently shot at very close range. The scents of damp soil and blood lingered in the air.

The sight left Birkir mostly unmoved, which surprised him. Seeing a corpse in this condition was, after all, not an everyday experience for him. It was just that his connection to the dead man felt so impersonal. He knew, however, that this would change over the coming days as the team pieced together all they could find out about this man. Maybe that would lead them to his killer; maybe not.

They approached one of the two forensic officers, a short woman clad in white disposable coveralls with elastic cuffs, and wearing rubber gloves. They knew Anna Thórdardóttir. Though she was not yet fifty-five, she looked at least seventy, her thin, wrinkled face and tired, dark-ringed eyes bearing witness to forty years of heavy smoking. She was the most experienced member of the forensic team, and though some of her colleagues found her pigheaded, she was, in Birkir's opinion, the best. He was pleased to see her here. She didn't often venture far from her laboratory, never mind all the way out in the country.

She greeted them brusquely with her hoarse smoker's voice and lit a cigarette.

"What can you tell us?" Gunnar asked.

Anna took some deep drags before replying. "There were a number of shots fired here in a small area. Shotgun fire. Some of them hit this guy." She pointed to the body with her cigarette. "Some were from quite a long range, forty meters or more. The parka took most of those." She bent down and pointed to some small holes in the garment. "Then one close-range shot took his leg off, from between three and six meters away, I'd guess. We'll check that more thoroughly later. Finally, he was shot in the head from very close range, less than a meter." She flicked the ash off her cigarette into a small black plastic canister—the type used to store 35 mm film—which she held in her other hand.

"Coup de grâce," said Birkir.

"Coo de what?" Gunnar asked.

"Never mind," said Birkir. "It's French, I think."

"Then he took a souvenir," Anna said. "Or that's what it looks like."

"How so?" Gunnar asked.

Anna took a final drag from her cigarette and stubbed it out in the canister. She snapped on its lid and put it in her pocket.

"Look here," she said, leaning over the body. She pointed to an irregularly shaped hole in the parka, over the heart. The top layer was missing, exposing the white lining beneath. "The murderer must have cut out this piece from the fabric."

"What for?" Gunnar asked.

"I have no idea," Anna replied.

"The hole wasn't already there?" Birkir asked.

"No, the whole garment is covered in blood, but there's none on the lining," Anna said. "And it looks like a rather new parka; it hasn't been worn much."

Gunnar said, "Maybe he's taken this as a trophy, like when a hunter takes the tail of a mink that he's shot."

"Maybe," Anna answered.

Gunnar asked, "Can you picture the course of events?"

Anna pointed to the remnants of a ruined stone wall nearby. "That's where the hunter must have hidden while he waited for the geese. There's a camping stool there, and a shoulder bag for a shotgun. His decoys are still in the potato patch. It looks as if one of them was hit from long range. The person or persons then fired on the hunter from this ditch and also from the hillside up there." She pointed. "It was the shooting from the hillside that drove the man from his shelter. The shot that took his leg off must have come from the ditch, also the one that killed the dog. The attacker was either very quick on his feet or there were two of them."

"Do you know what kind of shot was used?"

"Yes, we found some spent shells both in the ditch and on the hill. They're all the same type: red Federal Premium 12 gauge. We should be able to work out if they all came from the same weapon. If we find a gun, we'll probably be able to determine whether it's the right one. The firing pin makes a mark on the primer when you fire. The mark is always the same and it's distinctive for each gun."

"What about the victim? Did he fire his gun?"

"Yes. There are a few empty shells around the ruin that probably came from him. They are the same type as the shells in his belt: green Remingtons. He also fired three emergency flares from there. Elías recognized their spent shells." Anna nodded toward her colleague kneeling by the ruin and added, "He says, actually, that nobody uses those flares anymore because they're bad for the gun barrels. The guy probably didn't care about that."

"Where's his gun?" Gunnar asked.

Anna shrugged. "It's vanished."

"What does that mean?"

"Someone needed a shotgun."

"Do you think that the killer took it?"

"Probably."

Gunnar looked into the ditch. "Any footprints?" he asked.

Anna lit another cigarette before answering. "There are no obvious prints, but the grass has been flattened both here in the ditch and behind the boulders where we found the shells. We have asked for a good tracker dog to be sent here. Maybe he can find some tracks leading from here."

"Anything else?"

Anna pointed the cigarette at her colleague, who was on his knees by the stone wall. "We're gathering up any loose shot to see if they can tell us more about the weapons. The size and composition of the pellets, for instance, could be significant. Maybe we can guess how many shots were fired."

There was a brief silence; all three seemed deep in their own thoughts. Finally Gunnar said, "It's an odd weapon to use for murder. It's not easy to kill a man with a shotgun, even with magnum shells. It's got to be short range. With a rifle you can easily kill from long range."

Birkir answered, "It probably shows it wasn't premeditated. Either that or the killer didn't have another weapon available."

"Then there's the leg," Gunnar continued. "You couldn't possibly inflict an injury like that with ordinary bird shot. And at close range, though the force is much greater, there's hardly any spread, so it would have just blown a hole through the thigh. The range has to be just right for the spread of pellets to act like the blade of a power saw."

"We might have to experiment with similar shot in order to determine the exact range," Anna said.

Gunnar looked around. "Whatever. This all demonstrates determined intention," he said. "We must find out if anyone apart from Gudjón had any grievance with the victim."

Anna added, "It looks as if the deceased returned fire without inflicting the slightest wound. There isn't a trace of the assailant's blood anywhere he's been. Of course, his clothing may have fresh pellet holes in it—if you ever find it."

She handed them a plastic bag containing a car key, a pocket-knife, and a goose whistle. "This is all we found in the guy's pockets," she said and returned to her task.

Birkir and Gunnar watched her for a while as she photographed the body from all angles, and then photographed the severed leg and the dog. They felt confident that she would not miss anything of significance in this place, but they also knew it might take a day or more to finely comb the whole area.

They turned and walked back to the cars. This far north the sun was already sinking, and there was a chill in the air. The sheriff and the local cop were waiting for them in the patrol car, and Birkir and Gunnar got into the backseat.

"Can you tell us any more about the deceased?" Gunnar asked.

"I understand that he was quite wealthy and enjoyed the outdoor life a lot," said the sheriff. "It seems he was planning to knock down the old farm buildings and build a summerhouse here."

The patrolman added, "I was told he was going to bring in a bucket loader to demolish these shacks as soon as he evicted the occupant. Can't see what the hurry was, just before winter."

"What can you tell us about this court-ordered auction of the land?" asked Gunnar.

The sheriff replied, "That in itself is a tragic story. Old Gudjón is a widower. He has one daughter, whose son lives here with his grandfather and goes to the local school. The daughter lives in Reykjavik. Her life's been a struggle. She married an American before she was twenty and had the boy with him. Apparently they lived in various places in the United States until they divorced and she moved back to Iceland. She then bought a small convenience store in Reykjavik with her new boyfriend, and I understand they did quite well when they started out. Old Gudjón helped them by underwriting some loans, which shouldn't have been a problem except that her boyfriend hit the bottle and cleared out, having by then squandered large sums that should have been used to pay loan installments, sales taxes, and so on. After this everything went downhill. The daughter couldn't pay her debts and the creditors were ruthless; she lost everything and the guarantees were called in. Old Gudjón had no money to pay the debts, and the banks issued a distraint warrant."

"Was there no room for negotiation about this?" Gunnar asked.

"A younger man would probably have found a way to finance a composition settlement, but Gudjón just ignored it. It was as if he thought the problem would just go away."

"Was nobody able to help him?"

"I tried everything in my power. I even got him a lawyer, but the old man wouldn't let him in the house."

"What happened then?"

"The court ordered a forced auction; I managed to postpone the execution a few times to give Gudjón a chance to put his affairs in order, but it made no difference, and in the end the auction took place. There were some unpaid mortgage debts, as is common among farmers, and those loan companies sent their lawyers to bid for the land against Ólafur, who represented the principal claimants; they were only interested in covering their own losses and were happy to sell the land to Ólafur at what was a very low price. There was nothing leftover for the old man."

"Were no local people interested in the property?"

It was the patrolman who replied. "No. This is not good farmland. The hay fields are small and impractical, difficult to work with machinery, and there's not much else you can do here. The buildings are falling apart, and it's remote. It's mainly of interest to hunting enthusiasts from the city, although it's so far away that not many would be interested."

"What will happen to the old man when he has to leave the farm?" Gunnar asked.

This time the sheriff replied. "The local authority is looking into that. He will probably get a place in a nursing home if he can be persuaded to accept it. But the boy is going to be a problem, as is the daughter; the farm is still her registered domicile, and I understand she has been living here from time to time. The community will probably have to find a solution to their problems, too."

15:00

The time had come to speak to the occupant of Litla-Fell, and Birkir and Gunnar decided to walk back to the farm so they could assess the surroundings as they went. They followed the track down to the dirt road, which had shallow ditches on both sides full of yellowing grass; beyond them were small, tussocky hay fields where a few sheep grazed.

They met a vehicle coming from the direction of the farm, an old Ford Econoline with big wheels, marked as a school bus. They stepped aside, and as it drove past, they caught sight of the driver's inquisitive gaze and the faces of the children pressed against the side windows.

They watched until it disappeared beyond the bluff.

"The grandson must be back from school, then," Gunnar said and walked on.

Birkir stopped and looked back toward the old bit of ruined wall.

"This is a very peculiar murder, it seems to me," he said.

Gunnar stopped, too, waiting for more to come. Birkir finally continued. "If you were planning to kill a man with a shotgun, how would you go about it?"

"As I said before, I wouldn't use a shotgun. I'd use a rifle."

"Why not a shotgun?"

"A shotgun is for killing small animals at short range. You use a rifle to kill people."

"Right. What if you only had a shotgun at hand?"

Gunnar thought for a moment. "A shotgun is a very powerful weapon at short range but it's useless at a long distance. If I were going to kill a man with a gun like that, I'd shoot him in the belly from the shortest possible distance. Then in the head."

"Why go for the stomach first?"

"That's the easiest place to hit him. And he wouldn't defend himself after that if he was also armed."

"I see. But what if he was alert and expecting danger?"

"Then I would sneak up to him as close as possible to reduce the range. And I'd use slugs rather than pellets, if I could."

"Slugs?" Birkir said. He had handled a shotgun and learned to load it and fire a few shots, but he wasn't particularly familiar with this kind of hunting gear.

"A slug is a shell with a single large bullet instead of many small pellets. You can kill a polar bear with it at long range."

"So that's a theory we must consider. The lawyer must have had reason to be wary of the attacker. That's why he tried to defend himself. They must have known each other."

"Why?"

"If a stranger approaches you as you're hunting geese out here in the sticks, your first thought isn't that he's here to shoot you, even if he's carrying a weapon. Not unless you're involved in something very shady, or you know that this particular person means to do you harm."

Gunnar shrugged. "Maybe this was someone who also wanted to shoot geese here without a license. Maybe the lawyer meant to just shoo the guy off his newly acquired land, and the confrontation ended up taking a nasty turn. It wouldn't be the first time that two guys have fought over good hunting grounds, although these things don't usually end in a bloody gunfight."

"That's also a valid theory. We'll see."

They were quiet as they walked the last length of the dirt road that led steeply up to Litla-Fell. A few minutes later they found themselves in the farmyard.

An old man stood by the wall of an outhouse, skinning the carcass of a fat lamb. He had tied its back legs to the lifting boom of an old tractor and hauled it up to a convenient height. The head of the animal lay on the ground, and blood dripped from the carcass's headless neck into an old steel bucket. To the side was a wooden tub containing the entrails. Several dogs had been shut out of the way in the outhouse, where they could be heard barking.

A young boy stood beside the tractor, watching Gunnar and Birkir approach; they stopped a suitable distance from the slaughter. They could smell entrails, blood, and raw meat. Not unlike the smell from the dead man, only considerably stronger.

The old man did not look up from his labors. Obviously tall and strong at some time in the past, he was now shrunken, with bent shoulders, a crooked back, and bowed legs. He wore rubber boots, brown wool pants, an old and worn traditional wool sweater, and a light-brown cap.

"Good afternoon," Birkir said.

The man squinted at them and then resumed his work.

"Are you a Greenlander?" he asked Birkir, who had now moved closer.

"I can be a Greenlander if necessary."

The old man looked at him suspiciously. "Greenlanders are good people," he said. "They understand life."

"Well," Birkir said. "Then I'm probably not a Greenlander."

"We're from the Reykjavik detective division," Gunnar said impatiently. "We need to ask you a few questions."

"Ask away, but make it quick. You can see I'm busy," the old man said. He dried the bloody knife on a leg of his pants and took a small whetstone from his pocket.

"You're the one who found the body, aren't you?"

The old man spat at the stone and began to rub the blade of the knife against it. "Yes."

"When did you find it?"

"This morning."

Gunnar and Birkir moved closer, and the old man looked up from his work. His face was peculiarly pale, he had a gray beard, and his red-rimmed eyes were bloodshot and rheumy; a trail of spittle, black from tobacco, dribbled from one corner of his mouth.

"What time was that?" Gunnar asked.

"Just after nine." The old man looked toward the sun. "It's after three now, isn't it?"

Gunnar looked at his watch. "Yes, fifteen minutes past."

"I don't wear a watch; I can't read it without my glasses. But I can see things in the distance fairly well," the old man said.

"How did you find the body?"

"What do you mean?"

"What were you doing out there?"

"Seeing if he was all right, of course."

"Were you beginning to wonder about that?"

"Yes."

"Why?"

"He'd been out there much longer than usual."

"How do you know that?"

"How do I know? Do you think I'm deaf? The damn shooting woke us up this morning, there's such an echo here against the fell. I assumed he'd found a lot of geese because there was such a racket. It went on a long time."

"When was this?"

"At dawn. But he just stayed out there."

"Was that unusual?"

"No, perhaps not. But there'd been more shots than usual. He doesn't usually hang around. He'll take three or four birds in the morning flight and then make himself scarce. He knows I don't like all this shooting because it frightens the animals."

"Does he look in here on the farm to ask for permission to shoot?"

"He doesn't need to, I guess."

"How did you know he hadn't left?"

"He leaves his car here, down below the road. I can see it's still there." He pointed to the Nissan. "The school bus arrived here at seven thirty as usual to pick up young Gutti, my grandson here. That was when I first saw the car. Then I was seeing to the sheep for about an hour and a half, but when I came out of the shed, I saw the car hadn't been moved."

"Was that when you went to look for the man?"

"Yes. None of my business, of course, but I did go out to look for him."

"Then what did you do?"

"Well, I saw what had happened and I came back to call the sheriff."

"Did you touch anything at the scene?"

"I only touched Ólafur and realized he was stone cold. So he had been dead some time. Half his head was blown off and the leg, too. I reported this to the sheriff."

"Did you see a gun?"

"No, there was no gun there."

Birkir now took over the questioning. "Were you aware of any traffic here this morning?"

"No."

"Did you hear Ólafur arrive?"

"No."

"When did you hear the shots?"

"I just told you. They woke me at dawn."

"At what time?"

"I didn't look at the clock. Perhaps it was getting on toward seven. I got up and made porridge for the kid. He had to go to school."

"How many shots were there?"

"I didn't count them."

"Would you say you heard more or fewer than five?"

"More."

"More or fewer than ten?"

"More."

"Twenty?"

"More."

"Thirty?"

"Maybe."

"Did you see any emergency flares?" Gunnar asked.

"Did I see what?"

"The deceased seems to have fired some emergency flares. They give off a bright red light."

"We didn't look outside during the shooting. I was still in bed."

"Have you got a gun yourself?"

"I suppose so."

"What sort of a gun?"

"I've got an old side-by-side. I use it on vermin."

"Have you ever shot geese?"

"Only when there was nothing else to eat. It's not proper food." The old man turned back to the carcass, wielding his knife.

"May we have a look at your gun?" Gunnar asked.

"No."

"Why not?"

"What right have you got to see it?"

"We can get a warrant."

"You'd better get one, then," the old man said. He turned and took two steps toward them, pointing his knife at Gunnar, and said, "I'll tell you this here and now, my friend: I will not let go of my gun, however much you try to get it. A man must have the means to kill himself." He lowered the knife and added, "In case they bring the bulldozers in and start to demolish all this."

15:40

Birkir unlocked the Nissan with the key fob and opened the front passenger door. The car seemed to have been cleaned recently, both inside and outside; it was spotless. On the backseat lay a full thermos of coffee and a wrapped sandwich. The glove compartment contained a cell phone; an opened cigarette pack; and a leather billfold containing a few bills, a number of credit cards, and a receipt from a self-service gas station.

"He filled the tank at Ártúnshöfdi a little before four this morning," Birkir said.

"He must have allowed two hours to get here, then," Gunnar said. "He would have wanted to arrive before six to be sure to catch all of the morning flight."

"But why did he leave the vehicle so far from where he planned to settle in?"

Gunnar was opening the tailgate. "He knew exactly what he was doing. Geese are so set in their ways, and the flocks that come here know the surroundings. A car in the wrong place can scare them away."

He scanned the vehicle's cargo area. Two large coolers occupied most of the space; they were empty and more or less clean, with some reddish-brown stains indicating they were containers for game. There was also a large kennel strapped to the floor; inside it was a bag of dog food and a bowl.

"It doesn't look like a felony murder," Birkir said. He took the cell phone out of the glove compartment and checked the recent calls log.

"The last call is to a foreign phone number," he said.

He wrote the numbers down in a notebook, put the phone into a bag, and labeled it with the case number.

Gunnar looked longingly at the sandwich on the backseat. "We should have brought provisions," he said.

Birkir looked up toward the highway. "The killer must have arrived by car and left it somewhere nearby. After the attack he would have returned to it on foot and then driven back up to the main road and turned one way or the other. Maybe someone will remember having seen him."

Gunnar shook his head. "We passed a few cars after we left Route 1 at Borgarfjördur, but I don't remember anything about them. Do you?"

"No," Birkir admitted. "All the same, we'll have to talk to all the people who live on farms nearby. They may have noticed something unusual."

Gunnar looked around. The nearest farms could be seen in the distance, too far off for him to detect the presence of cars or people. "The Búdardalur cop can do that. He knows the area. The local guys will have to put some work into this investigation."

"So, what's our next move?" Birkir asked.

"This vehicle needs to be transported back south. Arrangements are already in place to collect the body. We need to have a look at the old man's shotgun; we'll talk to the sheriff about that when we get a moment."

After some thought, Birkir asked, "What's our opinion of the old farmer?"

"He's got to be at the top of the list of suspects."

"Do you think he's strong enough to pull off a shooting like this one?"

"Maybe the old man could manage to shoot a few rounds, but I wouldn't put money on him having a lot of stamina. Perhaps there were two of them. Perhaps the boy helped him."

Birkir looked at Gunnar and shook his head.

Gunnar added, "I mean, before he went to school this morning."

"I don't think so," Birkir said.

Gunnar took out his cell phone and looked at the screen. "There's a signal here," he said and dialed.

While his partner talked on the phone, Birkir walked around the car and then along the dirt road, away from the farm. He examined the side of the road carefully, looking for tire marks. If someone had arrived here by car, they would have had to turn around somewhere; the road was so narrow it seemed inevitable that impressions would be visible in the soft earth. He continued up as far as the exit off the highway.

Gunnar had fetched their car and now drove up behind him.

"Nothing here," Birkir said as Gunnar rolled the window down.

"Magnús is going to send a truck to pick up the Nissan," Gunnar said. "He said that Dóra and Símon have spoken to the family. Ólafur was apparently married to a younger woman but also had children from two previous marriages. The team also stopped by his office. There will be a briefing when we get back to town this evening."

A black car from a funeral parlor approached from the south; the driver pulled over and looked at them questioningly. Birkir nodded toward the turnoff and said, "You'll have to wait a bit; the forensic team is still at work."

17:30

Twilight was descending when a small station wagon appeared on the road below Litla-Fell and eventually made its way to a stop beside the patrol car. A tall uniformed cop got out, greeted Birkir cheerfully, and opened the hatchback to reveal a metal cage. The large yellow Labrador inside it got up awkwardly from its bed and yawned.

The policeman opened the cage and called to the dog, "We're here! Come on out!"

The dog shook itself and jumped out of the car. It ran around, urinating here and there.

"His name's Bingo," the policeman said, and the dog barked twice, as if in agreement.

As they walked toward the crime scene, Birkir described the situation to the cop. The body had been removed, and all that was left was a dark pool of blood and the outline Anna had drawn with white spray paint. Nearby, another mark indicated where the severed leg had lain; and a third mark showed the position of the dead dog, which the local patrolman had taken away.

They began by taking Bingo to the edge of the ditch where the gunman had probably hidden. The uniformed cop, clearly an experienced dog handler, gave the order to track, and the dog began nuzzling the turf with his snout; then, as the cop made encouraging noises, the dog ran around in circles for a while. Birkir watched from a suitable distance, doing his best to note the dog's movements. Finally the dog raced up the hillside toward the boulders, where he nosed around, stopping the longest behind the boulder where they had found the spent shells. Here the yellow grass was partly trodden down; the area would have provided a good view of the ruined wall, making it a likely spot for the gunman to have positioned himself. After further prompting, the dog turned back and made a beeline for the road, running along it all the way up to the highway, where he stopped and barked furiously; in the distance they could hear the dogs at Litla-Fell joining in.

Birkir came to the conclusion that there had probably been a single gunman, who had fired at the ruin from two directions. Having completed their task, the cop and his dog departed.

While Birkir had followed the dog, Gunnar had helped the forensic team chart the area. After they'd measured distances with a long tape, he'd recorded everything in his notebook. They'd also positioned numbered markers on all the places where shots had made impact, most of which were in and around the ruin. They'd noticed that the victim had directed some of his fire up toward the hillside; these shots appeared random, as none had landed near the place they now assumed the gunman had been hiding.

Anna had little luck finding footprints. For several days, the weather had been dry, and the earth was hard and empty of marks. She knew the ditch was the best place to look, since any person walking along its muddy bottom would have left some imprint; but oddly, although the ground was disturbed, there were no footprints.

"I think he must have tidied up after himself," she said, looking at her colleague. "It's as if he covered up all his tracks with some sort of a tool. Maybe with the butt of his weapon."

After she had measured and photographed the disturbed area, her colleague took a plastic mold of an impression that was possibly made by a shotgun butt.

21:00

The police headquarters on Hverfisgata was quiet as the members of the investigating team filtered in one by one. The building was almost deserted and most of the rooms were dark. A young woman was washing the floor in the corridor, listening to music on her headphones and singing along, apparently unconcerned with how terrible she sounded.

In the violent crime squad's section, all the lights were ablaze, and Birkir detected a certain tension in the air. The first meeting in a murder inquiry was always like this. Everybody was waiting to see if the data could be assembled into a coherent whole. Would they find something that would bring them closer to solving the case, or would the puzzle pieces not fit together? There were seven of them involved in the investigation, and, apart from Detective Superintendent Magnús, they all looked rather tired. The "Super" had not left the building all day, but he had kept in phone contact with the team, organizing and coordinating their operations while dealing with questions from the media as news of the incident spread quickly. And, of course, there were also other ongoing investigations to supervise.

Magnús still had a bit of a tan leftover from his vacation the month before, which looked good against his tidy gray hair and thick mustache. Usually he looked cheerful, but now the wrinkles between his eyebrows indicated he was worried. Two years shy of sixty, he looked fit for his age, and only the slightest bit of belly fat protruded over his belt. He'd managed to squeeze in a swim after work, at about five, when he'd realized that this briefing would take up most of his evening.

Gunnar did not look as alert as his boss. He was visibly tired, his clothes were rumpled and stained, and when he stood up his colleagues could see that he hadn't tucked his shirt into his pants. Leafing through his notebook, he described his and Birkir's investigation at the crime scene. As he spoke, he wrote bullet points on a whiteboard with a blue marker.

- *Incident takes place at dawn, 6:00–6:30 a.m.*
- *Weapon: a powerful shotgun.*
- *Farmer Gudjón reports the incident 9:30 a.m.*
- *The attack is focused and brutal.*
- *The assailant is probably quick on his feet.*
- *The victim tried to defend himself.*
- *Gudjón and a young grandson are at home.*
- *They hear a number of shots, probably about 30 in all.*
- *Farmer Gudjón says he owns a shotgun but refuses to produce it.*

Birkir also had his notebook open in front of him; he sat and listened to his colleague with critical attention, adding his input when he felt it was needed, which, actually, was not that often. Birkir looked in much better shape than his partner; his clothes were still clean, the creases in his pants were still visible, and his face looked alert.

After Gunnar finished his report, it was Anna's turn to cover the forensics. Large prints of the crime-scene photographs had been stuck up on the wall. But either the computer settings had been wrong, or the printer had been faulty, because the pictures were marred by too much blue ink. The blood wasn't red; it was purple. But maybe that was actually an improvement—it made it all seem slightly less real.

Anna pointed at the pictures with a cigarette as she detailed each item, her voice hoarser than ever. In the absence of an ashtray, she flicked the ash from the cigarette into her trusty film canister. Predictably, smoking was banned in the conference room, but Anna had special dispensation—she had a certificate, signed by a distinguished psychiatrist at the National University Hospital, saying that she should be permitted to smoke at work.

She exhaled cigarette smoke and summed up her findings. "We have completed a preliminary investigation of the spent shells found on the hillside and in the ditch and concluded that those shots were, in all probability, fired from the same gun. That means that the murderer was probably acting alone, using a single weapon."

Opposite Gunnar and Birkir at the conference table were detectives Símon and Dóra. They had been busy gathering background information about the deceased and had interviewed as many of his family, friends, and coworkers in Reykjavik as they'd been able to track down.

Dóra described their visit to the widow.

"She's around my age, late twenties. It was all a bit dramatic," she said.

"Too dramatic?" Magnús asked.

"No, just suitably dramatic, given the circumstances. She had no part in this incident, if that's what you're asking," Dóra replied. "I think," she added, after a pause.

Birkir had been expecting this addition. Dóra was very conscientious but prone to hesitation. He chalked it up to her inexperience, which would wear off as the years passed; learning how to correctly interpret people's facial expressions when they were confronted by the police took time. Some detectives, in fact, never got it, as they were too wrapped up in their own egos. Dóra was not one of them.

"I stayed with her until her mother arrived," Dóra said. "She was beginning to recover by the time I left."

Dóra was a sturdy young woman with red hair and freckles; she was short and powerfully built but well proportioned. On her left cheekbone she bore a horizontal scar that, although prominent, somehow didn't look bad on her.

She had originally been part of the uniformed division; during her rehabilitation after a car accident, she had been drafted to spend time in the detective division for a short trial period. Her superiors there found her to be organized and precise, attributes that were handy in doing detective work. Then two detectives retired, and she was appointed to one of the vacancies.

Símon had gotten the other position. He came from the crime prevention unit, where he had been pretty useless; this had something to do with his interpersonal skills, the rumors went. This flaw didn't matter as much in the detective division, but he had, all the same, signed up for a leadership-training course with the hope of improving his people skills. Símon was thirty-five, with short black hair and dark five o'clock shadow. What people usually noticed first about him, however, were his prominent ears.

"I went to the deceased's law office," he said. "They knew nothing."

"Nothing?" said Magnús. "Whom did you speak to?"

"I spoke to the chief executive and Ólafur's secretary. The chief executive was going to call a staff meeting and announce the death."

"How did the staff react?"

"I don't know. I had to go to the course."

"The course?"

"Yep, Dale Carnegie. You told me to go, remember?"

"Couldn't you skip a session?"

"No. They strongly recommend against that. But we should take a closer look at the farmer, don't you think?" Símon said, trying to change the subject. "We need to search the farm buildings for the gun, don't we? Shouldn't we have done that already, earlier today?"

Gunnar and Birkir looked wearily at one another.

Magnús thought it over and then said, "It's not advisable to apply for a warrant on such flimsy grounds. We need better reasons."

Gunnar said, "In that case it seems to me we should ask the sheriff to persuade the old guy to show us the shotgun, rather than force him. If he's guilty and has taken Ólafur's gun, then he will definitely have hidden it somewhere safe. We'd need to demolish the whole place to find it."

"Isn't that going to happen anyway?" Símon asked.

Birkir looked up from his notebook. "Whoever shot Ólafur isn't going to leave the gun under his bed for us to find. Some thought has gone into all of this," he said.

23:30

It was past Birkir's usual bedtime when he got back to his little apartment on Bergstadastræti in the center of town. There was nobody waiting up for him; he lived alone, as he had for many years. The apartment was on the second floor of an unusual old house; it was cramped and oddly laid out, but had high ceilings and a homey atmosphere. It had a living room and a bedroom of similar size, a long and somewhat narrow kitchen, and a small bathroom tiled in a sickly pale green. The place looked just as it had when he bought it; he hadn't gotten around to making any improvements. At this point he was used to it. All the walls were painted white, the ceilings gray-green, and the floor was covered in dark parquet. The living room had an ivory sofa and a glass-topped steel-frame coffee table, along with several big, lush potted plants that added ambience. The framed pictures on the walls, which included oil paintings, watercolors, and photographs, all depicted the same subject, if in different ways: people with stringed instruments. There was a watercolor depicting a sad clown with a violin; a black-and-white photograph in a beautiful old frame of the string section of a symphony orchestra; and a vibrant, stylized oil painting of a string quartet.

Birkir switched on the light in the living room and opened a cupboard containing CDs. He picked a disc he had compiled with adagio sections from classical works, and put it on. He stood still for a little while, listening to the opening notes of the intermezzo from Mascagni's *Cavalleria Rusticana*; it was Semyon Bychkov conducting the Orchestre de Paris. He turned up the volume and went into the bathroom, where he undressed slowly and took a long, hot shower. Afterward, he dried himself with a large white towel and put on navy-blue cotton pajamas.

Birkir Li Hinriksson was a loner. He had probably always been a loner, but nobody knew much about his childhood. Even his own memories of his early years were very limited. Originally known simply as Li, he'd been born toward the end of 1970 in Vietnam, when that country was still in the throes of a horrific war, and most of its inhabitants lived a precarious existence. His parents were tradespeople of Chinese origin, and by the time the war ended in 1975, they were living in extreme poverty. The extended family owned a battered old riverboat; twenty-three of them used it to sail out to sea in the hope of finding a better life in another country. This was how young Li became one of the boat people—one among thousands who, in the years after the war, drifted around the South China Sea on any manner of makeshift craft.

His family actually had more luck than most. On their fortieth day at sea, they were picked up by a French freighter that was heading for Malaysia. By that time only eleven of them remained alive, the others having perished from hunger, thirst, or disease. Both of Li's parents were already dead and his brothers and sisters were gone; his earliest memories began with what came after the freighter arrived in Malaysia. He was taken in by a family living in a refugee camp near Kuala Lumpur. It was a life of poverty, but he didn't know anything else and he rarely suffered from hunger.

In 1978 foreign visitors arrived at the camp—white people wearing badges with a red cross and speaking a very strange language. Li's adopted family was invited to go live in a new country they had never heard of. The head of the family looked at a map that the foreign people carried with them and saw that it was an island, not far from the country he had always dreamed of going to, the United States of America. He had relatives there, and that was where he wanted to live, so he accepted the invitation to move to this northerly island, determined that he'd build a boat as soon as he arrived and travel to America with his whole family. The Red Cross had registered Li as a member of the family, so he was going with them.

The group of twenty-nine refugees arrived in Iceland in pitch darkness on January 10, 1979. Li thought he would never see the sun again. But then it started snowing and that brought him happiness. At first, they all lived together in a big house and tried to learn Icelandic, but before long the group dispersed, and Li moved with his foster parents and four siblings into a small apartment in Kópavogur, where they shared three cramped rooms. Li had not learned any Icelandic during their first months in the country, so there was no point sending him to school. He did, however, meet Hinrik and Rúna, an old couple who lived in the same apartment building. Each morning the old man drove south to Vatnsleysuströnd, where he kept sheep; Li was allowed to go with him, and soon his Icelandic began to improve.

Li's foster father scanned the sea from the shore and came to the conclusion that it was not really advisable to travel to America in a homemade boat, so his big plans came to nothing. He did, however, manage to get in touch with his relatives in Minnesota, and the family decided to go for a visit, using their new Icelandic passports. Li was allowed to stay behind with his friends, Hinrik and Rúna, supposedly for two weeks—but his foster family never returned from their visit to America.

Li continued to live with the old couple and became increasingly fluent in Icelandic. Hinrik taught him the language using the only method he knew; he made Li memorize the work of the classic Icelandic poets. Hinrik himself knew most of Einar Benediktsson's verse and much of Jónas Hallgrímsson's writing, in addition to the work of other poets. They spent the day in the old man's jeep, in the sheepfolds, or in the kitchen, with Hinrik continuously reciting poetry that Li had to repeat; the boy loved doing this. In time, he learned to read, starting with the poems. Many years later he realized that he only needed to read or hear a poem once to know it by heart; the same was true for song lyrics, however inane.

In the fall of 1980 Li started school, at which point he spoke very good, if somewhat old-fashioned, Icelandic. Although by now nearly ten years old, he was put into a class with eight-year-olds; nobody knew exactly how old Li was, but he was the same height as an eight-year-old Icelander. This worked quite well, since he had never attended school before, but as a result the national register listed Li as having been born in 1972; the officials decided on January 10 as his birthday, that being the day in 1979 when he had arrived in Iceland. Asked to select a new name for himself, he chose Birkir as his first name, and based his patronymic on old Hinrik's name to convey the only lineage he really knew. Birkir Li Hinriksson, as he was known after that, lived with the elderly couple until 1992, when he turned twenty, according to the official records. Old Rúna died that fall and Hinrik put his last sheep down and went into a nursing home. Two years later he died, too.

Birkir recalled very little of his time in Malaysia. There, every day had been much the same and he had mostly been left to his own devices. He remembered nothing at all of the years before that, during the Vietnam War. Occasionally, if he detected the smell of something burning, strange fragments of memory would surface—but they were always too vague to make much sense. He hadn't heard his native tongue for twenty-five years, and at this point, had no idea whether he would understand a word of it. Yet he hardly ever gave this any thought. He knew that a large community of people from Vietnam lived in the Reykjavik area, but felt no urge to look them up. He had no wish to revisit the language he had once spoken, and was, in any case, not at all gregarious. He simply liked his own company.

Birkir graduated from Kópavogur High School and embarked on studies at the Iceland University of Education. Around this time, the Reykjavik Police got in touch and offered him a job on a trial basis; some Thai youths had been causing trouble, and senior officers at the police department had decided that it might be sensible to recruit an officer who was also an immigrant. It was a good idea, although not for the reasons the department had intended. Birkir turned out to be an excellent policeman. As for the Thai immigrants, Birkir looked just as alien to them as any other cop who tried to make contact—the only difference was that he looked more Chinese than Icelandic.

Birkir spent some years with the uniformed police in Reykjavik before he got a position in the detective division, where he concentrated on violent-crime investigations. He was good at the job, and it proved to be a bonus that he sometimes had a different way of looking at things than his colleagues who had spent their whole lives in Iceland. He tended to be generally suspicious, and never jumped to conclusions. People's appearances or facial expressions hardly ever fooled him.

Birkir had two hobbies: classical music and long-distance running. The music kept his soul happy and the running kept his body fit. There was good balance between the two. He had started this particular day by running ten kilometers before his shift. He would try to repeat this the following morning, preferably going a bit farther.

Birkir returned to the living room after his shower and sat down to listen to Jean Fournet's recording of Gabriel Fauré's *Pavane*. Then, craving something warm and rich, he went into the kitchen to fix himself a hot chocolate topped with whipped cream.

There was an ironing board in the living room—not one of those common, lightweight boards that are folded up after use and put in a closet, but the kind that remains permanently installed. Birkir stepped up to it now, removed his pants from the hanger he'd hung nearby, and began to press them. He listened to the Adagietto from Mahler's Symphony no. 5 as he carefully ran the iron over the creases in the pants, pausing every so often for a sip of hot chocolate. All the while his thoughts were on the man who had been shot down on the edge of a potato field in Dalasýsla in the early morning hours, and why his death had come so suddenly.

CHAPTER 2

09:30

"This is it," Gunnar said.

Birkir slowed the car and swung into a parking lot. All around them towered modern commercial buildings, one of which housed the law office where Ólafur Jónsson had worked.

On the high-rise in front of them a large digital billboard flashed advertisements in quick succession, and featured a clock with huge red neon numerals that read 09:32. Then 09:33.

"Time's getting away from us already," said Birkir. "Shall we split up?"

"Okay," Gunnar replied, struggling to extract the last jelly bean from its bag with his thick fingers.

"I'll go talk with the widow, you deal with the coworkers," Birkir said.

Gunnar dropped the jelly bean he'd finally managed to get a hold of and immediately started looking for it on the floor. "Where did the damn thing go?"

Birkir shook his head. "Get out, and then maybe you'll find it."

"Yeah," Gunnar replied, opening the door and easing himself out of the car. "Ah, here it is," he said, plucking the candy from the seat. "Will you pick me up afterward?"

"Take a taxi," Birkir said, putting the car in gear. "I might be some time."

"Okay. Right."

Gunnar entered the office building and looked around. It was an impressive space. Large windows let light into a soaring lobby that had a wide spiral staircase and a sleek glass elevator.

He studied the information board on the ground floor. The offices of the company Ólafur had worked for, ICinnheimtan, were on the fourth floor.

Gunnar looked longingly at the elevator but decided to walk up the stairs; he needed the exercise and there was no hurry.

He spotted two surveillance cameras high up on the wall, one of which soundlessly directed its lens toward him. Better behave, he thought, nodding in the direction of the camera, and he started walking, slowly and steadily, up the staircase. He studied each floor as he climbed. This kind of modern architecture was all about glass and open spaces, and he wondered if the people who worked here minded the lack of privacy. The hushed silence around him was disturbed only by his own muffled footsteps. He heard the soft sound of a bell as the elevator started its ascent. It was empty, summoned by somebody on an upper floor.

Arriving on the fourth floor, Gunnar looked through the glass wall into the spacious reception area of ICinnheimtan, where a secretary in a black suit sat at a desk and worked at a stylishly designed computer. There was nothing else on her desktop, not even a pen. Behind the woman was a dark-gray partition wall with four office doors.

"Good morning," said the secretary as Gunnar opened the glass door and walked in.

She had flowing black hair and wore black square-framed glasses. Even as she directed her attention at Gunnar, her fingers continued to work the keyboard.

"Good morning, I'm from the detective division." He showed his ID. "I need to talk to your boss."

She made no reply, her fingers still tapping away. A door opened and a man appeared. He wore a dark-gray suit, a white shirt, and a black tie. His black hair was combed straight back, and although his face was good-looking, it lacked expressiveness. A dummy in a shop window, Gunnar thought, trying to assess what type of man he was dealing with.

"My name is Tómas Benediktsson. Please follow me," the man said, opening a different door. "We have been meeting to discuss our reorganization."

Gunnar looked back at the secretary. She must have announced his arrival through her computer. They seemed to be people of few words.

Tómas said, "Ólafur's death is obviously a dreadful blow for us all. He was a key member of the team and a much-liked colleague."

They entered a small conference room that had a glass-topped table and black chairs. No cabinets, but there was one classy painting on the wall that featured strong colors and rough brushstrokes.

"Any news on the investigation?" Tómas asked.

Gunnar shook his head, "Unfortunately, no. Nothing yet."

"Is that so? Well, what can I do for you?"

"You can tell me about what Ólafur was working on. Did he have enemies?"

"He had many opponents, like almost everyone in our profession does, but enemies? Hardly."

"What was his job here?"

"Financial claims, foreign and domestic. The IC part of the firm's name stands for *International Collectors*. We work in collaboration with a multinational conglomerate."

Gunnar was trying to write the English words in his notebook. "I-N-T…How do you spell that?"

Tómas spelled the two words slowly and clearly.

"What can you tell me about his purchase of the farm?" Gunnar asked.

"It was a small job he undertook on behalf of a relative of his. Collecting an overdue personal surety. He actually referred the case to another law firm that we use for small claims. A million is our usual threshold for—"

"Hang on," Gunnar interrupted. "One million krónur—that wouldn't get you a decent secondhand car. Was the claim less than that?"

The lawyer smiled politely. "I meant that in this firm the minimum is one million *euros*. The claim was considerably less than that."

"Ah, I see." Gunnar grinned. "Then what?"

The unexpected sight of the gap between Gunnar's front teeth put the lawyer off his stride momentarily, but then he went on. "Though, as I say, another firm was actually handling the claim, Ólafur kept oversight of the matter on behalf of the claimant, and when the farm was put up for auction he bid for the property against the loan fund representatives, seeking to safeguard his relative's interests. He himself had been looking for a farm with hunting resources, and this property suited him reasonably well despite its distance from Reykjavik. The price was also acceptable."

"Did he go there often?"

"He tried to go whenever he could. There's a trout stream there, as well as good hunting, especially for geese and ptarmigan. If the forecast was good, he would sometimes leave town at four o'clock in the morning, bag a few geese on their morning flight, and then drive straight back to town and be at his desk by eleven. I went with him twice on trips like that. He invited me to come yesterday but I was busy, unfortunately—if that's the right word."

"What sort of gun did Ólafur have?"

"Wasn't it found next to him?"

"No. It had been taken."

"He had a decent gun, a Remington 870 Wingmaster pump-action. I was actually trying to get him to buy an automatic, but he wanted to stick to his Remington. He was a very good hunter, too."

"I heard that there had been some disagreement with the tenant of the farm."

"Yes, that's right. The former owner seems to be a bit strange in the head, if I can put it like that. Ólafur let him stay on as tenant and work the farm. Some people would have been grateful, but that man was not."

The lawyer paused, got up, and looked at his watch.

"What do you mean by that?" Gunnar asked, not moving.

"He was supposed to pay a small amount of rent to help cover property tax and other official dues. But he never coughed up anything to speak of, and then he actually began to be abusive and indulge in vandalism."

"Vandalism?"

"Yes. Damage was done to cars belonging to Ólafur and friends he'd invited to come hunting on the farm. Two cars were scratched up, and one had its tires slashed. At one point some game was stolen."

"Did Ólafur report this?"

Tómas sat back down. "Oh yes. Ólafur contacted the sheriff, but the tenant denied it, and of course it wasn't possible to prove anything. There were no witnesses and the authorities were not particularly interested. So in the end Ólafur gave the guy formal notice to quit."

"How did that go?"

"It's in the hands of the sheriff. Ólafur got a lawyer to serve an eviction notice when the man refused to leave the farm."

"How did the original claim come about?"

"I'm not familiar with the case. I'll give you the name of the lawyer who dealt with it." Tómas wrote something on a piece of paper that was lying on the table.

"Has the tenant ever threatened Ólafur?" Gunnar asked.

"He used violent language when they spoke with each other, some of which could probably be described as threatening."

"Do you think that the man is dangerous?"

"I wouldn't like to test that myself. It's impossible to guess what a guy like that might do if pushed. I assume he's a suspect. Is he?"

Gunnar ignored this question and asked, "What will happen to the farm now?"

"It will become part of the estate. The division will be complicated; Ólafur was married for the third time, and there are children from both previous marriages. There is a marriage settlement covering the properties. I assume that an administrator will be appointed. I might make an offer for the farm to simplify that part for the family. They are hardly going to want to keep it after this dreadful incident."

"No, probably not," Gunnar said. "Where were you yesterday morning between five and eight o'clock?"

"Me?"

"Yes."

"I was…at home asleep."

"Can anyone verify that?"

"My wife—ah, no, she's in London, so I was alone at home."

"Children?"

"No. You don't really think that I had anything to do with this?"

"These are questions that all of the staff here will have to answer. I have to start with someone, don't I?"

"I see."

"You knew that Ólafur was going hunting yesterday morning, and where. Did anyone else here know?"

"He most certainly would have told the front desk secretary he was going to arrive late. A few of the staff here know where he hunts. But it's out of the question that any of us had anything to do with this."

"That's good to know," Gunnar said. "But now I'd like to talk to the others. Please send them in here one at a time, in alphabetical order."

10:05

Birkir drove to the Grafarvogur district and found the address where Ólafur had lived with his young wife. It was a newish house, unpainted, with large windows. The garden was only partially planted.

There were no spots near the house, so Birkir had to park some distance away and walk back. He rang the bell and had his police ID ready when a young woman opened the door and peered out.

"My name is Birkir. I'm from the detective division," he said by way of introduction. "Are you the wife of the late Ólafur Jónsson?"

"No, I'm her sister," the woman replied, taking shelter behind the door.

Birkir looked at his notebook and found the name. "Is Helga available?" he asked.

The young woman looked at him suspiciously. "She's resting," she said.

She turned to look at someone behind her and said, "Mom, there's a foreigner asking if Helga is in. He says he's from the police."

A woman in her sixties immediately appeared.

Birkir said, "It's really important that I get to ask Helga a few questions. It's related to the police investigation."

"What is there to investigate?" the older woman asked. "Haven't you arrested that wretched farmer yet?"

"No. Nobody has been arrested."

"Oh, are you waiting for him to shoot more people?"

"There's nothing yet to indicate that the tenant of Litla-Fell is responsible for Ólafur's death, if that's what you mean," Birkir said. "May I come in?"

The two moved aside and showed him into the living room, where several well-dressed women sat drinking coffee. A couple of the women looked inquisitively at Birkir, but the rest pretended not to notice him.

"Do you have a specific reason to suspect that Gudjón committed this crime?" Birkir asked. "Anything that might assist us in our investigation?"

The older woman answered, "Ólafur told us to watch out for that fellow. The situation was so bad that he'd stopped taking the children up there. He was just waiting to get him off the farm."

"Was Gudjón threatening him?"

"Ólafur wouldn't have warned us against him without good reason. He said he wasn't scared himself, as he never went near the farm. And he was armed. It just wasn't enough. That man is an animal and he lives like a wild beast in that hovel."

"Did Ólafur not have other enemies?" Birkir asked.

"No, of course not. Everybody was really fond of him. And now my little girl is a widow at the age of twenty-five."

The woman's voice cracked, and tears flowed.

"May I speak to her?"

"I can tell you all we know," the woman said, sniffling and straightening up. "I gave Helga a sleeping pill and she just fell asleep, finally. She didn't sleep a wink all last night."

Birkir gave up. "I'll be back later," he said, and stood up to take his leave.

11:45

At the station the detectives reconvened in the incident room.

Gunnar was the last to arrive. He had walked back from the law office, stopping at home to fry three eggs and half a pack of bacon. It took him a while to get going again after this meal, as he had managed to get yolk on his shirt. His attempts to remove the stain with lukewarm water only made it worse, but trying to change his shirt had proved to be a problem since he had recently gone up a size and didn't have a clean one that was large enough. He was forced to squeeze into a too-small button-up, leaving the top button undone and skipping a tie.

The team reviewed its progress so far and discussed its next move. Magnús decided that Gunnar and Birkir should return to Dalasýsla to search the farm. Having seen the incident report, the district judge for Western Iceland had issued a search warrant for the house and all the outbuildings at Litla-Fell. There were clear grounds for a thorough examination of the premises and a full investigation into Gudjón's version of events. The evidence of an argument between him and Ólafur was the only lead the police had as of yet, and it was noted that the farmer had refused to show his shotgun to the officers on the scene despite explicit requests to do so.

Magnús accompanied his men down to the parking lot. He urged them to conduct the search tactfully and wished them a good journey. A four-man team of SWAT officers followed in a second car; since there was at least one firearm at the farm, they didn't want to take any risks.

They traveled in convoy as far as Borgarnes, where Gunnar insisted on stopping to buy a sandwich while their companions went on ahead.

The sheriff and the policeman from Búdardalur were waiting in the patrol car at the Litla-Fell turnoff. Gunnar and Birkir arrived at three o'clock, but they had to wait another forty minutes because the SWAT team had gotten lost and taken the road to Snæfellsnes. It took several phone calls to direct the men back on the right track.

Gunnar was bored and restless. He didn't expect the trip to yield any results, and he wanted to get the search over with so they could return to town. Birkir, on the other hand, sat there silent and expressionless. He was never impatient.

It began to rain. Threatening clouds were approaching from the south and an easterly wind was kicking up.

When the others finally arrived, they had a short discussion on tactics and then drove slowly toward the farm, where they parked all three cars in a line in the farmyard. They all got out, and the sheriff, Birkir, and Gunnar approached the house.

The sheriff knocked firmly several times. They heard somebody moving around inside and were surprised when a woman answered the door.

"What's all this goddamn banging for? You want to break it down or what?" she said, stepping outside and shutting the door behind her. "What the fuck do you want?"

She was a sturdy, tall, reasonably shapely woman in her thirties. Rather broad hips, thought Gunnar, but that didn't have to be a drawback in a woman. One could have described her sharp-featured face as pretty had her nose not been flat and badly broken. Her dark hair, with the remnants of a blonde rinse, was combed back off her face and held in place with a headband.

The sheriff explained their business and showed her the warrant.

"Where's Gudjón?" Gunnar asked.

The woman looked at him. "What business is it of yours? Is there anything on this piece of paper that says he has to be here today?" Her front teeth were crooked and one of the lower ones was missing.

"Who are you?" said Gunnar.

"Kolbrún. I'm Gudjón's daughter. Who the fuck are you?"

Gunnar showed his police identification.

She examined the card thoroughly, as if to memorize the name, and finally said, "Dad went looking for sheep this morning up in the highland pasture. Gutti, my son, got leave from school to go with him. Thank goodness, that's all I can say," she added, glaring in the direction of the SWAT team waiting by the cars.

"Anybody else with them?" Gunnar asked.

"No. It's just the two of them, and four horses. They'll be back this afternoon. Hopefully not too late; there's a storm brewing."

The sheriff directed the patrolman to take the SWAT team with him to search the outbuildings, while he led Gunnar and Birkir into the farmhouse itself. A faint musty smell was everywhere. They walked down a narrow corridor into the kitchen, where a bucket of warm soapy water stood on the table. The floor was damp.

"Don't you dare mess up my clean floors," Kolbrún said, taking the bucket off the table.

"We're only looking for guns here. It won't take long," the sheriff said. "Big objects like that should be easy to find."

Kolbrún emptied the bucket into the sink. "Why don't I just show you Dad's gun?" she said. "Then you can stop this crap and fuck off home."

Gunnar asked, "Is it at all possible your father got into a fight with Ólafur?"

Kolbrún seemed to have expected this question. "In the past, Dad might well have gone after that fancy dude and given him a whack with whatever came to hand. That wouldn't have surprised me in the least." She looked fixedly at Gunnar. "But he never would have attacked anyone with a firearm. Dad didn't shoot the guy. You can forget that idea."

"Why might your dad have wanted to tangle with Óla-fur?"

Kolbrún hesitated briefly. "Dad's bitter as hell over the way he was cheated out of the land. It may all have been legal, if you can call it that, but people took full advantage of our shit situation. Legal theft would be the right word for it."

She turned and pointed to a pantry just off the kitchen. "Dad's gun is in there on the top shelf to the right."

Birkir disappeared into the pantry and returned with a shotgun, which he handed to Gunnar butt first.

"Now you've got what you came for," Kolbrún said. "This is the only gun in the house."

Gunnar examined the weapon. "I think it's an old Spanish AYA," he said, opening the action and sniffing the barrels. "And I don't think it's been used for a long time."

Kolbrún nodded and said, "Dad's eyesight is so bad these days that he couldn't shoot anything, fox or fowl, let alone a human. You should have saved yourselves the trip."

She looked at the three men. "Is that it for today, then, assholes?"

"I think we should have a look around anyway," the sheriff said, leaving the kitchen. Birkir followed him.

Gunnar pointed at the empty bucket that Kolbrún had set down on the floor. "Doesn't your dad get domestic help from the parish?" he asked.

"No, and he can't see well enough to clean properly himself. I always give the house a good scrub when I come to visit."

Gunnar asked, "Were you here yesterday?"

"No, I arrived this morning."

"How? I didn't see a car outside. Did you take the bus?"

"I came on my motorcycle. It's in the barn."

"Why did you come now?"

Kolbrún looked at Gunnar in surprise. "Why now? What sort of a question is that? What do you think?"

Gunnar shrugged. "To see your son?"

"Yeah, and my dad, too. My menfolk need me just now. They're in shock over what happened. I mean, a man was shot dead within shouting distance. They aren't totally without feelings, as some seem to think."

Gunnar nodded. "How come your dad lost the farm?"

Kolbrún hesitated. Finally she said quietly, "It was, of course, mostly my fault. I made a mistake and nobody could, or would, help us. There were, on the other hand, many who wanted to make it worse."

"What happened?" Gunnar asked.

Kolbrún seemed to be of two minds about whether to explain further.

"It might help to eliminate your dad from our investigation if we know the full story," Gunnar said.

"Okay, then. I've been particularly unlucky with the men in my life and have probably made a number of wrong decisions over the years."

She turned back to the sink and filled a glass with water before continuing.

"Four years ago I began living with a guy who was a recovering alcoholic. We bought a little store in a new suburb of Reykjavik and things actually went quite well in the beginning. Of course, we had to take out a loan, which Dad underwrote. I worked in the store from seven in the morning until three in the afternoon, when my partner took over and worked until eleven thirty. He did the buying and the finances and I looked after the housekeeping. Since he'd been declared bankrupt, due to his drinking, the business was actually in my name; I had to sign everything he gave to me, and often I just didn't have time to look carefully at what I was signing. That's what led to all my troubles later on."

Kolbrún took a sip of water. They could hear Birkir and the sheriff moving around on the upper floor. She looked up at the ceiling and shook her head.

"What troubles?" Gunnar asked.

"The shop was going well," Kolbrún said, as if she hadn't heard the question. "There was a lot of construction going on in the neighborhood, and the workers on the sites were good customers. I cooked soup at lunchtime and it became very popular, along with the sandwiches. Business was quieter in the evenings, and we decided to add slot machines and the national lottery to attract customers. Unfortunately, my partner turned out to be a compulsive gambler. At first, he just played the machines in the evenings, and sometimes did the lottery and the football pools. But it wasn't long before he was spending practically all of his time on it. He acted totally ecstatic when he won and seemed to completely ignore the large amounts of money he paid out to play. In the end, his gambling got way out of hand, and one month we couldn't pay our business loan installment because he spent so much. Then I found out that there was nothing left to pay the sales tax or any other debts with, either. He hit the bottle and took off with what was left of the money. That was the last I saw of that asshole."

Kolbrún gave a wry smile and set her glass down on the counter. "It took me some time to work out the financial situation, but by then it was all too late. The beneficiary of the guarantee that Dad had signed spotted a chance to make some profit. He'd sold us the shop for a pile of money, but now had a chance to get it back for next to nothing, even though we'd already paid back a large part of the loan and established a good business."

She reached up to a cupboard for a pack of cigarettes and a lighter, and lit a smoke.

"By the end of that month, I didn't have a króna to pay what was owed to the lottery company or anyone else. Because the business was in my name, I ended up in prison for withholding sales tax. So Dad lost the farm for a pittance. There was no way for me to help him while I was inside, and when I got out it was all over. The only thing I can do now is to work like a maniac and hope I'll get the chance to buy the farm back. Maybe that can happen now, with the new owner dead; his wife will hardly want to build a house here after what's happened."

Gunnar did not mention that he knew of another potential buyer.

"Where do you work?" he asked.

"I work in a seafood store during the day, and then I work as a cleaner at the City Library in the evening," she said. "I'm looking for extra work every other weekend. Do you know of anything?"

Gunnar shook his head. "Do you think it's good for you to work so much?"

Birkir and the sheriff entered the kitchen before Kolbrún had a chance to reply.

"What the hell are you looking for?" she said. "I showed you Dad's only gun." She blew cigarette smoke in their direction.

"We're looking for another weapon. Whoever shot Ólafur took his gun," Birkir replied.

"What a bunch of jerks." Kolbrún shook her head.

The policeman from Búdardalur entered.

"Did you find anything in the outbuildings?" the sheriff asked.

"No, but we had a call from Reykjavik on our car radio." The policeman was very agitated. "Another goose hunter has been shot. Down south in the Rangárvellir district. It happened this morning."

19:30

By the time Birkir and Gunnar neared Rangárvellir the wind was roaring, it was pitch-dark, and rain lashed against the car. They had no problem, however, finding the place they were looking for—the blue flashing light of a patrol car was visible across the flatlands from miles away.

They knew they were getting close when a policeman dressed in rain gear and a reflective vest waved them down with a flashlight and demanded identification. After passing the checkpoint, they drove on and stopped when they reached a small cluster of parked patrol cars. Just beyond they could see three large rescue vehicles with lights blazing, and they could hear the drone of their powerful diesel engines despite the howling wind and thundering rain of the storm.

Birkir peered through the windshield into the darkness; the wipers struggled vainly against the downpour. He could hear shouts and dogs barking. A man in a yellow raincoat appeared in the beam of their headlights, edged his way along the side of the car, pulled the rear door open, and got in. They recognized Thorlákur, the Selfoss detective.

"The body's out there in the meadow, about two hundred meters from the road," he said, skipping the formalities. "Screw this weather."

"Have we got a name?" Gunnar asked, notebook ready.

"Fridrik Fridriksson."

"What else do you know?"

"The guy parked his vehicle nearly five kilometers down the road from here. Then he must have walked about a kilometer to a known goose-hunting ground and taken cover in a ditch. The decoys he placed were untouched. He seems to have sustained a gunshot wound right there in the ditch—we found a substantial amount of blood spatter in that area, along with his abandoned gun. Then he got to his feet and tried to run toward the nearest house; his footprints are deep and show that he was covering ground quickly, at least to start out with. The tracker dogs followed the trail until it ended here, where the body was found. The assailant must have chased Fridrik on foot and, after catching up to him, shot him at close range. We haven't touched the body yet. We're waiting for better lighting so we can do a thorough investigation and take some decent pictures."

"He hadn't been missing long when you started the search. How come you didn't wait to see if he turned up? Why did you start looking for him right away?"

"One of his relatives called emergency services around noon to say that he hadn't been in touch and wasn't answering his cell. Everyone is jittery after that hunter in the west was murdered—not without reason, clearly. We thought it would be easy enough to take a look around. It didn't take us long to find his car, and then his gun nearby. Those clues seemed suspicious enough to justify a large-scale search."

He unzipped his raincoat and fished out a digital camera.

"We should be able to find decent tracks left by the killer in the mud," Gunnar said.

"I don't know about that," Thorlákur replied. "Four guys from the rescue team followed the tracker dogs and trampled all over the area around the body."

He leaned forward and held out the camera so that Birkir and Gunnar could see the screen. "There. That's what it looks like."

The picture showed a man lying facedown on waterlogged earth. There were two large black holes in his back. Thorlákur flicked through a few more pictures of the scene. The muddy ground surrounding the body was covered in deep footprints.

"Must have been very close range," Gunnar said.

"Yes, the first shot came from a distance of a few meters. The guy must have fallen, and the second shot hit him lying down. The killer had to be standing over him."

Birkir peered at the screen. "Is that a hole in the outer layer of the parka?" He pointed with his little finger; a white patch was visible on the man's back next to the entry wounds.

Thorlákur looked more closely. "I hadn't noticed that."

"We'll check that," Birkir said. "Have you got his wallet?"

"Yeah." Thorlákur dug into another pocket, and drew out a bag.

Birkir donned rubber gloves and extracted the soaking-wet wallet from the bag. He opened it and examined the contents: credit cards, cash, receipts.

Birkir said, "Here's a receipt from the gas station at Ártún-shöfdi, time-stamped at four twenty-five this morning."

"Hey," said Gunnar immediately, "just like yesterday. Could it be the killer intercepts his victims at gas stations?"

"Perhaps," Birkir replied. Then, turning to Thorlákur, he said, "Can we see where the attacker parked his vehicle?"

"It'll have to wait until dawn," Thorlákur replied. "But given what's happened, there's an earlier case we need to reopen and take a better look at."

"What's that?" Gunnar asked.

Thorlákur coughed a few times before starting his account. "Just over a year ago, a young man presented himself at the Selfoss county hospital. He'd been hunting geese in the Landsveit area to the north of here and had been hit in the chest and face. His clothes protected his chest, but a few pellets had gotten deep into his face and one eye. The doctor who examined him notified us right away and we did an immediate incident report. In fact, I typed it up myself," he added, tapping his chest to emphasize the point.

"The guy's story was that he'd been creeping along a ditch toward some geese when some shots hit him. His reaction was to run back to his car and drive straight to the hospital. Apparently, he'd been hunting without a license. Later, we wanted to carry out a closer examination of the location, but he couldn't find the exact spot where he'd been."

"Do you think there's a connection between these cases?" Birkir asked.

"I don't know," Thorlákur replied. "We investigated it as best we could, but we never found anything of significance. There were plenty of footprints and spent shells in the areas he showed us, but that's no surprise since it's one of the most popular goose-hunting grounds in the county. The guy stuck firmly to his story throughout. I actually suspected that he'd been out hunting with a friend who'd ended up shooting him by accident, and was lying to avoid trouble. The guy was young, and immaturity often accounts for a certain lack of honesty, so to speak. Maybe I was wrong, though; maybe someone did actually try to kill the guy. I don't know. But he lost his eye as a result."

"Do you have his name?" Birkir asked.

Thorlákur dug out his cell phone and dialed a number. After a brief conversation he turned back to Birkir. "Jóhann Markússon. Not long before this happened, he'd moved from Akureyri to Reykjavik. I contacted my colleagues up north last year, but they didn't have anything bad on the guy. He had a valid gun license and all his stuff was above board. His only misstep was hunting illegally down here, it seems."

They heard a car approaching, and Thorlákur turned to look out the rear window. "Ah, here are the forensic guys from Reykjavik. I hope they've brought some decent lamps. Do you want to get a closer look at the scene?" he asked.

Gunnar peered out into the rain and darkness. "Let them check the area first—they've got all the gear for that. We'll go eat in the meantime. Then we'll need to speak to the landowner."

23:55

It was raining in Reykjavik, too, when Birkir and Gunnar finally got back to town, and it was just as blustery as it had been in the east. Their drive over the Hellisheidi pass had been slowed by sleet and poor visibility. No question—fall had arrived.

Gunnar gathered his things as Birkir pulled up outside an old apartment building on Skúlagata.

"Good night," Birkir said.

"See you in the morning," Gunnar replied. He got out and slammed the car door shut behind him.

Inside the house the wind whined through the drafty front door and echoed around the ice-cold stairwell. Gunnar tiptoed up the stairs and slipped into the little apartment he called home. He shut the door gently behind him and crept along the hallway without switching the light on.

It had been a long day, and the homicide investigation had not yielded any useful results—they'd gotten another body, and that was all. Gunnar and Birkir had gone to speak with the local farmer, who said he'd given Fridrik—and no one else—permission to shoot geese on his land that morning. There was nothing more to learn there, so they had driven back to the crime scene and sat in the car for a half hour, watching the forensic team's lights out in the meadow and listening to the rain hammer the roof. They knew they couldn't do much just now; they would only be in the way out there in the dark, plus they would get wet and dirty. After a short debate, they'd decided that going home was their best option. The case wasn't going to be solved right away no matter what.

A voice came from the living room. "*Gunnar, bist du da?*"

He stopped and turned.

"*Guten Abend, Mutter,*" he said.

A stout, white-haired old woman sat in an armchair in front of the television; she looked as if she'd been dozing and had just woken up. She was dressed in a worn housecoat and gray woolen socks. On the table in front of her was an empty beer bottle and a small liqueur glass containing a few dregs of Jägermeister; smoke coiled up from a cigarette glowing in an ashtray.

It was a small room, with a made-up sofa bed against the wall and two old chairs on either side. The table stood in the middle, and the television was by the window, whose yellow-brown drapes were stained with damp at the bottom.

Gunnar's mother, Maria Ludwig, had come to Iceland from Lübeck, Germany, in the spring of 1947, at the age of twenty-five. She had responded to an advertisement inviting German women to go to Iceland to work on the land. It seemed a sensible proposition, as the employment prospects for young, uneducated females in Germany after the war were very poor. She had lost her fiancé right at the end of all the fighting. After surviving four years of military service almost unscathed, he lost his life during the Allies' final offensive in northern Germany. By that time, he'd been a lieutenant in charge of a small team of teenagers who had been ordered to fight to the last man in defense of some bridge or other near Hamburg.

Upon her arrival in Iceland, Maria was employed by an old couple in the Húnavatn district in the north. They were nearly as poor as she was, and they couldn't afford to employ Icelandic workers. Maria was not unhappy in the job, but life was hard work for all three of them. She learned only a little Icelandic; there was not much unnecessary conversation in this particular household. She stayed on with them for four years, until the old couple had to retire from farming. After that, Maria took whatever work she could. With no remaining close relatives alive in Germany, Maria decided to take Icelandic citizenship; this meant adding an accent to her name, becoming María instead of Maria. It wasn't a major change, but even so, she felt she had lost something of herself. By 1959 she was in a relationship with a seaman from Siglufjördur, and in the fall of 1960 her son, Gunnar, was born. The relationship with the seaman didn't last, and in 1963, María moved to Reykjavik. Gunnar never saw his father again, and when it became permissible for children to take their mothers' names, he changed his patronymic, Sigurdsson, to the matronymic Maríuson. He got a job in the Reykjavik police force in spring 1982.

"*Warum kommst du so spät?*"

"I had to go out of town. There was a murder."

"*Schon wieder ein Mord?*"

"Yeah. We're up to our necks in this investigation."

"*Ach so.*"

"*Gute Nacht, Mutter.*"

"*Gute Nacht, mein Schatz,*" María said, grinning toothlessly. She had begun to feel old age taking hold of her, and knowing she wouldn't always be there to look after Gunnar caused her anxiety. She had a habit of challenging all females between the ages of thirty and sixty with the same question, "*Sind Sie verheiratet?*" But since old María was beginning to confuse German with Icelandic, most of the women she tried to interrogate didn't realize that she was asking them about their marital status and never even replied.

Gunnar turned and stepped into the kitchen. He paused, battling the urge to have a glass of beer and a shot of ice-cold bitters. Both were in the fridge, but he'd set himself a goal to go to bed sober at least three evenings every week—and preferably four. He had also become much too fat, and he knew the excessive beer drinking was partly to blame. He came to a decision and shoveled several spoons of cocoa into a cup, mixing it with boiling water and some milk. Then he buttered three pieces of bread and topped them with thick slices of cheese.

As he snacked, Gunnar glanced at that day's newspaper. The killing in Dalasýsla occupied the whole front page and three pages inside. The coverage included photos of the farmhouse and outbuildings at Litla-Fell and the investigators working in the fields. They'd evidently been taken with a powerful telephoto lens; nobody had been allowed near the crime scene, and the Búdardalur patrolman had kept everyone well away while the police had scoured the area. Gunnar recognized himself in one of the pictures. His shape was unmistakable.

There would be blazing headlines in the days to come, now that there had been another killing. Gunnar decided not to read any newspapers while the investigation was still ongoing. When it came to his job, he was like a sports enthusiast who liked to read the sports pages closely when his team was winning, but flipped through them quickly when there was a loss.

He got up to return the milk and cheese to the fridge, resisting—not without struggle—the temptation of the beer bottle within. He managed to overcome the craving, and he retired to the apartment's only bedroom and went to sleep.

CHAPTER 3

06:30

Birkir woke a few seconds before the alarm clock rang. He switched it off and peered through the window. He could tell from the poplars in the garden that the east wind had mostly subsided, but the wet windowpanes showed it was still raining. The thermometer showed five degrees Celsius. A chilly dawn was creeping in.

He fixed himself a quick breakfast: a glass of orange juice, a piece of toast, and a cup of strong loose-leaf black tea without milk or sugar. As he ate he donned light running gear and good shoes. He was out on the sidewalk before seven o'clock, and for the next hour he jogged gently through the Thingholt area, heading west over to Sudurgata, and then turning south toward Skerjafjördur. He had run six kilometers and was passing to the south of Reykjavik's airport when his cell beeped to tell him that he had received a text.

It read: Meeting at nine.

Succinct and clear, the message from Magnús confirmed they would be working over the weekend. Birkir had assumed this

71

would happen—the two unsolved homicides made it inevitable. It was not yet eight o'clock, so he had plenty of time, and he continued into Fossvogur; it was ten past the hour when he turned back toward home on Bergstadastræti, increasing his speed and running the last two kilometers in just under eight minutes.

Upon reaching home, he had a quick shower, shaved, and dressed. A freshly pressed suit was ready, as usual, on the hanger next to the ironing board in the living room. He held up a gray shirt against the jacket and chose a tie that went well with both. It was very important for him to be neatly dressed. He frequently sensed suspicion—sometimes even enmity—from strangers because of his race. Cleanliness and well-tailored clothes seemed to tone down these types of prejudice; that was the reason he bothered. He didn't think of it as letting other people's stupidity and lack of sophistication dominate his life. He simply found it easier to do his job when he felt respected. Besides, it didn't feel like a burden to him to dress nicely. He felt a lot better when he was wearing clothes that he liked.

09:00

At police headquarters, more pictures had been put up on the wall of the incident room. The principal difference between the photos from Dalasýsla and those from Rangárvellir was simply the light; the former were taken in daylight, the latter at night under bright artificial illumination. The details were similar—maimed corpses, purplish blood.

The investigating team was unchanged, apart from Anna. It was her day off, so her colleague in forensics, Elías, was there instead. Once everyone was assembled, he gave a short description of the Rangárvellir crime scene.

"There was mud all over the place, and it was impossible to carry out a proper examination. We set up the lights and took photos so the body could then be removed. We closed the area off to traffic; there should be a patrol car there now, from Hvolsvöllur, taking care of security. We'll go back when it stops raining and things dry out a bit. They're forecasting better weather later today. Maybe then we'll be able to find some footprints, and possibly even spent shells."

The victim's clothing was laid out on a plastic cloth covering a table. Every part of it had been soaked, either by water or blood. An old camouflage parka, pants, a fleece jacket, long underwear, and woolen socks. The parka lay facedown. Two blackened holes of different sizes passed through the back and front of the garment, and on the back someone had roughly cut a patch from the outer layer, revealing the white lining.

Elías said, "The killer pulled the fabric up and cut the circle with a knife. He did the same to the victim in Dalasýsla."

Gunnar measured the patch with a tape. "Diameter is about ten centimeters. The murderer likes to take a trophy," he said.

Magnús read a description of the victim from his notebook. "Family man, about forty years old. Works as a freelance electrician. In the habit of going goose hunting on land belonging to relatives several times each fall."

"Other interests?" Gunnar asked.

"Active member of a nonconformist Christian congregation. It doesn't look as if he has anything in common with Ólafur Jónsson," Magnús replied.

"Apart from goose hunting," said Gunnar.

Magnús nodded. "We must, nevertheless, find a connection between them. Let's ask the relatives to make a list of family members, friends, colleagues, neighbors, and any others who those two guys have had any interaction with. It should be possible to find the name of a mutual acquaintance—unless, of course, they were chosen completely at random, in which case, we have a psychopath who will murder just about anybody, and it all becomes more difficult. Shall we make up a name for this killer?"

"Let's call him the Gander," Gunnar replied, "as in Goosey Gander."

Magnús wrote "the Gander" on the board and asked, "What do we know about the Gander?"

"He kills people," Gunnar replied.

"Why?" Birkir asked, not addressing anyone in particular.

Gunnar replied, "Maybe he's a fanatical wildlife activist who's finally lost it."

"You mean someone who's against goose hunting?" Magnús asked.

"Yeah."

Birkir said, "Well, nobody is likely to risk going hunting this fall—not now."

Magnús looked at him. "I wouldn't be too sure about that. I've heard about hunters banding together. They're going to put guys with rifles on guard in the hunting grounds. I think some of them are quite ready to take on our killer. It'll probably end in disaster, with the hunters shooting each other."

Gunnar said, "I want to have a closer look at this debt-collection agency. It's possible the Gander needed Ólafur out of the way for some reason. Then he kills another hunter to divert our attention."

"Have you got anyone particular in mind?" Magnús asked.

"No, but I want to pursue this."

"Okay," Magnús said. "But we must also keep the family in Litla-Fell in mind. They had the opportunity, a possible motive, and, perhaps, the desire to murder Ólafur."

Gunnar shook his head but said nothing.

"One thing came up yesterday," Dóra said suddenly. "I almost forgot it when the second murder was reported."

She blushed a little when the others looked at her. "I went and spoke to Ólafur's attorney, the guy who deals with his personal affairs and who will be looking after the estate and the will and all that. He told me Ólafur called him last Tuesday to consult with him about divorce proceedings."

"Really?" Magnús said. "He was intending to divorce his wife?"

"Yeah," Dóra replied, "that's what it looks like. But the attorney told me also that Ólafur's death didn't change anything for the wife. The terms of their prenup were that she'd get the same share of the assets whether the marriage ended in divorce or Ólafur's death."

Magnús was visibly relieved. "So we don't have to worry that the wife resorted to desperate measures because of a possible divorce," he said.

Dóra shook her head. "No, not because of the money, anyway."

10:30

Birkir's task was to visit Fridrik Fridriksson's family, and he took off as soon as the meeting at headquarters was over. Inside their apartment building on Kleppsvegur, he found their name on the directory; they lived on the fourth floor. He rang, and a woman's muffled voice came over the intercom: "Hello, who's there?"

She buzzed him in after he introduced himself. The stairwell was clean, but it was painted dark brown and was rather dimly lit. Birkir stepped briskly up the stairs—perhaps a bit too fast, for on the landing of the third floor he walked straight into a tall young woman who was on her way downstairs. She wore jeans and a T-shirt, and he knew she was not wearing a bra the moment his face ended up between her breasts.

Birkir was used to meeting women who were taller than he was and hardly ever thought twice about it. He was quite happy being only five foot five, even though that surely made him at least a head shorter than most of the men in Reykjavik—natives of Iceland tended to be tall, not compact like Birkir's own Vietnamese ancestors. In his view, height mattered less than being strong and quick, physical qualities he maintained through a disciplined exercise regimen. Still, the sudden, intimate contact with this unfamiliar woman on the stairs made him feel strangely small.

"I'm sorry," he gasped. "I didn't see you."

"That's okay," she said. "I'm not hurt."

She was shapely and nicely proportioned, despite being well over six feet tall. She was blonde, with short hair, and she had a pretty, if unusual, face. She disappeared down the stairs.

Birkir continued on his way until he spotted an open doorway on the fourth floor occupied by a woman holding an open Bible to her chest. She was dressed in black from head to foot, and a large, golden crucifix hung on a chain around her neck. Her silvery hair was pulled into a knot at the back of her head.

Birkir introduced himself, and she invited him in.

"Are you Fridrik's widow?" he asked.

The woman nodded.

"Allow me to offer my condolences on your husband's death."

"Thank you," the woman whispered.

All the drapes were closed, and the apartment was dark but for a few lit candles. On the walls hung framed reproductions of paintings, some more famous than others, all with biblical subjects. Some were familiar to Birkir; he owned a large book filled with classic paintings depicting scenes from the Bible. He'd received it as gift for his combined christening and confirmation, which had taken place on the same day when he was fourteen years old. For some years afterward, he had occasionally leafed through this book in the hope that it would help him to better understand the Christian message. In that respect it had not been of much help, but now he recognized a few of the reproductions hanging on the walls: *The Sacrifice of Isaac* by Caravaggio; *Madonna of the Fish* by Raphael; *The Last Supper* by da Vinci.

Utter silence reigned in the apartment. At first Birkir thought the woman lived alone, but as he entered the living room he saw four children sitting together on a sofa—three boys and a girl. The girl was in her early teens; she wept quietly. The boys looked to be about four, seven, and ten years old. Although their eyes were red-rimmed, all were silent.

A man got up from a chair, approached Birkir, and introduced himself.

"I am the leader of the congregation this unhappy family belongs to. I am here to try to provide support and solace through prayer and invocation to our father God Almighty and our Lord and Savior Jesus Christ."

The man was stout, looked to be around fifty years old, and sported a black wig and a small mustache.

Birkir introduced himself, and the man took his outstretched hand. His hand was soft and his fingers stubby; Birkir had the chance to notice the details since instead of releasing his hand immediately, the man took it in both of his, bowed his head, and said, "May God Almighty be with you in your work and give you His guidance in your search for the evil that exists amongst us, and in its eradication. Amen."

He finally let go of Birkir's hand and looked up.

Birkir stared at the preacher bemusedly and then turned to the widow and asked, "Was your husband an avid hunter?"

The woman did not reply and looked instead at the preacher. He said, "Yes. Fridrik liked to go hunting. He considered it his calling to avail himself of God's bounty, in moderation, to provide for himself and his family. He hunted both fish and fowl. The scriptures say: 'Be fruitful and increase in number; fill the earth and subdue it. Rule over the fish of the sea and the birds of the air and over every living creature that moves on the face of the earth.'" The man's voice rose in pitch as this speech proceeded, as if he were preaching to a mighty congregation.

Birkir waited until he was sure the man had finished, and then asked, "Who knew that Fridrik was planning to go hunting this particular morning?"

At this, the woman finally had something to say. "Only us— me and the children, I mean. And his cousin out in the country. Fridrik called him the evening before last and asked for permission to hunt in the pasture, the same as usual."

"Did Fridrik have any enemies?" Birkir asked.

Once again, it was the preacher who spoke up. "Satan is everyone's enemy. His followers hide in many places, and they are also our enemies."

The preacher crossed himself and continued. "Fridrik always upheld the sign of the cross, and he never flinched from such tasks as God Almighty has entrusted to our congregation."

"Are you saying that he sometimes quarreled with people about religious matters?"

"We pray for those who encounter serious troubles and setbacks in their lives. Sometimes our prayers are not gratefully received. Sometimes people resist and retreat. But once they experience the wonder of the living faith, they kneel down and pray with us."

"Can you think of anyone in particular with whom Fridrik might have quarreled?"

The preacher looked at the widow. She shook her head.

"Perhaps you'd like to think about it," said Birkir. "We need you to make a list of everyone that Fridrik was in any way connected to, starting with family, friends, and colleagues. All the groups are listed on this sheet of paper," he added, taking a folded sheet from his pocket and handing it to the woman. "Please also include the names of people you have prayed for recently. I'll pick it up tomorrow, if that's all right."

11:00

Gunnar was driving west to the Dalasýsla district for the third time in as many days, only this time he was by himself. The weather had improved considerably, traffic was light, and the journey was not unpleasant. Now and again the sun broke through the bank of clouds, and once when he glanced up, a rainbow had formed in the west where showers were still falling. Beautiful fall colors were beginning to emerge in the countryside, and Gunnar took pleasure in his unhurried progress.

His first stop was at the roadside kiosk at Búdardalur, where he bought a Coke and a couple of hot dogs and loaded them up with ketchup, mustard, and raw onions. Having satisfied his appetite, he presented himself at the sheriff's office, where he had a long conversation with the cop who had taken on the detective work in the district. The man had visited all of the farms in the vicinity of Litla-Fell and talked to their occupants, but nobody had noticed anything unusual the previous Thursday morning. None of the people he'd talked to had heard any shots or seen any emergency flares. The driver of the school bus said he had not seen anyone when he'd driven along the fork toward Litla-Fell at seven thirty in the morning; he did say that he would certainly have remembered, because there was never any traffic on that part of the route.

The policeman had turned up one thing, however: he'd contacted the Roads Administration and gotten a transcript of the data from a computer at Brattabrekka that did automatic traffic counts at ten-minute intervals throughout the day. It showed that traffic had decreased by midnight Wednesday night, and that after two o'clock only one or two cars an hour passed along the road. At five forty, two cars had passed in a ten-minute period, then no traffic had turned up for a full thirty minutes. One of the cars could have been Ólafur's, but who was in the other? Gunnar wished the computer data could tell him that. After six o'clock in the morning, traffic had quickly built up again.

"Could any of the vehicles possibly have been a motorcycle?" Gunnar asked.

"I don't know if the counters are able to detect the difference between cars and motorcycles," the policeman said. "I'll check it with the administration. I'm also going to put out the word that we want to talk to anyone who drove over Brattabrekka that night."

"Maybe that will turn something up. We'll see," Gunnar said, getting up and taking his leave.

There was nobody around at Litla-Fell as he drove into the yard, apart from two barking dogs. Kolbrún opened the door when he knocked.

"What is it now?" she asked and looked over his shoulder at the farmyard. "No guns today?"

Gunnar replied, "I need to debrief your boy. Then the case is closed as far as you're concerned. I hope."

She ushered him into the kitchen.

"Gutti is doing his homework. Dad is seeing to the animals in the outbuildings; if I know him right, he won't come in until you've gone. Do you have any business with him?"

Gunnar shook his head. "No."

"Good." Kolbrún called her son, who moments later appeared in the doorway holding an exercise book and a pencil.

"I can't work this multiplication problem out," he said. "It's got fractions."

"You'll have to get your teacher to help you on Monday," his mother said. "I've forgotten all my math."

She nodded toward Gunnar. "This man needs to talk to you about what happened on Thursday. You must tell him the whole truth about everything he asks you."

"Can we go on living here now that the bad guy's dead?" the boy asked Gunnar.

"That I don't know," Gunnar said. "Can you remember Thursday morning?"

"Yeah, I woke up when I heard guns. There were lots and lots of bangs." He pointed his finger into the air and made shooting noises.

"Where was your grandfather?"

"He was awake, too, of course."

"Do you sleep in the same room?"

"Yeah, we sleep upstairs."

"What happened then?"

"The shooting finally stopped, and I went back to sleep for a bit."

"What did your grandfather do?"

"He made porridge and woke me up again."

"You didn't see a car?"

"The school bus came to pick me up."

"You didn't see another car?"

"No. I only saw the bad guy's car. It was parked below the hay field."

Gunnar thought a moment before asking the next question. "Have you been baiting the hunter?"

"The bad guy?"

"Yeah."

"No."

"The sheriff says that someone scratched the man's car, and that something was stolen."

The boy shook his head emphatically and replied, "The black ram butted the car once and there was a tiny scratch. Grandpa and me didn't do nothing. Grandpa told the sheriff. Once the guy reversed into a fence post, and then he said we'd damaged his car. Grandpa had to put a new fence post in."

"But did someone cut the tire of his car?" Gunnar asked.

"That's what the bad guy said, but Grandpa said he'd driven over a sharp stone."

"Did you ever steal anything from the man?"

"No."

"Not even game?"

The boy shook his head. "Lappi, one of our dogs, once ate a big trout that the guy had caught and left by his car. He said we'd stolen it, but Grandpa says people should know better than to leave food around when dogs are on the loose."

The boy looked firmly at Gunnar. "Grandpa also told me to watch out for the bad guy, because he was tricky and a liar. I kept away from him when he was here."

Gunnar jotted something in his notebook.

"What did you do yesterday, you and your grandfather?" he asked.

"What did we do? We went looking for sheep. Some stragglers were missing, and me and Grandpa rode up onto the heath to look for them."

"Did you have a day off from school?"

Kolbrún replied, "I spoke to the teacher. We agreed it would do both Gutti and Dad good to go for a ride. It's like all you people think this incident hasn't affected them in any way. You should have offered them trauma counseling. That's what would have happened back in town."

"You're probably right," agreed Gunnar.

The boy said, "We found three yearlings, and a ewe lying on her back. Grandpa slaughtered her because she was so poorly. Then the weather got really bad, and I was soaking wet when I got home. But I wasn't terribly cold."

Gunnar said, "Right, okay, that's it. Thanks for your help."

He hesitated a moment and added, "Let me just have a look at this math problem that's bothering you."

15:15

Birkir pulled out the address and cell phone number of Jóhann Markússon, the man who'd lost an eye after being shot while hunting geese. His cell was off, so Birkir left a message and then sat down at his office computer and played Solitaire until Jóhann called back around four o'clock. After Birkir explained what it was about, Jóhann said, yes, if it was that important, he could come right away. He hung up, and Birkir turned back to the computer. He was just about to solve the game when the front desk notified him that he had a visitor.

The man was in his twenties, rather tall, dark-haired, and fit. He was wearing the black uniform of a security guard.

"Will this take long?" he asked. "My night shift is about to start."

His face was handsome, but he had divergent pupils that gave him a slightly strange expression. He wore small, elegant glasses that mitigated this effect somewhat. He had a few small scars on both cheeks.

"I won't hold you up," Birkir promised and showed him into an interview room.

"Tell me about what happened last fall," Birkir said when they had both taken a seat.

"When I was shot at?"

"Yes."

"Do you think it's got something to do with these killings?"

"Maybe."

"I don't think so."

"We'll find out."

"Well, I hope it's not related. Anyway, it was like this: I'd just moved to Reykjavik from Akureyri. By October, I still hadn't found work, and one day I just decided it would be cool to go goose hunting—the weather forecast for their evening flight was good. I'd always lived in the north and done a lot of hunting in the countryside around Eyjafjördur, but I was not very familiar with the hunting grounds here in the south. So, I headed off one afternoon and drove just east of Selfoss. I wasn't sure it would work out with the geese, but that didn't matter, because I was mainly in the mood to get outdoors and see the country. But when I got to the Landsveit district I saw some geese. They were quite a distance from the nearest house, so I didn't bother to get permission. My plan was just to bag two or three birds, if I managed to get within range. I know it's not right to do that, and I'm not usually a poacher. The circumstances just prompted me to take the chance."

Jóhann looked at Birkir as if he was expecting him to say that he understood, but Birkir simply asked, "What happened then?"

"I drove as close to the place as I could and then parked and continued on foot for a couple more kilometers. Finally, I found a ditch I could sneak along. I still had about a half-kilometer to go, and I knew that my route wasn't going to be easy. I'd gotten within about a hundred meters of the geese when I decided to peer up from the ditch to work out what to do next. But as soon as I raised my head I heard a shot and felt pain in my face. I jumped back down into the ditch and ran back to the car as fast as I could. I assumed I'd gotten into the line of fire of someone who'd seen a bird closer to the ditch than I'd been aware of."

"Why did you run away? Why didn't you yell for help?"

"I don't know. Probably just panic. I was there without permission, and I was embarrassed. This was probably a hunter who was licensed to be there, and I'd gotten him in trouble by sneaking around the place like that. I didn't know at the time how badly my face had been hurt; it was painful at first but it quickly went numb."

"Were you badly injured?"

"No, not very, although it hurt like hell getting shot in the face. I think I had a lucky escape, given the circumstances. The shooter must have been in a range of about forty to fifty meters, given the spread of the pellets. Most of the shot that hit me in the face penetrated the skin and stuck, but my clothing protected me from the rest. The doctor removed seven pellets from my face. The one that hit my eye was, of course, the one that caused the most damage. It hurt a lot the following day, and the wound wouldn't heal. I got an infection and my eye had to be removed a few weeks later. I got an artificial eye to replace it." Jóhann pointed to his left eye.

"So you never saw anybody?"

"No."

"Is it possible someone followed you and wanted to hurt you?"

Jóhann seemed so surprised at this question that he forgot to answer, and Birkir asked again, "Have you got any enemies?"

"No," Jóhann replied finally. "Definitely not."

"Did anybody know you intended to go hunting?"

"Yeah, I talked to a few people about it the previous evening—they knew I wanted to go hunting. I hadn't decided exactly when, though. I do remember asking if anybody knew of a good place. But I can't see what that has to do with my accident."

"Did someone suggest a place?"

"No. Nobody in the group knew anything about hunting."

"Have you been goose hunting this fall?"

"No." Jóhann shook his head firmly. "I don't hunt geese anymore."

17:45

The last task on Birkir's list for the day was to pay another visit to Helga, Ólafur Jónsson's widow.

This time he was able to park right outside the house, and the widow herself answered when he rang the doorbell. She wore jeans and a pink shirt, and her hair was tied back in a ponytail. She was a petite woman with a big bust.

Birkir introduced himself. "Can I ask you some questions?"

"About Óli?" she asked, as if he might have come on a completely different errand.

"Yes."

"Come in. Excuse the mess. I'm packing."

"Oh?"

"Yeah. The executor of the estate contacted me on behalf of the other beneficiaries. Meaning Óli's kids. They wanna sell the house."

"Immediately?"

"Yep. It seems there's a lot of demand for homes like this just now."

The young widow seemed to be pretty well composed, considering everything that had happened and the disruption it had caused, so Birkir decided to get straight to the point, "We've established that Ólafur was planning to divorce you."

"Yeah, that news seems to be all over town. That's why they don't feel the need to postpone the sale."

"They? You mean the children?"

"Yeah, or their mothers. They're all ganging up."

"What about you? Don't you also inherit?"

"We signed a prenup and made wills. I get about half a million krónur for each month of marriage. Whether ended by divorce or death. Not a fortune, but the good thing is it's in US dollars—four thousand a month."

"Why did he want a divorce?"

"Everyone seems to know the answer to that, too. I cheated on him a few times when he was abroad."

"How did he find out?"

"He got someone to spy on me. Some goddamn private eye who does work for the law firm. The fucking asshole put a camera in my bedroom."

"A video camera?"

"Yeah, digital. Internet ready, he said."

"Who said?"

"Óli."

"Are you saying that there are video recordings of you committing adultery?"

"'Committing adultery'? What planet do you come from? Yes, there are videos of me fucking in my own bed."

"Where are they now?"

"All the original discs were in Óli's safe-deposit box. The executor is probably jerking off to them right now."

"Who is with you in the videos?"

"My boyfriend, of course."

"Who is he?"

"I don't suppose there's any point in keeping that a secret now. It's a guy who works at the law firm. Tómas Benediktsson."

"Did Ólafur know who he was?"

"Sure. The camera had autofocus and excellent resolution and everything. These are classy movies."

"Was Ólafur going to discuss this with Tómas?"

"He said he was going to deal with the matter in his own way."

"What does that mean?"

"I've no idea. Wanna see the pictures?"

"Yes, if you don't mind."

She beckoned him to follow her into a study, where she turned on a computer. They waited while it booted up.

"He hid the camera on a shelf next to my bed," she said. "It was in a box that looked like a book. I didn't catch on until Óli brought the video home. A compilation of the best shots, he told me."

A moving image appeared on the screen. A man and a woman having sex. You could also hear the accompanying noises. Birkir had not seen the man before, but there was no mistaking the woman.

Silicone, he thought.

"Great soundtrack and all," Helga said. "Does it turn you on?"

Birkir looked at Helga and said, "Once I had to watch seven hundred porn tapes that the police confiscated from a video rental. Since then I've been immune, but thanks for asking."

"No problem."

"Do you know the name of the guy who spied on you? The private eye who does work for the law firm?"

"No. Óli never told me."

21:20

Birkir met up with Gunnar at the police station.

Gunnar had arrived in town about eight o'clock and was writing up his visit to Dalasýsla. He was lazy about taking notes, but he knew he had to get the details down on paper before he forgot them. It was not a long report, but it took him a good while to tap it into the computer using his two pudgy forefingers. It didn't help that, on his way in, he'd bought two hamburgers, a large portion of fries, and a two-liter bottle of Coke from the nearby kiosk. After consuming all of this at his desk, his keyboard was as greasy as it was sticky.

Birkir told Gunnar about his visit to the widow who was so well endowed with silicone.

"We need to have a chat with this Tómas guy—tonight if possible," he said.

Gunnar had finished the second hamburger as he listened, and now he nodded, his mouth full.

"The two of us need to go together," Birkir added.

Gunnar nodded again. He pulled up the national register on the computer and found the address they needed.

"He lives on Skúlagata, just like me," he grinned. "Not in the same house, of course."

It turned out that despite the shared neighborhood, the two addresses had little in common. While Gunnar's apartment was in an old house on the east side of Snorrabraut, Tómas lived in a brand-new high-rise on the corner of Vatnsstígur.

Birkir and Gunnar chose to go on foot, which meant they wouldn't have to return a police vehicle to the station afterward. It wasn't a long walk, and the weather was okay. Birkir planned to go straight home when they finished, but Gunnar fancied going for a beer; he knew he'd be able to call for a squad car if the need arose.

When they got to the building where Tómas lived, they decided to hang around in the hallway awhile to see if they could get inside without alerting him they were on their way. It was a twelve-story building with more than one apartment on each floor. Somebody was bound to show up.

A list of the building's residents was posted in a large frame on the wall. Next to the number of an apartment on the eighth floor they saw the names of Tómas Benediktsson and his wife; there were no children listed.

A security camera in the corner focused on them, and Birkir pressed his cell phone to his ear in the hope that their presence would seem less odd if he were seen to be calling someone.

"I would have liked to see the video of the widow," Gunnar said, scratching his balls.

"You watch more than enough porn already."

"It's more fun when there's a hidden camera. You know, like more real."

"You're a pervert," Birkir said.

They detected movement inside, and Gunnar got ready. An elderly woman leading a dog unlocked the door and was about to open it, but Gunnar jumped in.

"Please, let me help you," he said, holding the door open for her.

The woman smiled gratefully and went on her way.

They took the elevator up to the eighth floor.

If Tómas was surprised to see the policemen on his doorstep, he concealed it well. As he invited them in, he called into the apartment: "Darling, there are some gentlemen from the police who want to talk to me about Ólafur." He didn't wait for a reply before showing them into a spacious study and closing the door behind them.

There were three chairs, and they all sat down. There were also a desk with a computer, and crammed bookshelves lining the room.

Gunnar began, "When I interviewed you yesterday, you implied that you and Ólafur had been friends."

"Yes, we were friends."

"Right to the end?"

Tómas studied Gunnar pensively, then his demeanor changed suddenly and he smiled coldly. "No," he said, sharply. "We fell out. You've probably heard about it. That's the reason for this visit, isn't it?"

"Why did you fall out?" Gunnar asked.

"You've probably heard about that, too. I understand it's all over town. Ólafur found out that I'd been seeing his wife."

"And he didn't like it?"

"No, but he should've been grateful to me for showing him what a slut she was."

"So your purpose was to demonstrate that to him. You felt this was your duty?"

"Not exactly, no."

"How did Ólafur react to this information?"

"He threatened me."

"With what?"

"He wanted me to leave the firm and never show my face there again."

"Was he in a position to fire you?"

"No."

"What was he going to do if you refused?"

"He had a video of me and Helga. He threatened to put it on the Internet."

"How did you feel about that?"

"Obviously I couldn't let that happen. And I couldn't let him be the only one to make secret recordings, either. So I managed to record our conversation on my cell, and I told him that I'd report him to the police for extortion if that footage showed up on the Internet. There are laws that deal with conduct like that."

"Nevertheless, this confrontation had you on the defensive. It would not have been very good for you if this affair had been made public, would it?"

"No. That's certainly becoming clear now."

"Do you know who supplied Ólafur with the video?"

"Our firm has access to a company that provides security services. Installing surveillance equipment like this is their everyday work."

Birkir leaned forward in his seat. "The picture quality is much better than what an ordinary security camera can provide," he said.

Tómas transferred his gaze slowly from Gunnar to Birkir. "Have you seen this material?"

"Yes."

Tómas looked intently at Birkir, whose face remained expressionless.

Finally he said, "The company we use delivers the highest quality. It can be an advantage in some cases. Do the police have a copy of this recording in their possession?"

"No." Birkir shook his head.

"Just as well. That might have been bad for you. The law punishes that kind of invasion of privacy."

"We can get hold of a copy if needed," Birkir said.

Tómas was silent, but his cheek muscles betrayed that he was grinding his teeth.

Gunnar spoke again, "You told me yesterday that Ólafur had invited you to go hunting with him on Thursday. That was a lie, wasn't it?"

"Yes, it was a lie."

"But you did know he was going hunting?"

"Yes. I have access to his calendar on the office network."

"Did you follow him?"

"No."

"Why did you tell me that he had invited you?"

"It just popped into my head. I wasn't under oath or anything when I was talking to you. My mistake, nevertheless. I apologize."

"Where were you that morning?"

"Last Thursday?"

"Yes."

"I was here at home, asleep. I told you that yesterday."

"So you're saying some of what you said was true."

"Yes. Everything else was true."

"Were you alone?"

"Yes. My wife was in London."

"And where were you yesterday morning?"

"I was also here at home."

"Alone?"

"Yes."

"And this morning?"

"Also here at home, but this time with my wife."

"Does she know about the affair?"

"Yes. I told her today. I gather everybody knows about it now—our families and friends. We're going to start seeing a marriage counselor next week to try and fix things."

"Do you have a shotgun?"

"Yes."

"Are you prepared to hand it over for inspection?"

"My guns are not here."

"Guns? How many do you have?"

"Two shotguns and one rifle for hunting reindeer."

"Where are they?"

"They are in safe keeping at my parents' house in Seltjarnarnes."

"Do you mind if we fetch the shotguns from there this evening? We'd like to check them out."

"Go ahead, if it makes you feel better."

Tómas picked up the phone and dialed. While he was talking, Gunnar called headquarters and arranged for a uniformed officer to go collect the guns.

23:00

After the visit with Tómas, Gunnar was finally free to go out for a beer. He was looking forward to drinking with a fairly clear conscience, having completely abstained from alcohol for the previous two evenings. Birkir, on the other hand, went straight home.

Gunnar's favorite bar was on the lower end of Smidjustígur; it was his habitual haunt partly because its regulars were, he felt, suitably mature, especially those who frequented the place during the week. You could even have an intelligent conversation with some of them.

But the main reason he returned to the place again and again was the canvas-walled patio out back, which was always thick with cigarette smoke. Smoking had been banned inside bars and eateries for ages, but the proprietor had rigged up a cover for the outdoor space so people had somewhere to go when they needed to light up. This was where Gunnar preferred to hang out. He'd smoked for fifteen years, but had been forced to give it up after a persistent cough began to torment him. Since he couldn't smoke his own cigarettes, he became an enthusiastic passive smoker. In particular, he craved the mixture of beer and tobacco smoke; when he found it difficult to do without, nursing a beer on the smoke-filled patio gave him a boost. Even though his old mother lit a cigarette now and again, she never managed to produce enough smoke to satisfy this addiction.

The bar was filled with a boisterous weekend crowd when he walked in. Most of the regulars who appreciated the quiet weekday evenings avoided Friday and Saturday nights, when the crowd's loud chatter, laughter, and pushing and shoving disturbed the peace. A game of chess would have been impossible in the midst of the uproar. Gunnar recognized only a very few faces among all the young people, but he was determined to have his beer. He hoped they would leave him alone.

He elbowed his way through the press of people and rapped twice on the counter to attract the attention of the bartender, who nodded in acknowledgment and, as soon as he had finished serving another customer, disappeared into the back room, returning with a half-liter bottle of Holsten beer and a small square bottle of Jägermeister bitters. Neither of these was officially on sale here, but the landlord always kept some especially for Gunnar.

Gunnar handed over a credit card and poured the beer into a glass while the machine printed out the bill. Then he poured the bitters into a shot glass and placed the empty bottle on its side on the counter. Finally he signed the bill and nodded to the bartender. In all this noise, it was handy being able to do business without too much talking.

Taking a glass in each hand, he turned toward the room. There was an empty chair at a table for two, under the slope of a staircase; the other chair was occupied by Emil Edilon, who sat with a half-empty glass of whisky in front of him. Or was it half full? Gunnar needed to find out. Whether or not Emil could be bothered to chat would determine that. If he was in good form, sitting with him would be entertaining; if he wasn't, his sullen silence would be anything but fun.

Emil was a renowned writer in his sixties. Gunnar suspected he was gay, but the man didn't flaunt it. His generation was still mostly in the closet. In the early seventies, he had written a postmodern novel based on Dramatic Situation Number Twenty-Three of Georges Polti's famous book *The Thirty-Six Dramatic Situations*; it focused on the necessity of sacrificing loved ones. The novel had attracted attention in several countries. It had been translated into four languages. Not that sales had been impressive—from what Gunnar knew, it had sold all of twelve hundred copies.

Pushing his way through the crowd, Gunnar sat down opposite Emil, who did not look up. A slim man with long, wavy, silvery hair parted in the middle, Emil also had a neatly trimmed goatee and a pointed nose that made him somewhat striking. Thick glasses shielded his sad eyes.

"Half empty," thought Gunnar and he remained silent. He briefly lifted the bitters to his nose, and then emptied the glass in a single gulp. He closed his eyes and grimaced at the bracing sensation of the bitters going down. Finally he took a generous sip of the beer.

"You've got twenty minutes," Emil said without looking at him.

Gunnar looked up. He didn't quite understand what his companion was driving at. Over the previous six years, Emil had been writing a major crime novel, and, from time to time, they had debated the nature and conventions of this genre; apart from that, they did not discuss police matters.

"What do you mean?" Gunnar asked.

"The idiot Ginger Journalist made a deal that the Blue Baron would call him the minute you appeared." Emil nodded toward a bald man with a bushy gray mustache and a purple strawberry mark on one cheek, propping up the bar and staring with great interest at the sign over the emergency exit.

"The Blue Baron made the call as soon as you came in. The Ginger Journalist lives in Lower Breidholt, and it'll take him a half hour to get here. That was ten minutes ago. I assume you're not keen to give an interview tonight?"

"No," Gunnar said. "Preferably not. The superintendent deals with all media relations. I'm not allowed to say anything."

Emil looked at the clock. "Nineteen minutes," he said. "You'll never get rid of the Ginger Journalist if he nabs you."

"No, probably not," Gunnar said and sipped his beer. "How's the novel coming?"

Finally Emil looked at him, "There's a crisis, my friend. A goddamn crisis. I'm tearing up two pages for every one that I write. I need an interesting cop to write about."

He took out a long pipe and stuffed it with tobacco.

"You can write about me," Gunnar said.

"You?"

"Yeah, me and Birkir. You know him. We're good together."

"You and the slit-eyed show-off?"

"Yeah."

"It's impossible to make you two interesting."

98

Emil lit up, and the most disgusting tobacco smoke Gunnar had ever smelled filled the air. Emil was actually famous for the stench created by his favorite tobacco. There were many theories as to what additives were responsible for this stink; surely, none of them classified as health products.

A bouncer came over to the table. "Please smoke outside," he said.

"I'm going," replied Emil, and blew out a plume of smoke.

Gunnar coughed. "Do the cops need to be anything special?" he asked.

"Yes. Interesting policemen drive the story forward. You two, on the other hand, have the personalities of goldfish. You're still living with your mother, and the slit-eyed show-off gets off on pressing his pants. There's no pain in either of you."

He looked at the clock. "Fifteen minutes."

"I've had toothaches," Gunnar said.

"Toothaches! Jesus Christ. You think that gives you a dimension?"

Gunnar did not reply, instead asking, "But why do the policemen in a crime novel have to be so interesting? Why can't they be more like dentists, for example?"

Emil looked up from his pipe. "Have you ever read an exciting story about root canal work?"

Gunnar refused to give up. "Another character in the story can provide the driving force—for instance, the victim or the murderer. Use one of them to add depth to the story. Use the police to simply convey information."

Emil shook his head and said, "The policemen in my story must show initiative and some intellectual process. They must outmaneuver the criminal and lay a trap for him. They must have something between their ears."

Gunnar reflected in silence. "That's a thought," he finally said. Then he drained his beer glass, got up, and went home.

23:30

"*Hakuna Matata.*" A catchy melody sang out from the television, which was turned down low. Onscreen, lively cartoon figures danced to the beat of the music.

Detective Anna Thórdardóttir had finally arrived home after a difficult day at work. Her weekend had been ruined shortly after lunch, when she was called out to deal with a case. All her colleagues in forensics were occupied with the goose hunter killings, so when an unrelated matter came up, it was inevitable that she was called in. That was how things sometimes panned out; weeks might pass without anything important for the team to deal with, and then a load of cases came along all at once, usually right before the weekend.

This case involved the suicide of a forty-year-old stockbroker who had lost all of his money, together with that of many of his clients, thanks to unsuccessful dealings in foreign currency forwards. He had driven his SUV to an old gravel pit out of town. The vehicle was worth seven million krónur, but the stockbroker didn't own it—he'd been leasing it, or trying to, anyway. But he missed payments and the company had sent him a letter requesting its immediate return, which he left on the passenger seat to avoid any confusion over the car's ownership. He also brought along a thirty-meter-long rope. He'd tied one end of it to the front axle of a rusting industrial-size digger with flat tires that had been abandoned in the pit. He'd fashioned the other end into a wide noose, which he passed through the opened tailgate and looped over the driver's headrest. Having drunk a quarter of a bottle of brandy and smoked three cigarettes—leaving the stubs on the ground next to the car—he got behind the wheel and put the noose around his neck.

It's impossible to say how long he sat in this position, but he gave himself enough time to call the national emergency number and report a suicide, while carefully describing the location. He then put the phone aside without breaking off the call, so that on the emergency service's recording you could hear him start the car, step violently on the gas, and then brake hard a moment later. Between the rev of the engine and the sound of the brakes you could hear—if you played back the recording very slowly—a kind of cracking noise.

The patrolmen who arrived first at the scene turned the ambulance back and called the detective division. Símon, least busy of the violent crime team at the time, was sent to the scene. When he had finished vomiting behind the digger, he called for assistance from forensics, and as everyone else was busy, Anna had to report for duty. Her task was to establish that the man had acted entirely alone.

The body sat bolt upright, seatbelt fastened, and the head lay neatly in its lap. The fingers gripped the steering wheel so tightly that they had to use tools to loosen them. The right foot had pushed the brake right down to the floor.

What surprised the cops most was that the braking marks began five meters farther away from the old digger than the length of the rope allowed. It looked as if the man's last reflex had been to brake when he felt the rope tighten around his neck, but the car had continued moving for five meters before his foot reached the pedal. By that time, the head had been severed from the body and fallen into the man's lap. The ABS brakes then stopped the car at eight meters—a good thing, actually, as otherwise it would have careered off into the rough moorland and probably been trashed. The only thing the rental office needed to do so they could lease the car out again was to clean up the blood. Then again, it was a lot of blood.

There was not much Anna could do except take fingerprints from the car's door handles and gearshift. She took a number of photographs and measured the area, and lastly picked up the man's head with both hands and placed it carefully on one end of the stretcher the morticians had brought. Men stronger than she lifted the body and set it down next to the head.

Having completed the crime scene investigation, Anna went to the detective division's headquarters to write up the suicide and upload the pictures onto her computer. Then she checked the progress reports on the goose hunter killings. She dreaded going home. Keeping busy at work kept the memory of what she had just witnessed at bay; but she knew that as soon as she relaxed, it would be difficult to banish the gruesome crime scene from her thoughts.

When she finally forced herself to go home, sometime after eleven o'clock, her husband had already gone to bed. That was okay; she never discussed her work with him, anyway. She took the vow of confidentiality that came with her job seriously. Besides, he had always been a lousy listener when she needed an outlet for her emotions. He was a straightforward man who drove a large concrete mixer and loved watching soccer on television. He watched crime thrillers, too. Preferably not the news.

Anna had her own method for forgetting her day. She had collected a stack of Disney videos to watch when she spent time with her grandchild; she watched them on her own sometimes to unwind. She put on *The Lion King* while her supper cooked in the microwave. It was a TV dinner that had reached its sell-by date, and to make it more palatable she opened a two-liter bottle of Coke. When the food was done cooking, she settled onto the sofa with her dinner, glancing around to make sure she had a sleeping pill nearby, just in case she didn't fall asleep easily. A pack of cigarettes rested next to the ashtray by her side.

"*Hakuna Matata*, what a wonderful phrase."

CHAPTER 4

03:10

Birkir was awakened by the ringing of the telephone. It took him a few seconds to emerge from a strange dream: He'd been surrounded by dancing white creatures, but they weren't ghosts. They were snowmen, he realized—snowmen with top hats and carrot noses—that had been whizzing through the air as he tried to take them down with a shotgun. He never managed to hit one in his dream, even though he loaded and fired the gun, over and over.

He lay still for a long time with his eyes open, puzzling over this while the phone continued ringing relentlessly. Finally he picked up the receiver.

"This is Birkir," he said, looking at the clock. The illuminated dial showed that it was the middle of the night.

A familiar voice said, "Hi. It's Gunnar. I've been thinking."

"Go back to sleep," Birkir said gruffly.

"No, listen. The weather's perfect for goose hunting just now."

Birkir coughed and cleared his throat. "Goose hunting? I don't hunt. And I thought you had more than enough on your plate."

"Yeah, well, we don't really go hunting, not exactly—more like, I get into my hunting gear and you hide in the back of the car. First, we'll stop and get gas from Ártúnshöfdi at around four o'clock. There won't be many people around, especially given what's been happening. If the Gander is waiting there for a victim, he might just follow us. We'll head for Borgarfjördur and see what happens."

"What if he shoots at us?"

"We'll be better equipped, and there are two of us."

"I think this is a bad idea."

"If you don't come with me, I'll go alone."

"That's an even worse idea."

"You coming, then?"

Birkir thought about it. "Oh, all right," he finally said. "It might be worth trying just this once. But I have a very bad feeling about this. Which car do we take?"

"Obviously not a squad car. I've borrowed a decent SUV from one of my friends who hunts. We can use that."

"Did you wake the guy up to borrow his car?" Birkir asked.

"Yeah."

"What did he say?"

"It was fine. He owed me a favor."

"What sort of favor?"

"Never mind. Just get ready. I'll be starting out soon." Gunnar hung up.

Birkir shivered as he crawled out of bed. He didn't know much about goose hunting, but he knew it involved standing still and feeling cold. He would have preferred to wear the old snowsuit he kept in the lumber room, but it was bright orange—probably not a practical choice for either goose hunting or hiding from a murderer in the backseat of an SUV.

During his conversation with Gunnar, it had occurred to Birkir to try to talk the man out of his idea—only briefly, though. He knew his colleague was serious enough about the idea to take the trip alone if Birkir chickened out. He was certain that Gunnar had been mulling over this plan ever since the investigation had turned up a time-dated gas station receipt on victim number two. Gunnar probably hadn't slept much of the last two nights as he'd thought it over. Once he'd made up his mind, he'd phoned. Birkir knew all this because Gunnar was his friend. Basically his only friend.

They had met when Birkir first joined the Reykjavik uniformed police force. Gunnar was quite a bit older, with years of experience under his belt. You could hardly imagine two more different characters, but they nevertheless got along together very well while on the job. Neither of them had extended family in Iceland, and both felt willing to take shifts during holidays when others preferred to have time off. These were often uneventful stints, and that allowed them time to chat or just be quiet together. They also complemented each other physically. Small of stature, Birkir could only offer limited help in situations where brute force was required, whereas Gunnar was strong enough to fight for them both if it was necessary. Birkir, on the other hand, was a good runner and useful in a chase. Finally, Gunnar tended to do the talking, while Birkir wrote reports. They had to split up, though, after Gunnar was appointed to the detective division. In his new position, he quickly began to miss his colleague. It wasn't long before he started pulling all sorts of strings with the police administration and, eventually, succeeded in getting Birkir reassigned to his new division.

Despite having such different interests, the pair also spent quite a bit of time together outside of work. For many years, Gunnar had been in the habit of having a beer as soon as he came home from his shift, followed by a Jägermeister to go with another beer after supper—a custom he had picked up from his mother, who'd needed the extra kick of the German liqueur to go with her low-alcohol pilsner during the many years when strong ale was prohibited in Iceland. This routine of his, however, created a bit of a transport problem for Gunnar if he wanted to go out later in the evening, since he wouldn't dream of attempting to drive under the influence.

He got into the habit of phoning Birkir instead. There was no danger that Birkir would be incapable of driving, since he couldn't drink alcohol. It made him ill—some sort of allergy. He could take one glass of white or red wine with food, but that was all. Birkir didn't see this as a drawback, since he had another source of intoxication: running. Every week he jogged a total of nearly ninety kilometers, with one run being at least thirty. The endorphins this activity released in his body provided the only high he needed. Birkir didn't mind driving Gunnar around town in his spare time, because the man was easy company when under the influence. The truth was, he never actually looked drunk. Their habit of driving around together turned into a habit of doing things together—going to movies, soccer matches, and concerts, preferably jazz. They went out like this a couple of times a week usually. Once a month, they would hang out at Gunnar's apartment and play rummy with old María, a tradition she cherished.

The first time Gunnar had shown up drunk for the evening shift, Birkir had driven him straight home and told everyone he was ill. The second time it happened, Birkir did the same but told his friend that if there was a third time, he would take him directly to the rehab center for treatment. Gunnar would not admit to being an alcoholic; he was merely doing what his mother had done all her life, and he only drank two types of alcohol, Holsten beer and Jägermeister bitters. But never again did he show up drunk for his shift; he even took it one step further and made it a goal to go to bed sober several days a week.

03:50

As Gunnar drove up to the house, he saw Birkir waiting on the sidewalk clad in dark-green Gore-Tex pants, a dark-blue quilted parka, and a black wool hat. That would do to conceal him in the dark, Gunnar thought. He was wearing his old camouflage hunting jacket.

Birkir climbed into the rear seat of the vehicle, a Toyota RAV4, and endeavored to make himself as inconspicuous as possible. The idea, after all, was to pretend that Gunnar was going hunting alone. Gunnar had thrown a dark blanket on the seat for Birkir to take cover under if necessary. In the back, he had stowed a shotgun in its bag, two decent rifles, and two pairs of high-powered binoculars. One of the rifles was his. The other belonged to his usual hunting partner, who had young children at home and no safe place to keep the weapon and so had asked Gunnar to keep it in the gun closet in his bedroom. The rifles were light and manageable, and Gunnar and his friend used them mainly for shooting seagulls—usually the black-backed variety—or for target practice. Both had telescopic sights.

Gunnar had thought ahead to bring a sack containing some foam-rubber decoys, and a picnic bag with a coffee flask and some sandwiches. He'd also packed two pocket-size walkie-talkies that he'd picked up from headquarters; each had a headset with an earpiece and a microphone so the two of them could easily stay in touch if they needed to take separate positions.

They stopped at the Ártúnshöfdi gas station, and Gunnar took plenty of time filling the tank at the automatic pump. He strolled around the car, wiping invisible dirt from the headlamps while glancing around. The area around the gas station was brightly illuminated on all sides, and there was a full moon, a clear sky, and good visibility, so anyone wishing to hide nearby would have had difficulty. There were no other cars at the station and very little traffic on the western highway at this early hour. The store was well lit, and you could see the attendant inside reading a newspaper. This place stayed open around the clock; drivers on their way out of the city often stopped here if they needed fuel or refreshments.

Suddenly a vehicle with a security company logo appeared. It drove in a circle around the gas station, and then stopped by the main door. The security guard got out of the car and disappeared into the store. A short while later he reappeared, carrying a paper cup of steaming coffee, walked toward the pumps, and examined the hoses. Voices came from the walkie-talkie clipped to his jacket, and he uttered a few words into its microphone as he continued with his task.

"Good morning," he said to Gunnar as he strode past. Getting into his car, he pulled quickly out of the parking lot and drove away.

Gunnar replaced the gas tank cover and got back into the Toyota.

"I met that security guard yesterday," Birkir said from his hiding place in the back seat. "He's the guy that got shot in the face back east about a year ago. I interviewed him just before his night shift."

"This city is extremely small," replied Gunnar.

They drove off, heading north through Mosfellsbær. Not far from the intersection with the Thingvellir road they met a police patrol car, which turned around just behind them and chased them, its blue lights flashing.

"What the fuck do these guys want?" Gunnar said, while Birkir sank to the floor behind the front seat and covered himself with the blanket. They had to keep up the pretense that Gunnar was a lone hunter on the move.

"There's no peace," Gunnar said. "First that security guard and now this."

He stopped the vehicle, and the patrol car pulled up behind them. An officer got out and walked toward the Toyota carrying a flashlight. Gunnar got out his wallet and extracted his driver's license.

"Where are you going?" the policeman asked, taking the license and examining it.

"I'm heading for Borgarfjördur," Gunnar replied. He did not remember having seen this cop before, and he hoped that was mutual.

"What for?"

"Goose hunting."

"Do you think that's advisable, given the recent killings?"

"I'll be careful."

"I have to ask you to turn around and go back to bed," the policeman said, handing back the license. "There's a dangerous guy on the loose."

"Are you authorized to stop me?" Gunnar asked.

"No, but I think it's for the best that you don't proceed."

"Well, I'll take responsibility for my own comings and goings, if you don't mind," Gunnar said. "Was there anything else?"

"Do you have a gun license?"

Gunnar had been expecting this question and had the right documents at the ready. The patrolman inspected them carefully and handed them back.

"Was there anything else?" Gunnar asked again.

"No."

"I'll be on my way, then."

The policeman stepped aside, and Gunnar drove off. A short while later, the patrol car caught up to them. It followed them closely. "Goddamn assholes. They've appointed themselves as a goose preservation society," Gunnar said. "The Gander is hardly likely to follow us while these bastards are on our tail."

A few minutes later, an eighteen-wheeler came zooming toward them—probably at a speed somewhat over the limit, for the patrol car slowed, switched on its blue lights, and turned around. It rapidly disappeared in the direction from which they had come, chasing down the truck.

Gunnar kept to ninety kilometers per hour. It was slow enough to allow anyone wanting to follow them to do so easily, but fast enough to appear normal. They went through the Hvalfjördur tunnel, stopping at the pay booth. Birkir studied the security cameras by the barrier while Gunnar offered a one-thousand-krónur bill and asked for the receipt.

"We should check on how those cameras work," Gunnar said, as they drove off. "I wonder if they're always on, with a time code showing, or if they just activate when a car runs a red light."

"I'll check that out when we get back to town. But they must at least take a picture when someone goes through without paying," Birkir said.

"I don't think the Gander is going to let himself get caught like that," Gunnar said as he turned east off the circle.

As they drove along the northern shore of Hvalfjördur, two cars overtook them at high speed.

Birkir raised himself up in the seat and looked through the rear window, using one of the pairs of binoculars. He saw no one behind them, but looking across the fjord he could see the lights from the cars on Kjalarnes.

"I don't know if we're going to get anywhere with this," he said.

Gunnar didn't reply immediately, but then said, "We'll continue as planned. If the worst comes to the worst, this may just turn into an excellent goose hunt."

They drove on toward the bridge over Borgarfjördur but swung right just before it and headed northeast up the fjord. Birkir had spotted the lights of a car a ways back on the highway, so Gunnar slowed down to make sure that whoever it was could see they had turned off. After driving on for a little over twenty kilometers, Gunnar turned onto a side track and parked in a spot where the car would be plainly visible from the road. They waited there for several minutes but saw no traffic. From this place there was a good view over the large meadows bordering Hvítá River; in the bright moonlight they could observe their surroundings almost as distinctly as if it were day.

"Let's go down there." Gunnar pointed to a spot a couple of kilometers away, where two ditches met in the meadows. "I've often bagged birds in that place, and the landowner's given me permission to work the patch anytime, because I did him a favor once. You take a rifle and sneak on ahead as fast as you can. When you're halfway there, lie down and keep an eye on me with the binoculars. I'll just stroll along like a regular hunter, not looking around. Use the walkie-talkie to let me know if you see anything unusual."

He motioned to Birkir to hand him one of the rifles, which he loaded and handed back to him.

"You know how to use this, don't you?"

Birkir examined the weapon. "Yes, I've used a gun like this."

They donned the walkie-talkies and turned off their cell phones to prevent the radio interference their signals would create.

"All ready?" Gunnar asked.

"Yes."

"Then go."

Gunnar switched on the internal car light as Birkir slid out the rear door facing away from the road; he extinguished the light once his partner had disappeared into the ditch below the track. He waited for five minutes, then got out, put the second rifle in the bag with the shotgun, and hoisted it onto his shoulder. He hung his binoculars on the other shoulder, took the sack of decoys, and got going.

"Testing, testing, one, two, three," he said into the walkie-talkie. "Are you there?"

"I'm ready," came Birkir's reply.

Gunnar stepped over a low fence and made his way through the long grass alongside the ditch. At one point, he had to climb down into a ditch that barred his path and jump across its water-logged bottom. After ten minutes he reached Birkir, sheltering behind an old hay bale and scanning the area around the car with his binoculars.

"There's definitely nobody following you," Birkir said.

"Stay there while I'm on the move, and then follow me," Gunnar said, walking on. When he got to the spot he had been aiming for, he stopped and set down his bags. He raised the binoculars and immediately spied the back of Birkir, who was still on the lookout. After checking the rest of the area, he said into the walkie-talkie, "You can come now, but stay out of sight in the ditch if you can."

He continued to watch from his position overlooking the ditch until Birkir arrived.

"Stay hidden down there," Gunnar said. "I'll put up the decoys and then join you."

"Where are you going to put them?" Birkir asked.

"I'll set up two groups within range, one on each side of us, with empty space in between. Geese aren't attracted to a landing place just because other birds are already there; it's about the grouping. They're smart enough to be frightened off if it doesn't look right. You have to have the correct spacing so that the geese will feel safe—and sense that because other birds are there, there's no danger."

Birkir smiled. "Do you think your decoys will also do that for the Gander?"

Gunnar didn't reply, but began arranging his decoys—eight in one cluster and twelve in the other. Each group included two birds with their necks stretched up as if on lookout. The others were grazing. All had their beaks facing into the wind.

Decoys deployed, Gunnar took the rest of his kit and crawled down to join Birkir. It was nearly six o'clock, and the two of them hunkered down as best they could in the bottom of the ditch.

"I'm cold," Birkir said after a while.

"You're a sissy," Gunnar replied.

They were silent for a bit then Gunnar heard Birkir softly recite something:

"In the pale light, absent words,
arcs a lone bird over moorland;
silence reigns: ashimmer here
scenes of beauty, sharp and clear."

"What the fuck is that?" Gunnar whispered. Ignoring the question, Birkir continued:

"Steepling fell-sides, stony gray
Stories tell of times long over—
heaviest on my heart lie yet
hurt, remorse, a deep regret."

"Where did you hear that bullshit?" Gunnar said.

"On the radio," Birkir replied.

"Is it a poem?"

"Yes, or, actually, more like the lyrics of a song."

"Right."

"It suddenly seemed to fit in with this morning."

"Yeah?"

"Yes, but there's a strange thing."

"What?"

"I can't remember the third and fourth verses."

"Right," said Gunnar, and he peered over the edge of the ditch.

"I'm sure I heard the other verses as well, but now I can't remember even one line. Odd."

Gunnar looked at Birkir and shook his head.

Daybreak is different in bright moonlight than when the skies are overcast. There is no slow build to dawn; just before sunrise, the light from the moon pales a little and morning simply arrives without any sudden explosion of light. Gunnar and Birkir noticed its arrival nonetheless. They watched as the compact shadows of the decoys, which had been cast to the east by the moonlight, were replaced by elongated shadows to the west as the first rays of the sun hit. Then they heard the geese. Gunnar picked up his shotgun and loaded it with three number two magnums.

"I'll watch the geese. You stay on lookout," he whispered.

The first gaggle they heard flew past, and silence descended again.

"Just keep calm. There'll be others," Gunnar said.

"I'm completely calm, and I'll stay calm even if we see no more geese," Birkir said, checking his watch.

Ten minutes later, they again heard the honking of geese, and this time the flock came closer. There were between ten and twenty birds, and they circled the site at a height of two hundred meters. Then they headed into the wind toward the gap between the groups of decoys. Gunnar fired the first shot when the birds were at a range of twenty meters. One goose fell to the ground, and he fired twice more, bringing down two more birds; the remainder of the flock dispersed to the north, honking their alarm. Gunnar was about to jump up to the rim of the ditch, but suddenly changed his mind.

"Are we alone?" he asked Birkir.

"Yes," his partner replied. He had been watching the other direction.

Gunnar clambered up and gathered the dead geese. He put them down next to one of the decoy groups, arranging them with their heads under their wings. Then he returned to Birkir in the ditch and reloaded his gun.

"Now it's your turn," he said.

"Mine?"

"Yeah. Have you ever shot geese?"

"No."

"But you know how to use a shotgun, don't you?"

"Yes, I took a training course."

"In that case you have to give it a try. I'll keep watch."

Birkir took the gun and held it at the ready. They could hear geese, but they knew it would be a wait before another flock decided to settle on the patch. Gunnar surveyed their surroundings through his binoculars, but Birkir had the feeling he was looking for geese rather than people. His suspicion was confirmed when Gunnar whispered, "The geese that come here have probably spent the night on the sand flats over by Hvítá River. They eat the sand to help with their digestion and then make for the hay fields in the morning to eat the grass."

"Are they here all year round?"

"No. They'll be migrating soon to the British Isles, when the high-altitude winds begin to blow from the north. They come back at the end of March. It's only the geese in downtown Reykjavik that stay here all winter, but I wouldn't want to eat them."

Half an hour later, things finally began to happen. A large flock of geese appeared and headed straight for them, flying into the wind. When the birds were directly overhead Birkir stood up and fired a single shot, and the leading goose fell to the earth like a stone. The other geese fled, turning sharply north after a moment's disarray, and disappeared, honking, into the mist that was now forming over the marsh.

"Why didn't you shoot again?" Gunnar asked, surprised. "You could have gotten two more."

Birkir was silent. "What for?" he asked finally.

"To fully experience the thrill of the hunt, of course."

Birkir looked at his partner. "I only need to shoot one goose to know what it feels like to shoot a goose."

Gunnar looked at him in disbelief. "And what does it feel like?" he finally asked.

Birkir thought for a moment. "I felt a kind of primitive pleasure when the bird dropped to the ground. Some sort of hunting instinct is probably intrinsic to the human animal, even though generations have passed since it was necessary for survival."

"So you didn't enjoy it?"

"It was, in some way, similar to the pleasure I experience when a criminal confesses to guilt after a long interrogation. That pleasure also has its roots in rather primitive urges that I'm not particularly proud of. So I don't think I'll be pursuing the 'thrill of the hunt' any further."

Gunnar looked at his partner and shook his head. "You are a bit peculiar, but I think I've told you that several times before. Let's call it a day. Let's go home."

Dividing the load between them, they walked back to the car. The sun had risen now and it was broad daylight; it wasn't likely anyone would try to ambush them now, but they nevertheless kept their wits about them. When they had stowed the weapons and their bag in the back of the car, they got in, and Birkir turned on his cell phone.

"Eight unanswered calls," he said. A beep indicated there was voice mail. He called the mailbox number and listened.

"Another hunter's been shot," he said.

"Shit," Gunnar said. "Where?"

"To the west of us—the Mýrar area—this morning."

"Goddammit, he took the same route as we did. Our plan almost worked."

Birkir continued listening to the voice mail messages. Then he said, "The victim wasn't alone. His companion got away and was able to call for help. They're setting up roadblocks. Now we have a chance of catching him."

10:15

This time it took Gunnar and Birkir a while to locate the area where the shooting had taken place. They turned off the

Snæfellsnes road at the wrong intersection and had to call the police in Borgarnes for guidance. But when they finally reached their destination, the crime scene looked similar to the others. And yet the details weren't exactly the same—not quite. This killing seemed to have happened faster, and the victim had not been alone. He was an older man, probably about seventy, and had been shot once in the center of the back at very close range. There was a fist-size hole between his shoulder blades, and the force from the shot had thrown the man forward onto his face. His hands were down by his sides—he hadn't even had time to try to break his fall. A newish shotgun lay by his side, and he had an ammunition belt around his waist. A large bag of decoys lay overturned at his feet.

The victim's companion sat in the backseat of a police car that was parked nearby with its engine running. His head was buried in his hands, and he was so shocked and shaken that he was scarcely able to speak. A patrolman from Borgarnes who was at the wheel of the car was trying to calm the man down, with little visible result.

"The Gander is getting more efficient," Gunnar said to Birkir. "One shot that kills his adversary immediately. No gunfight and no chase."

Birkir glanced over his shoulder at the patrol car. "Do you want to talk to the witness?"

"Yeah, leave that to me," Gunnar replied.

"Right now?"

"Yeah, it's for the best," Gunnar replied. "It will be interesting to hear what he has to say about this. Maybe now we'll find out more about what we're dealing with."

Gunnar went over to the car and got into the backseat.

"Good morning," Gunnar said, nodding to the driver.

"Morning," the cop answered. The distraught man merely nodded.

Gunnar studied him carefully. He was bald and had a small, delicate build, a trim mustache, and round glasses. He looked about forty. Gunnar was a bit surprised. The man hardly looked like the type to go hunting at all, let alone when there was a dangerous murderer on the loose who specialized in pursuing goose hunters. He was wearing a standard hunting outfit that hung loosely on his compact frame.

Gunnar offered his hand. "Gunnar Maríuson, detective."

With a limp handshake, the man replied, "Ragnar Jónsson."

As if saying his own name burst a dam, the man's words came out in a torrent. "I told my father-in-law we shouldn't do this trip. It wasn't worth the risk. But he was adamant, so I had no option but to go with him. Then suddenly, this happens. There was nothing I could do. Nothing at all." The man spoke so fast he couldn't catch his breath between words and was red in the face by the time he stopped for air.

Gunnar took out his notebook and a pen. "The deceased was your father-in-law?"

"Yes. Bára and I. We're married. Bára is his daughter, and my wife."

"What was his name?"

"His name is, I mean, was—" the man gulped and had to pause momentarily before being able to continue. "Vilhjálmur Arason. He is—I mean was—retired. He once owned a small fishing company."

Gunnar tried to soothe him. "Keep calm, my friend. I need you to tell me what happened right from the start, clearly and distinctly. Try to breathe deeply. When did you decide to go on this hunting trip?"

The man took some deep breaths before replying, this time a little more calmly. "We've gone hunting on this particular weekend every year since 1992. In 2002 we put the trip off due to the weather—you couldn't stand up, the wind was so strong—but apart from that it's always been the same Sunday."

"So everything was going along normally this time?"

"Yes. Everything was completely normal. Two weeks ago, my father-in-law started talking about the trip and making preparations. He wouldn't hear of putting it off, despite these killings. He arranged the hunting license with the farmer who owns the land. They are old friends—were friends, I mean."

"Do you go hunting often?"

"No. I just take this one trip each fall. My father-in-law goes much more often, but then, he's retired."

"Where do you both live?"

"In Reykjavik."

"When did you leave this morning?"

"I think it was just after four o'clock."

"Did you buy gas on the way?"

"No. The tank was full."

"Who did the driving?"

"I did, but it's my father-in-law's car."

"Did anybody follow you?"

"No. I don't think so. Do you think that somebody followed us? Is that possible?"

Gunnar ignored the question and continued. "Did the police stop you on the way?"

"No, of course not. I didn't drive particularly fast."

"When did you arrive here?"

"Sometime before six."

"What happened then?"

"We had gotten our things ready, and my father-in-law moved off ahead of me. I got caught up putting on my ammunition belt, and he'd gone on about a hundred meters when I heard a shot."

"What were you doing?"

"I was standing by the car, I was about to lock it."

"Where was the car?"

"More or less where it is now." Ragnar pointed through the window at an SUV.

"What happened then?"

"I looked up and saw my father-in-law lying in the grass. There was a guy standing over him holding a shotgun. I realized immediately what had happened and ran back to the car and reversed up the track as fast as I could. When I'd made it a safe distance I called the emergency number. It took me a while to press the right keys, I was so shocked."

"Did you see the man again?"

"No."

"Did you see another car?"

"No."

Gunnar turned to the policeman in the front seat. "Do you know this area?" he asked.

"Yes," the policeman replied.

"Any idea how the killer might have fled the scene?"

"No. I can't figure it out. The only drivable road in or out of here is this track that we're on. He must have come on foot and left his car elsewhere. When we got the call and heard what had happened, we immediately closed off the highway this side of Borgarnes. The police in Snæfellsnes also blocked it to the north at the

Heydalsvegur intersection. We've been tightening the noose over the past hour."

Gunnar turned back to the small, bespectacled man sitting next to him. "You say you saw the killer at a distance of a hundred meters. Have you got good eyesight?"

"It's not bad. I'm a bit nearsighted, but I had my glasses on." He pointed to the glasses sitting on his nose.

"How clearly did you see the guy?"

"I couldn't see his face at all, and he was wearing camouflage gear."

"What sort of shoes was he wearing?"

"I didn't notice."

"Pants?"

"Camouflage."

"What color was most prominent in the pattern—green, yellow, brown, or gray?"

"Green, I think."

"His parka. What was it like?"

"It was a jacket. Don't think it had a hood."

"How long was the jacket?"

"It came down well below his waist."

"Same color combination as the pants?"

"Yes, I think so."

"Hat?"

"Yes. He was wearing a baseball cap."

"Color?"

"Green, I think."

"Not camouflage?"

"I don't think so."

"The gun—was it single- or double-barrel?"

"I don't know."

"Height?"

"I don't know. Maybe similar to my father-in-law."

"How tall is that?"

"Six foot, maybe more. Even from that distance I could tell he was quite a bit taller than me."

"Slim or fat?"

"In between, I think"

Gunnar pondered this. "Male or female?"

This question surprised the man. "Male, I suppose."

"Not sure?"

"He looked like a guy."

"Hair color?"

"I couldn't see from that distance."

"Was he wearing an ammunition belt?"

"He had some kind of belt around his waist."

Gunnar looked at the words he had scribbled hastily in his notebook. Then he asked, "What did you do after calling the emergency number?"

"I tried to see if the guy was lurking somewhere around here."

"But you didn't see him?"

"No. He'd gone."

"What did you do then?"

"Waited for the police."

"You didn't go to check on your father-in-law?"

"No. I was too scared."

"So you didn't know if he was dead?"

"Yes, well, I figured he was."

Gunnar jotted this down.

"Anything else you can think of?" he asked.

"I don't think so. I'm just thinking it could well have been me."

"Meaning?" Gunnar asked.

"It could have been me who died," the man replied. "Maybe he would have shot us both if we'd been walking side by side as usual. Or maybe just me, if I'd been walking ahead."

"There's no point thinking like that," Gunnar said. "Life is full of risks. You had a lucky escape this time, but you might find yourself in just as much danger the next time you're in traffic."

"Maybe," the man replied wanly.

Gunnar glanced at his notebook again. There was not much there to work with, he thought, disappointed. Had he forgotten anything?

"Look, I've got to get home and tell my wife," the man said.

"The Reykjavik police will see to that," the patrolman said. "You shouldn't worry about it. They'll make sure she has everything she needs."

"She was very fond of her father," the man said sadly.

Gunnar said, "I guess that applies to most of us."

"I suppose so," the man replied.

"Your gun," Gunnar said. "Is it in the car?"

"Yes," the man replied. "I chucked it onto the passenger seat when I drove off."

"May I check it?" Gunnar asked.

"Yes, of course."

Gunnar got out and walked over to the SUV. There was a five-shot pump-action on the front passenger seat. He put on rubber gloves and opened the car door, cautiously picked up the gun, and examined the maker's name: Mossberg 500. He carefully opened it. In the magazine were two shells and a pin shutting off space for two more. Everything was regulation. In the chamber was a spent shell of Icelandic make: Hlad Original, 42 grams, 70 millimeters. Gunnar emptied the gun and put all three shells in his pocket. Then he examined the action carefully and sniffed it. He detected a faint smell of burned powder and gun oil. This weapon had been well looked after. He replaced it on the seat, shut the door, and returned to the patrol car.

"You fired your gun recently," he said to Ragnar.

The man gave Gunnar a surprised look. "Yes. I shot in the direction of the guy so he wouldn't follow me."

"You didn't mention that before."

"Didn't I?"

"No."

"That was clumsy of me. That's very important, of course, isn't it?"

"Yes, it's important."

"Yes, of course. I should've known. Now, let me see." The man thought.

"Take your time," Gunnar said.

"Yes. I remember," the man said. "I'd loaded the gun. Two shots in the magazine and one in the barrel as usual. I fired one shot when I saw the guy standing over my father-in-law and realized what had happened."

"Did you aim at the guy?" Gunnar asked.

"Yes, well, no—only really up in the air. The range was so far. Should I not have done that?"

Gunnar took time before answering. "It's not an unnatural reaction," he finally said.

"I didn't know what else to do," the man said weakly.

"Don't worry about it," Gunnar said. He tried to smile reassuringly, but it didn't seem to have any effect.

"Do you mind if I keep the shells from your gun? They will help us in the forensic investigation."

Ragnar nodded. Gunnar got out of the car and walked toward the body. A circle of yellow plastic tape had been placed on the ground around it at a radius of twenty meters. Birkir was standing nearby, talking on his cell phone. The deceased was clad in hunting gear that looked, it occurred to Gunnar, almost identical to Ragnar's description of the murderer's attire. Not that it meant anything. Camouflage was the current fashion as far as hunting clothes were concerned, and most hunters dressed the same. Gunnar looked down at himself, dressed in similar gear. He looked more like the victim on the ground than a detective at a crime scene.

"Goddamn bad luck," he said, walking over to Birkir. "We were so close to him this morning."

"It's not over yet," Birkir replied, still holding the cell phone to his ear. "We could still catch him. I'm sure that he's around here somewhere."

Gunnar surveyed the surroundings. The dry, tussocky ground was uneven and impassable by car except for the track they had taken to get here. The killer must have trekked some distance on foot to get here and back. Perhaps Birkir was right; perhaps he was still on the move somewhere nearby.

Birkir finished his call and said to Gunnar, "They're sending a helicopter and more men with dogs. The SWAT team will come with the helicopter. I think we may catch him this time."

"We can't let him get away again," Gunnar said.

"I don't think it's possible for him to hide, especially if he's driving. The cops at the roadblocks will be stopping all traffic going south or north, searching vehicles, and recording names. And getting everyone to explain where they are going."

They surveyed the scene in silence. Finally Birkir said, "The Super asked where we'd been this morning."

Gunnar looked at him. "What did you say?"

"I did some beating around the bush."

"Was Magnús happy with that?"

"I think so. We got here reasonably early, after all. We'd have been later if we'd come all the way from Reykjavik after the call out."

"Good. If he asks again we'll say it was a field trip—we were timing the drive to the Dales and checking when it gets light here. You with me?"

"Yes."

"Great."

"When?" Birkir asked.

"Eh?"

"When did it get light this morning?"

Gunnar looked at his watch. "About six, wasn't it?"

"Possibly."

"That's it, then. We'll time the drive on the way home," Gunnar said.

Birkir was looking at the body. "One thing is bothering me," he said.

"Oh?"

"This time the Gander hasn't cut out his trophy patch from the jacket."

Gunnar thought about this. "Maybe he got scared and beat it when he realized there were two hunters. The witness says he fired a shot at the killer before he took off."

"I'd say it's very unlikely the Gander got scared," Birkir said. "But maybe he tried to give chase."

"In that case the victim's son-in-law had a lucky escape," Gunnar said.

"Perhaps."

12:30

Any mail that arrives at Reykjavik police headquarters is opened immediately by a filing officer, who catalogs the content and assigns an appropriate case number for reference purposes. The filing officer also scans every document electronically so it can be processed in the local network; sends the original to the archive for filing; and then e-mails the relevant people to notify them that they can access the information on their computers. Over the years, this well-established protocol had proven to be a robust and secure system for managing all police department business. Every weekday delivery by the Iceland Postal Service was received by the filing officer on duty in the same brisk, efficient manner. Personal deliveries included. The mail never arrived on weekends. Or almost never.

On this particular Sunday, some mail did come: a brown envelope was slipped through the mail slot next to the entrance. The slot was rarely used, as the door was never locked and there was always a policeman on duty just inside. The envelope went unnoticed until an officer passing through the main entrance saw it and picked it up. It was addressed to "Detective Division, Violent Crime Unit."

The cop shrugged. He was on his way out to the kiosk to buy cigarettes after his lunch, and as he was somewhat late, he put the envelope on the desk of the duty officer who usually received personal deliveries. The envelope sat there for two hours because the duty officer was swamped helping organize things out west; he'd been charged with calling the owners of all of the summerhouses in the district to get permission to carry out interior searches.

By three o'clock things were easing off, and the duty officer finally noticed the envelope. He pondered it briefly, and then wrote "document archive" under the address and placed it in the tray for internal mail pickup.

17:00

The whole team was gathering in the incident room, which had been set aside for the investigation. The photographs from crime scenes one and two posted on the wall had been moved closer together to make space for the pictures from the third scene. Magnús had organized the images with painstaking care.

"There will be no more bodies," he said. "The justice minister has banned goose hunting for an indeterminate period. This situation cannot be allowed to continue."

He drummed the table with his fingers. His nerves were beginning to fray. "Things are getting crazy," he added.

"In that case we'll have to hope that the Gander doesn't develop a taste for other types of animals," Gunnar said, and he tried to stifle a yawn. He hadn't slept for about thirty-six hours, and it was beginning to show.

Birkir was last to enter the room. He carried a large map.

"Anything new?" Magnús asked. Birkir had been reviewing the search in the Mýrar area north of Borgarnes, where the old man had been killed in the early-morning hours.

"No." Birkir shook his head as he pinned the map on the wall opposite the photographs. There was ample space there, next to a large map of Iceland.

"We're still watching the roads up there and will continue to do so until we decide otherwise. The Borgarnes sheriff is in charge of the Mýrar area," Birkir said. "Our helicopter flew over the region today, and traffic was under constant surveillance. The police are now visiting all the farms in the area to ascertain the movements of people in the area over the last twenty-four hours. They are also searching the summerhouses."

Birkir hesitated briefly and then added, "I'm afraid, however, that he's gotten away, unlikely though it may seem."

The room fell briefly silent; disappointment was etched on all of their faces. Everyone's hopes for this search had been high.

Magnús broke the silence. "What were his possible escape routes?"

Birkir pointed to the map, which covered Borgarfjördur and Mýrar; it was large scale and showed the area in detail. He said, "If the guy is driving, there's only one possible getaway route—a track that runs along Langá River and joins Route 1 at Galtarholt." Birkir traced the track with a finger. "There wasn't any watch on this intersection until an hour after the call out. But the track is very slow, with many fences and gates that need to be opened. The helicopter was deployed over there as soon as it arrived in the area. They didn't see any cars on the track, and all the gates were closed."

"Could the Gander have escaped on a motorcycle?" Gunnar asked.

Birkir shrugged. "He would have been spotted from the helicopter if he'd been anywhere around. There was no sign of a motorcycle."

"On foot, then?"

"If he's on foot, he could easily still be hiding somewhere— the witness said he was wearing camouflage. But then we'd need to explain how he got there. There is, actually, one line of inquiry we could follow here. I checked today and found out that the control system in the Hvalfjördur tunnel photographs all the traffic that passes through. When the sensors detect movement, the cameras are activated. The pictures from last Thursday and from this morning are being copied for us. They'll let us know when they're ready, and then I'll send a car to pick up the discs."

"Are license plates visible in these pictures?" Magnús asked.

"Yeah, that's the whole point."

"So we can see if anybody was tailing Ólafur last Thursday? Or the pair from Reykjavik this morning?"

"Yes."

"Excellent. This might crack the case."

"Maybe."

"Okay, so what do we know today that we didn't know the day before yesterday?" Magnús asked. Not waiting for a reply, he answered his own question. "The Gander is very dangerous and reckless. He seems to have detailed knowledge of the goose hunting areas in the south and west, and is capable of making quick getaways after the killings. Anna, what can you tell us?"

Anna stubbed out her cigarette and stood up. "The ammunition used in all the murders is ordinary number two bird shot. That in itself is strange, since the killer is so focused on carrying out attacks specifically designed to kill people. It would make much more sense for him to use larger shot, or simply a powerful rifle. The conclusion must be that he doesn't have access to another weapon or to heavier shot. Maybe he doesn't have a gun license and isn't able to buy larger-caliber shells. In that case, he must have acquired a shotgun with ammunition illegally, perhaps in a burglary. He uses what he has on hand." Anna sat down again.

"He's certainly a marksman, though," said Gunnar.

"What about footprints?" Magnús directed his question to Anna.

"We have no pictures of prints yet. In Dalasýsla he seems to have tidied up after himself. As for the second killing, we're still waiting for the soil to dry out a bit more so we can examine that area better. In Mýrar the surface was too hard for any footprints to show."

Magnús drummed his fingers on the table while he pondered the matter. "We also have those lists of names to think about," he said. "If there's a link between the Gander and the victims he should feature there. We'll have three lists after today. Maybe four, if we include the guy from Akureyri. Hopefully there'll be an overlap somewhere."

"And we need to investigate Tómas, the lawyer, some more," Gunnar said.

Anna coughed. "I've checked his guns. They don't match the shells we found at Litla-Fell."

Birkir said, "Besides, I bet he's got an alibi for this morning. His wife is back home now."

"Are you sure?" Gunnar asked.

"Yeah, she was at home last night."

"How do we know that?" Gunnar said. "He just yelled something into the apartment. We never saw the woman."

"In that case, what weapon did he use?" Birkir asked. "We removed his guns yesterday."

Gunnar said, "Guys like him have no problem getting their hands on firearms. Don't forget that the Gander took Ólafur's gun. Could be that Tómas has a cache somewhere else, but only let us see those ones. Decoys."

19:00

Detectives Dóra and Símon were given the task of visiting Tómas to ask about his movements that morning. If he had been in bed with his wife, he was probably out of the picture. It was as simple as that. But they would need the wife to confirm his story.

On arrival at the high-rise, Símon did the talking over the intercom, and again when Tómas admitted them to the apartment and showed them into the study.

"Where were you between five and eight o'clock this morning?"

Tómas looked at Dóra as he answered, "Here at home, in my bed."

"Can your wife confirm that?" Símon asked.

Tómas was silent.

"Was your wife not at home?"

"She decided to stay with her sister."

"So you were alone, then?"

Tómas said nothing.

"Did you go out at all?"

"I was not alone."

"Was someone with you who can testify that you were at home?"

"Yes, I suppose so."

"Who?"

"Helga."

"Your mistress?" Dóra asked.

"That's too strong a word. More a bit of fun when there isn't anything else around."

"Did she come here on her own initiative?" Dóra asked.

"No, I called her when my wife left."

"Why?"

Tómas shrugged. "She was available. I have a very strong libido. Period."

"Where is Helga now?"

"She left at noon."

"Do you know where she went?"

"Probably home. I didn't ask."

Suddenly this conversation made Dóra feel sick.

"What a douchebag," she said quietly, as if to herself—although Tómas clearly heard her, and his face went white. "Who do you think you are?" he hissed. "You're just a police bitch who knows nothing about me. I don't forget language like that."

"Great. Then you'll remember you're a douchebag," Dóra snapped back.

Tómas took a step closer to her and said, "I think you're just envious of Helga because of what she gets from me. I'm free tonight, if you take a bath first."

Dóra looked Tómas up and down before replying. "I saw the video footage from Helga's bedroom. I couldn't see that you were particularly talented. It was all rather predictable and boring. Certainly nothing that would inspire envy."

Símon glared at his colleague and then turned apologetically to Tómas.

"Thanks for your assistance."

19:30

Birkir stopped by the headquarters of the security company, where he introduced himself to the supervisor on duty and showed his police credentials.

"I need some information about one of your staff members," he said. "Jóhann Markússon."

The supervisor tapped the name into his computer.

"He is not on duty at the moment," he said.

"When did he work last?"

"He was on the night shift yesterday."

"When did that finish?"

"Eight o'clock this morning."

"Where was he working?"

"He was driving. They go all over."

"The gas station at Ártúnshöfdi. Is it on his route?"

The supervisor tapped on the keyboard some more. "Yes. He goes there once a night to check the security system. They're open twenty-four hours, and it needs careful monitoring."

"Does he always go to the same places?"

"No. We move the staff around regularly."

"Could Jóhann have left his shift a bit early this morning?"

"Before eight o'clock?"

"Yeah."

"No. We're always in contact with the vehicles, and he finishes here. Returns the car and files his report."

"That's completely certain?"

"Yes. There would have been an entry in the daily log if he had left earlier. That only happens in emergencies. Illness, that kind of thing."

After this interview, Birkir went home.

He was exhausted after a long day that had delivered nothing apart from a third body and still more questions. He had also shot his first goose, of course, but that was not in his thoughts at all.

He didn't want to go to bed just yet but didn't know what he wanted to do. There wasn't even any reason to press his pants, because he had never changed out of the clothes he'd had on for their early-morning hunting excursion. His suit was hanging neatly in its place, ready for the following day, pressed and clean. He considered jogging a few kilometers but decided not to; it wasn't worth the trouble when he felt this tired. He hardly ever watched the television in the living room, and he certainly didn't feel like it just now. He decided to listen to some good music.

He put a CD in the player—*Evening Adagios*—and gazed through the window at the now dimly lit yard. It was a still evening, and a satisfying tranquility reigned outside; the trees were vibrant with fall color. As the music of Debussy, Barber, and Rodrigo resonated through the apartment, he began to feel somewhat better.

He thought about the murders. Three in four days, and the team was getting nowhere. He doubted that the lists of names would bring any further results. It could be the killer knew some of his victims personally—but certainly not all of them. Somebody was trying to confuse them. He sensed it. The killings were not logical and yet they were, somehow, carefully planned. He worried that there was some terrible madness behind this. Clever madness, if such a thing existed. They would not catch this murderer unless he wanted to be caught. Extremely sharp detective work was probably the only hope. Or a lucky coincidence.

Birkir tried to form an image of their opponent, a complete picture of the killer that might help him to focus. A picture he wouldn't have to rationalize or explain to everyone else. He went over the components one by one.

Age? The killer was definitely not very old. Unlikely to be over forty. Probably about thirty.

Physical abilities? At the very least, he was reasonably athletic. And he was tall, according to the description the Mýrar witness had given.

Psychological characteristics? Restless, excitable, not necessarily quick tempered.

Interests? Either an experienced hunter or a fanatical conservationist. Or neither.

Previous crimes? No criminal record, surely. Perhaps he had a case history with a psychiatrist.

Single? Yes, probably. Not likely to be a family man. Possibly divorced.

Working? Maybe, but hardly in a nine-to-five job. He was probably self-employed in some way and running his own business.

Nationality? Native Icelander—had to be. He was very familiar with the countryside.

Sex? Male...But Birkir had second thoughts. Was that certain? Could the killer be a woman?

He thought about this picture for a long time while the disc played. When the music stopped, he opened the door to the balcony and inhaled the evening air. A faint cooking smell came wafting in from the restaurant next door, and suddenly he was starving.

He had forgotten to eat supper.

21:00

This was the first murder investigation Dóra had taken part in, and now there had been three homicides in the space of four days. It was not a good start, and, for some reason, she felt responsible. It was their job to stop this, but Dóra and her colleagues seemed to be like helpless preschoolers in this business. What in heaven's name were they doing wrong?

She returned to the office after the visit to Tómas's place. One telephone call to the widow had confirmed the lawyer's account; Helga had readily admitted to spending the night with him. She hadn't had anything better to do, she'd explained.

Dóra was a bit embarrassed that she'd lost her temper during the interview with Tómas. Not all truths need be told—she'd learned that early in life—and Símon had gone ballistic afterward, he of all people, berating her for "unprofessional behavior." He'd asked where she'd seen the bedroom video and seemed disappointed when she admitted that she'd never laid eyes on the footage. Her comments on Tómas's performance had been mere speculation.

Well, Dóra decided, she wasn't going to let these assholes ruin her evening. She had plenty of other things to occupy herself with.

Dóra was from Bolungarvík, a small fishing village in the far northwest of Iceland. The fifth of eleven siblings, she had quickly realized it was necessary to show a certain determination to get what she wanted; she'd also learned about responsibility and independence. Her brothers, younger as well as older, had taught her how to fight. It had not been an easy childhood, and she had experienced plenty of loss: her oldest brother had died at sea working on a shrimper; another had perished in an avalanche in Flateyri; and her next-to-youngest sister had died in a car crash. Dóra was a passenger in that crash, and the scar on her cheek was a reminder of it. The scar on her soul was, however, much deeper.

She'd graduated from high school in Ísafjördur, the town next to her own, and then moved to Reykjavik with her boyfriend. He enrolled in a business administration course, and she got a job with the police. Three months later, the boyfriend announced that they had grown apart—she was unable to sustain conversations that fulfilled his needs as an intellectual and an academic, he claimed. The relationship ended and he moved in with a girl that he'd gotten to know during his university seminars.

Dóra enrolled in the police academy and came in third from the top in her year. After that she was offered a permanent post in the uniformed division. That job suited her well. It wasn't particularly well paying, but previously she'd always been broke. The paycheck allowed her to buy a cheap studio apartment in the Hlídar district; it was only twenty-five square meters, but it was comfortable. She'd never had so much space to herself. At home in Bolungarvík, she had shared a room with her two sisters; at lodgings in Ísafjördur she had shared a room with a girlfriend; and during the first months in Reykjavik she had lived with her boyfriend in a tiny student apartment.

Dóra's chief asset was her energy. Not afraid of hard work, she tackled everything that came her way, however unpleasant, with speed and efficiency. Her superiors quickly noted this and even took advantage of it, frequently sending her to disorderly domestic situations where alcoholic excess and violence were the norm. Places where mothers were tyrannized and children neglected. Places where the problems were difficult to resolve or ameliorate. Yet in such situations, Dóra was in her element. She had a natural ability to handle drunks, and was quick to identify the correct tactics for each case.

On one occasion she had to remove a baby from a home in the middle of the night. The blind-drunk husband followed her out of the house, got behind the wheel of the family sedan, and accelerated into the side of the patrol car. Dóra was sitting in the backseat with the baby, and the impact snapped her femur; the baby sustained only scratches from the broken glass that showered from the side window.

When she was more or less back on her feet, Dóra got a temporary office job with the detective division. It was only meant to keep her busy during her rehabilitation, but a permanent position came up, and she applied for it. She had already demonstrated her fine organizational abilities in the department and was given good references by her supervisor in the uniformed division. Her boss was actually very sorry to lose such an efficient employee, but couldn't find an excuse for hanging on to her and was honest enough to write a glowing recommendation. As a result, she had become a detective.

Dóra sat in the squad room, reading carefully through all the reports that had been written about the three murders. She considered the sequence of events and tried to picture the circumstances. She looked at timing, distances, and methods in due order, taking notes the whole time. There had to be a clue somewhere.

She read the report she had written after visiting Helga the previous Thursday morning. The encounter was the closest she had gotten to talking with an actual victim in this case, and she pondered whether her assessment had been sufficiently professional. She had, in fact, followed it up by making discreet inquiries among the couple's friends and neighbors about their matrimonial situation. Then Birkir had shown up at a progress meeting with a completely different picture of the widow than the one she had constructed.

At half past ten, a uniformed officer showed up bearing a small package addressed to Birkir. Dóra signed for it and phoned Birkir for authorization to examine the contents. It contained DVDs with the security-camera images from the Hvalfjördur tunnel.

CHAPTER 5

MONDAY, SEPTEMBER 25

09:30

The investigating team's morning meeting began with Magnús listing the day's tasks for himself, Gunnar, Birkir, and Dóra. Item one on the agenda was looking at the photos from the Hvalfjördur tunnel security cameras. Dóra had already found images that confirmed when the two victims had driven through: Ólafur at 04:21 on Thursday, and Vilhjálmur at 04:34 on Sunday. She'd also noted down the license plate numbers of all of the cars that had passed through the tunnel within thirty minutes of the victims. Naturally, traffic had been very light, but there were a few cars that merited further investigation. There was also a motorcycle that had gone through on both days—04:27 on Thursday and 04:50 on Sunday—but unfortunately, she couldn't decipher its license plate from the pictures. What she could tell was that the rider appeared to be wearing black leather gear and a white helmet. He didn't seem to be carrying anything that looked like a shotgun. But they needed to find a way to contact this guy and interview him. They would also have to get anyone who'd driven a car through to explain their movements; that was a simpler task, since all of the license plates were clearly visible in the pictures. This particular job went to Símon.

Item two was doing a follow-up interview with Ragnar, the son-in-law of Vilhjálmur Arason, who had witnessed the murder. They needed to ask him for a list of names of relatives and friends, along with some other questions. Assuming he was now in a more balanced state mentally, they also hoped to get from him a better, more detailed description of what had happened. Birkir took on that task.

Suddenly, there was an interruption.

"Magnús, what am I supposed to do with this?"

A slim man of about sixty barged into the room clutching a brown envelope in one hand and a sheet of paper in the other.

"I can't scan something like this into the archive. There's no identification," he continued. "You have to give me a case number."

"We're in a meeting," Magnús said.

"Right, you're in a meeting and so you send stuff like this down to me, and I'm just supposed to sense what to do with it."

"What stuff are you talking about?" Magnús said. "I haven't sent you anything. Not lately, at any rate."

The man thumped the envelope and the piece of paper onto the conference table. The envelope was addressed, "Detective Division, Violent Crime Unit." Below this, someone else had added, "Document archive."

Magnús said, "I didn't send you this."

The paper bore the words *Monday, September 25, 10 o'clock. oldfarts@hotmail.com—password shotgun123.*

The e-mail address told them nothing, but the objects stapled to the sheet immediately captured their complete attention: two small pieces of camouflage material with dark brown spots.

"Where's Anna?" said Magnús.

Dóra replied, "In the lab."

Magnús grabbed the sheet of paper, got up, and stormed out with the others in hot pursuit. The archivist was left abandoned.

"What on earth is going on?" he said, addressing an empty room.

09:50

In the northern district of Thingey, the weather was pretty good—the morning was overcast but dry. There was a slight breeze from the north and the temperature was just above freezing. On a barren plain near the western route to the Dettifoss waterfall, a little to the north of Route 1, a mechanical digger was excavating. In the shelter of an old Land Rover nearby stood a thin man wearing a well-worn sheepskin parka and a wool hat. He leaned on a shovel and peered at the dirt being dug out. The arm of the digger disappeared further and further into the ever-deepening crater, scooping up heaps of wet gravel in its jaws as groundwater trickled from the sides of the hole and collected in the bottom.

The man in the wool hat was a geologist, Fróði Bergkvist. He was a graduate of the University of Iceland and had post-graduate degrees from two foreign universities. His specialty was construction material technology. On this particular morning, his work was to look for a new gravel pit for the Icelandic Roads Administration.

His firm, Bergfróði—of which he was CEO and also the only permanent staff member—had been tasked to prospect for extraction sites that contained material that could help build a new road. Its starting point was east of Lake Mývatn, and it was slated to run northward, west of Jökulsá River and through to Axarfjördur. This new road would, among other things, improve tourist access to a national park that included Europe's most powerful waterfall, Dettifoss; the hiking trails at Hólmatungur; and the echoing rocks of Hljódaklettar. The road was to be properly leveled where necessary, and paved. The existing track was a low-grade dirt road and suitable only for SUVs and large vehicles; it simply wasn't adequate for the region's ever-increasing traffic.

In his office Fródi had examined aerial photographs of the region, identifying and marking potential sites. Then he had spent a few days exploring the area on foot—checking out the landscape, taking photographs, and collecting small soil samples. Over many millennia, Jökulsá River had frequently changed its route within an area several kilometers wide, and it was very likely they would find suitable material in one of the many dried-up sections of riverbed. But first they'd have to get to it through the thick layers of dirt and vegetation that had covered the gravel deposits over thousands of years.

Fródi's research had now reached the stage where he had hired a digger to do test excavations at a few selected sites. They had dug in five places this morning, but all of the results had been disappointing. In two of his chosen locations, the layers of dirt had been too thick to remove, while in the others the hard rock substrate was too close to the surface.

Things looked hopeful, however, where they were now. The earth layer was, admittedly, more than a meter in depth, but beneath it they had found fine gravel as far as the arm of the digger could reach. It promised to be a very productive source once the earth and vegetation were bulldozed out of the way.

The gravel that the digger had piled up seemed to be excellent road-construction material, with good size distribution. Best of all, it didn't seem to contain too much fine grit.

Fródi signaled to the digger operator that the hole was now deep enough. He would have to come back with a drill to check out the depth to solid rock. Hopefully it would be several meters.

The operator got down from his rig, stuffed his pipe with tobacco, and watched in satisfaction as Fródi shoveled gravel samples into three strong plastic bags.

But the job was not finished. Fródi wanted to get down into the hole to check for stratification of the gravel deposits; it might be necessary to take samples from individual layers. He was prepared for this. He had brought his trusty five-meter wooden ladder, which the digger operator helped him to get down from the roof of the Land Rover and slide down the hole. It protruded above the edge of the hole by about a meter; Fródi climbed down, rung by rung, scrutinizing the gravel. It seemed to be pretty uniform all the way down to the bottom. It wasn't until he was on his way up again that his attention was drawn to the earth layer. It occurred to him to look for ash deposits formed during major eruptions in the north of Iceland. This natural phenomenon had been his chief interest during his geology studies at university, and the subject of his final dissertation. You could use the ash layers to date the various strata. Investigating that type of detail had no practical value for the current search, but he could never resist doing so when he was in holes like this.

He spotted something black half a meter from the surface, and probed it with his fingers. To his great surprise, he found it was plastic. He tried to scrape the earth away to work out what it was.

"A plastic bag?" he said to himself. Was he digging in an old garbage dump? Surely not. Not here.

"Pass me the spade," he called to the driver, who was smoking his pipe by the edge of the hole.

He took the spade and scraped the earth away to reveal what seemed to be a long bundle wrapped in black plastic. He tore a small hole and pushed a finger through, touching something soft and yielding. He withdrew his finger, sniffed it, and instantly recoiled from the nauseating smell of putrefaction. Hastily wiping his finger on his pants, he sprang like a shot from the hole, yelling at the driver, "There's something dead down there!"

09:55

"It's the same color."

Anna held the scrap of camouflage material with a pair of steel pliers and compared it carefully with Ólafur Jónsson's parka, which was laid out in front of her on an examining table. The piece fit neatly into the hole in the outer layer—or, rather, half of the hole, as this was a section that had been snipped from the original missing patch.

"He's sending us a message," Gunnar said, pointing at the sheet of paper. "Date, time, and e-mail address."

They all looked at their watches.

"It's two minutes to ten," Gunnar said.

"We can use my computer," Dóra said.

They hurried back to the squad room and clustered around Dóra's desk. With practiced fingers, she tapped in the address and password, and the inbox immediately appeared.

"There's no e-mail here," she said.

"What's the time?" Gunnar asked.

"Ten o'clock," Magnús replied.

"Hang on. Here's something," Dóra said. An e-mail arrived with the subject line: GOOD MORNING COPS. The sender's address was iamhunting4u2@hotmail.com.

Dóra opened it, but there was no text.

"What should I do?" she asked nervously.

"Let me." Gunnar almost yanked Dóra out of the chair and threw himself down in front of the computer. Selecting Reply with History, he typed with his pudgy fingers a single word— WHY?—and clicked Send.

They all held their breaths. Nothing happened for what seemed like ages, and gradually tension relaxed and groans of disappointment could be heard.

Suddenly there was a beep. Gunnar opened the new e-mail and began to read aloud: "*You ask why. I don't know if it's possible to answer or explain it…*"

10:15

Birkir had gone to bed at ten thirty the previous evening, woken up fully rested at five thirty, and run thirty kilometers in two and a half hours. This speed of twelve kilometers per hour, or five minutes per kilometer, was not up to his average performance for running the 42-plus kilometers of a marathon course; but it was a very good training run under the circumstances. His best time in a marathon was three hours twenty-seven seconds, and his next-best time was three hours thirty-four seconds. His goal was to someday do it in less than three hours.

When he had showered after the run, he'd felt really good, and that feeling remained as he left his colleagues in front of Dóra's computer. There were other things to be done this morning, and he was quite content to review these e-mail exchanges later. His immediate task was to have a talk with Vilhjálmur's son-in-law about the events he had witnessed the previous day.

Ragnar Jónsson lived in a trim little apartment building in the Fossvogur district of Reykjavik. Before going in, Birkir appraised the house and its surroundings. Rarely had he seen an apartment building with such an attractive and well-kept lot. The yard was well looked after, with thick green grass and neatly trimmed trees and shrubs. The flowers in the beds were, truthfully, a little faded because of the recent frosty nights; the leaves had taken on the colors of the fall. Suddenly he felt rather sad. Perhaps the feeling was owed to the incomplete line of verse that suddenly came to him: *Autumn of my mind, night feeds my fear.* He wasn't sure if the words came from a poem he'd once read, or if he'd improvised them.

He didn't dwell on the origin of the phrase; he had long since given up trying to do that. Usually when something popped into his head like this, he imagined it was something he'd once read, or poems he'd recited during his Icelandic lessons with old Hinrik. It was always just a line or two, never a whole poem. At times he recited such things aloud, to the wonderment of those present, but usually he just kept the snatches to himself.

He entered the hallway and pressed the buzzer. The door opened, and Ragnar met him at the door of his ground-floor apartment in stocking feet but wearing a jacket. A bit like a visitor who, in the usual Icelandic fashion, had taken his shoes off on arrival, Birkir thought.

Ragnar showed Birkir in.

"This is Bára, my wife," he said. "It's difficult for her to get up."

A very large woman sat in a deep armchair with a stool under her feet. Her face seemed lost in the rolls of fat that encased her neck and shoulders; it bore no expression, but now and again a fat hand brought a handkerchief up to her eyes to wipe away invisible tears. A dark-blue dress covered her immense body like a tent.

"We are completely beside ourselves with grief," Ragnar said. "My wife was my father-in-law's only child."

Birkir turned to the woman and said, "My condolences to you both. I know that this is a very difficult time for you. I do, however, need to ask you some questions."

There was no reply from the woman.

"What sort of questions?" Ragnar asked.

Birkir turned to him. "Can you describe to me the events leading up to the hunting trip?"

Ragnar looked surprised. "But I told the other policeman all that yesterday. Isn't that enough?"

"You may be able to remember more detail today," Birkir said. "Please, just go over it again. Step by step."

"Very well, I'll try," Ragnar said. He hesitated a moment before beginning. "For many years, my father-in-law and I have made it a habit to go on an annual goose-hunting trip in September. We always try to go on the last Sunday of the month, to be exact. My father-in-law's relatives own a farm in the Mýrar district, and he always has permission to shoot birds on their land. I'm not really much of a hunter myself, but my father-in-law was fond of it and he enjoyed having companionship. We began to prepare for the trip two weeks ago, but when news came of the murders I wanted to call it off. Isn't that right, darling?"

Bára's nose appeared to move up and down in her face. This was the only perceptible indication that her head was nodding in agreement; her chin and jaw were hidden beneath her voluminous double chins.

Ragnar continued. "But my father-in-law wouldn't hear of putting off the trip. We're not going to let ourselves be scared off, he said. But then it happened, just like that, as you know."

"Did many people know of this hunting trip?" Birkir asked.

"Yes, although everybody naturally thought that we'd call it off. But my father-in-law was so determined, wasn't he, love?"

The woman's nose moved up and down again.

"Is it possible that someone followed you?"

"If they did, I wasn't aware of it."

"Is the area where you were a popular hunting ground?"

"It's private land, so only people who get permission can hunt there—not many do."

Birkir checked his notebook before saying, "The landowner says you were the only ones with license to hunt yesterday."

The son-in-law nodded. "Yes, that's correct."

"Is it possible that you encountered somebody who was hunting there illegally?"

"I don't know. Isn't that most likely?"

"Yes, unless someone followed you."

"Who could that have been?"

"Did anybody have a quarrel with your father-in-law?"

"No, not at all."

"What about you?"

"Good heavens, no."

"How old was your father-in-law?"

"Sixty-five in July."

"What was his occupation?"

"He used to own a small fishing company, but sold it and retired when he turned sixty."

VIKTOR ARNAR INGOLFSSON

Birkir checked his notebook. "He was single, wasn't he?"

"Yes. His wife, my Bára's mother, died eight years ago. She suffered from hypertension."

"Was Vilhjálmur an enthusiastic hunter?"

"Yes, he used to do a lot of salmon fishing, and in the fall he would shoot birds, both goose and ptarmigan. He had plenty of time, of course, after he retired."

"Are you sure he didn't have any enemies?"

"None, so help me God. Why would you think that?"

"He was killed, wasn't he?"

"Yes, that's true, but who would these enemies be?"

Birkir decided to change the subject. "What's your occupation?" he asked.

Ragnar relaxed. "I'm an elementary school teacher. The head teacher granted me leave for a few days because of our loss. He was very kind; he brought flowers from the school and the rest of the staff. He said he would arrange a substitute for me."

Birkir got up and looked out the window at the yard.

"It's a nice place you've got," he said.

"Yes," Ragnar said, adding somewhat proudly, "I take full responsibility for the garden. Our neighbors are all happy to leave it in my hands."

He was visibly relieved to be able to talk about something other than the murder, and continued enthusiastically. "I always have plenty of time during my summer vacation to putter around in it. It suits me to be outside, and I love seeing how the plants thrive. There is a particularly beautiful *Rosa moyesii* here by the south wall. The spirea has also flowered beautifully for me in recent years. We've got a number of fruit bushes—red currants, black currants, and gooseberries. We always have a lot of berries, but the kids sometimes pick them before they're ripe. The birds

152

are also always after them. Around the perimeter I've got a *Salix pentandra* hedge that I trim every year. On the whole it's all very successful, but I'd really like to increase the number of beds on the south side, and have a small greenhouse here by the east side of the house."

"Can't you do that?"

"No. I haven't been able to get consent from the others for that. Also, the children in the building need somewhere to play. But they can be a bit boisterous and careless."

Birkir felt sympathy for this meticulous gardener who seemed to have a lot to put up with. But it was time to return to the business at hand.

"I need you to make a list of everybody your father-in-law knew," he said. He passed Ragnar a sheet of paper listing the various categories—family, friends, neighbors, and so on.

"I'll try to put this together," said Ragnar. "Bára will help me with it."

"Do you have you a photograph of Vilhjálmur that I can borrow?"

"Yes." Ragnar took down a framed picture from the wall and handed it to Birkir. "This one is relatively recent."

11:35

Kristján, a detective from Akureyri, gazed in disbelief, first at the endless wilderness that surrounded them, and then at what lay at his feet—a human body wrapped in filthy black plastic. Brown tape had been wound several times around the bundle, but by now it was beginning to come apart, making the contents partly visible. The smell was appalling.

The men who had discovered the body had scooped it up with a digger and deposited it here. In retrospect, it would have been better to examine the body in situ, but Kristján let that pass. He hadn't quite gotten his head around the fact that something like this could happen. That some geologist looking for road-building material could root up a half-rotten body wrapped in plastic, especially in this uninhabited vastness. Whoever dug this grave cannot have expected its contents to ever come to the surface. Sure, it had been buried just half a meter deep, but in ordinary circumstances that would have been enough to keep it from being discovered, even taking into account the considerable erosion caused by surface drying and constant wind.

Fródi Bergkvist and the digger operator were waiting in the Land Rover, which they had moved a good distance upwind of the excavation pit. They clearly didn't want to remain anywhere near their find, nor to be exposed to the stench it emitted.

Kristján had already done a preliminary report after obtaining from Fródi a detailed explanation of what the two men had been doing in this place, and what had led Fródi to select this precise spot for his soil sample.

"Geologically speaking, this area is quite promising," Fródi had said. "There is also good vehicular access from the track down there. Other than that, it was pure chance."

"The odds must be one in a billion to find a body this way," Kristján declared to his colleague from the Húsavík police, who were responsible for this district. "We won't hit another jackpot like this in our careers," he added.

They were waiting for the hearse to arrive from Akureyri, bearing a hermetically sealed container for the remains. A forensic scientist from the Reykjavik detective division was on the way to Akureyri to open up the plastic bundle in the mortuary there. They would carry out further crime scene investigation at a later date if necessary. Actually, there was nothing to be seen on the ground here—no footprints or the like. The wind erosion in recent months had seen to that.

12:00

"...*My nature is to kill. I hunt men and I never let go.*"

When Gunnar finished reading the Gander's e-mail, Magnús called the computer specialist from the economic crime division to ask for assistance. It was noon before the man turned up, and while they waited the team didn't do much apart from stare at the screen and bite their nails. Over and over they read the reply to the question why. What on earth were they dealing with? What was in the mind of a person who could write something like that and then follow it through? *I hunt men.* Was there no reason for the murders apart from the instinct to kill? Was this just some horrifying game? Had the victims' only crime been that they went hunting? Why did the Gander choose to kill hunters?

When the expert finally arrived, Magnús straightaway pointed at the computer screen. "Is it possible to trace this to the user?" he asked.

"Hotmail address," the computer guy said, peering at the screen through thick glasses.

"Meaning?"

"It's a mailbox that anybody with Internet access can create from anywhere."

"But can it be traced, like a phone call?"

"It's possible we could find an IP address, but it's a long process that might take some time. It'll go through a string of foreign servers."

"How long?"

"For us? Probably days. It's not a simple task. Best thing would be to keep him talking, try to get some more mail from him. Maybe he uses more than one computer."

Magnús patted Gunnar on the back and said, "Do something."

Gunnar again tapped at the keyboard: WHO ARE YOU? After a brief interval a reply arrived, but not with an answer to the question Gunnar had asked.

> Distinguished opponents. It is your turn to answer
> some questions. We are going to play a little game.
> I shall pose you a riddle to solve, and you will reply
> within the time limit I set. If you give the wrong
> answer, someone will die. I may either choose the
> victim carefully or just pick at random. It depends
> how I feel. So there is much at stake. Let us begin
> with a few easy literary questions. The first is as fol-
> lows: Whose eyes have all the seeming of a demon's
> that is dreaming? Time limit 30 minutes. Good luck.

Magnús read the quotation aloud. "How do we find this in thirty minutes?" he asked despairingly.

The computer guy answered instantly, saying to Gunnar, "Do a Google search on the text."

Gunnar did as he was told, and immediately a number of hits came up. Tensely the team scanned the screen.

"It's a poem by Edgar Allan Poe," said Gunnar, seeing that name mentioned in most of the results shown.

Magnús clapped his hands and said, "Great! Send him our reply."

Gunnar looked at the clock. "No. We need to know whose eyes he's writing about."

He clicked on one of the sites listed and urgently began reading. "It's a metaphor," he said finally, "comparing the raven's eyes to those of a demon."

"We've got it, then," said Magnús. "The Raven."

Taking Gunnar's place at the computer, the specialist forwarded all the exchange of messages to his own mailbox. "I'll try to do what I can with this. Copy me on everything that passes between you. Don't CC me on the e-mails, just forward them," he said and left.

Magnús heard his cell phone ringing and disappeared into his office. He quickly came back and said, "That was the police in Akureyri. They found a body."

12:30

Birkir was in the car outside Ragnar Jónsson's home when his cell rang. It was Gunnar.

"Listen, a corpse has turned up near Mývatn. It was buried. Magnús wants you to go help the guys from Akureyri deal with the situation."

"Why? Don't we already have enough to deal with here?"

"Yeah, but the thing is, the victim's been shot with a shotgun. Many times."

"A shotgun?"

"Yeah, like all the others. Could be connected."

"Is the body in reasonable condition?"

"No. It's far gone—just over a year, we think. The guy was in his twenties, name of Leifur Albert Rúnarsson."

"How do you know that?"

"He had some ID in his pocket."

"A stroke of luck," Birkir said. "Has he been missing? I can't remember having heard about it."

"It is actually a bit peculiar," Gunnar replied. "He was declared dead about a year ago. Suicide. The media didn't make much of it."

"Hang on a minute. How so—suicide?"

"The Akureyri guys thought he had thrown himself into Dettifoss. His car was discovered by the falls, and there was a handwritten farewell note. It all seemed to be clear cut."

"I see."

"So, Elías from forensics flew up north this morning. He already removed the body from the plastic they found it in and took a preliminary look. Now he needs to go look around the place where it was buried. Can you get on the next flight?"

"Me?"

"Yeah."

"What about you?"

"I'm busy playing a quiz game."

12:45

Two minutes before their time was up, Gunnar typed in the answer: The Raven. Then he clicked Send.

The Gander replied quickly.

> Well done. You are evidently well versed in the magic of Google search. Now we can get serious, with questions that the computer can't manage. Question two: Which book's final sentence asks the question, "What about Solitaire's back?" You have

four hours to solve this. Remember that a human
life is at stake. We'll communicate again at five
o'clock. Bye.

Gunnar did a search on the word "Solitaire," but got well over a hundred thousand hits. Then he tried "What about Solitaire's back?" with quotation marks, which produced no results. He tried again, without quotes, and there were more than forty-seven million choices; scrolling through the first hundred, he found no book references. They added "a book" to the search string, then "end of a book," but were still no nearer to an answer.

"What can we do?" Magnús asked, sounding desperate.

"We could just ignore him," Gunnar said.

"What if he kills someone?"

"I think he'll do that anyway if we don't catch him soon."

"But we'll win time if we find the answer, right?"

"Yeah, but we'll also lose time looking for it."

"Can we get some help with this?"

Gunnar gave it some thought. Finally he said, "Maybe we could try to enlist help from guys that are used to this kind of question-and-answer thing. The bar I go to has a quiz night every Friday. There always seems to be some geek there who knows practically everything. I'll run this question past the crowd over there. Maybe someone will know the answer."

14:00

Birkir caught the one o'clock flight to Akureyri, landing an hour after take-off. Elías, his colleague from forensics, was there to meet him in the company of the local detective officer, Kristján.

Kristján was short and stocky, with close-cropped hair, a round face, and, Birkir found as he shook his hand, stubby fingers.

"What a goddamn mess," the man said in an emphatic northern accent. "We were sure we had it all wound up last fall when the guy went missing. It's true we didn't come across the car until day three of the search, but this letter seemed to explain the whole thing." He waved a photocopy of the handwritten note.

Elías took over. "The letter was sent to us in Reykjavik at the time. Anna examined it and pronounced it genuine."

Birkir took the note from Kristján and read, "*My dearest Mom. Life has become unbearable over the past few months. I haven't been able to sleep and everything seems so hopeless. This will no doubt come as a surprise to you, as I have tried to spare you these tribulations of mine. But now I have decided to put an end to it all, and when you read this you will know that all is now well with me. Your son, Leifur Albert.*"

"Anna got hold of something that the guy had written earlier," Elías explained. "She compared it with this note and confirmed it was the same handwriting. She's the only one of us who has specialized in handwriting analysis."

"Anyway, who else would have written it?" said Kristján defensively.

Birkir took out his notebook. "When was the disappearance reported?"

Kristján replied quickly. "Saturday, October second. The same day that we lost the Cup Final in Reykjavik. A very bad day."

From the airport, the three of them drove to the Central Hospital. In the mortuary, Leifur Albert's earthly remains had been laid out on a slab.

"We'll send him to Reykjavik tomorrow," Kristján said, covering his nose and mouth. "We have no forensic pathologists here."

Birkir studied the body and its clothing. The man was dressed for hunting, in green, yellow, and brown outdoor gear. A shotgun blast, obviously from close range, had taken off two fingers of his right hand—the thumb and index finger. There was a big shotgun wound to his left groin, and the top part of his head had been blown off with another close-range shot. Putrefaction had rendered his face unrecognizable, so there was no point in asking anyone to identify him. A mercy for the family. Besides, they had other ways to establish that this was Leifur's body, like through DNA analysis.

"I took care unwrapping the plastic that covered the body," Elías said. "It's possible there may be fingerprints on the inside of it. We'll check it in the lab back in Reykjavik. We've got better facilities there."

Birkir continued looking at the corpse. "Isn't the body unusually intact considering it's been there twelve months?" he asked.

Elías nodded. "That's not necessarily abnormal. He was only half a meter down in the ground, out in the middle of nowhere. I think he was probably frozen solid for most of the year."

14:45

Emil Edilon never used a cell phone, and he rarely spent much time at home during the day, so it was only after some searching that Gunnar found him at Café Mokka.

The writer was scribbling something on a paper napkin with a pencil stub. Next to him was an empty coffee cup.

"It'll take you a while to finish the book if you don't use better paper," Gunnar said, taking the seat opposite him.

"I'm working," Emil said. "Shouldn't you be doing something useful somewhere?"

"I have a question for you."

"Have I advertised myself as some kind of information service?"

"No, but it's very important."

Emil looked at his empty coffee cup. "I've finished my refill," he said. "I'll listen to you for five minutes if I get a fresh cup of coffee and a slice of apple cake with cream."

"I need the name of a book," Gunnar said.

Emil cut in before he could say another word. "Coffee and apple cake."

Gunnar rose and made his way to the counter, where he ordered coffee and apple cake for two.

He retook his seat. "We've been given a riddle we need to solve. Have you ever heard the line 'What about Solitaire's back'? Apparently it's the last sentence of a book."

"Solitaire…" said Emil. "Somewhat unusual female name, I think. Can also refer to a card game—the British call it Patience. It's also a big diamond—more than one carat if I remember correctly."

"Can you remember it appearing as a name in a book?"

"Not at the moment."

"Could you talk to the guys who do your Friday quiz every week? Some of the smarter ones? Don't tell them I'm the one who needs to know. Also, I need you to stay at home for the next few days. I might need to get you on the phone at short notice."

Emil, about to transfer a piece of apple cake from plate to mouth, stopped abruptly. "I'm supposed to wait at home for you to call me?"

"Yeah."

"I think you're going to have to explain this a bit more."

Gunnar thought it over. Emil was not likely to give anything away. He was, in fact, famous for being able to keep secrets, and had many confidants. Many a sinner took comfort in being able to open his heart to Emil when the conscience pricked.

"This is confidential," Gunnar said.

"I have kept secrets before."

"Okay," Gunnar said. It took just a few minutes to explain where the riddle had come from.

Emil took a long time to think over the situation and finally said, "All right. I'll try to help you. But you'll have to get a cell phone for me to use. I really don't care to be stuck at home any more than I have to be."

"Agreed," Gunnar said. "Who can you get to help you?"

Emil pondered this. "I'll start with the Crippled Critic, the Blue Baron, the Cross-Eyed College Teacher, the Red-Nosed Researcher, and the Ginger Journalist. They know all manner of things."

"You mustn't tell them what it's all about," Gunnar reiterated.

"I won't."

"What are you going to tell them?"

"I'll make something up. That's easy for me."

Emil took his pipe from his pocket. Glaring at it in disgust, Gunnar said, "You never mention anybody by name, and you're always using these weird compound nicknames. Why?"

Emil said, "I can't remember people's first names. It's some kind of malfunction in my head. So I make up these sobriquets, usually by combining an adjective and a noun. It's easier for me to remember. The made-up name also gives me a link to the real name, which I can remember if I think it over long enough. The Red-Nosed Researcher is called…" Emil hesitated. "…Rúdolf. He works at the Agricultural Research Institute."

"So the first letter in the nickname is the same as the letter in the real name?"

"Sometimes, but not always. The Blue Baron is called…" He closed his eyes and tapped at his forehead. "…Brúnó?"

Gunnar nodded. "That figures."

"The Cross-Eyed College teacher is a woman. Kolla."

"What do you call me when I'm out of earshot?" Gunnar asked.

"You're the Germanic Giant."

"That's not too bad."

"Nope."

"The question about Solitaire. Will you remember it?"

"Yes, I'll remember. What will I get as a reward for this?"

Gunnar grinned. "I'll go to bed with you," he said.

Emil put his head to one side and gazed silently into Gunnar's eyes for a long time.

"My friend," he finally said. "Maybe one day you'll come across some miserable woman somewhere who just might sleep with you if you pester her long enough. But you'll never get a guy to agree. Ever." He smiled and added, "But don't let it bother you. It's not your fault that you're ugly."

Gunnar grinned again. "What do you want as payment?" he asked.

Emil thought for a long time. At last he said, "Last month, the Blue Baron was unfortunate enough to mistake some guy's wallet for his own. He only realized his mistake when he'd been drinking for three and a half days using some plastic cards he found in the wretched thing. It would give our little group some peace of mind if the police report was inadvertently mislaid."

Gunnar wrinkled his nose. "If you produce the goods I'll take a look at the file."

15:10

It fell to Kristján and Birkir to visit Leifur Albert's mother in Akureyri. She lived alone in the ground-floor apartment of a duplex not far from the police station and, as luck would have it, was at home when they stopped by. She worked as a nursing assistant at the Central Hospital, but happened to be off duty that day.

She was a chubby, dark-haired woman of about fifty. When she opened the door, Birkir thought she looked somewhat sad. Perhaps that was to be expected.

She recognized Kristján and invited them in.

Kristján shook her hand and said, "This is Birkir Hinriksson from the Reykjavik detective division."

"Sólveig Albertsdóttir," she said, acknowledging Birkir's greeting.

Birkir glanced around the apartment. It was tidy, but the furniture was old and worn. Framed pictures hung on the walls—reproductions of paintings, photographs of landscapes, family pictures. Their arrangement demonstrated good intention but not much taste.

Sólveig asked the policemen to be seated in the living room.

Kristján did the talking, "We think we may finally have found your son Leifur's body."

The woman caught her breath.

"The thing is, the circumstances are not quite what we were expecting," he continued.

She exhaled with a low moan.

"We seem to have been mistaken in concluding that he committed suicide."

"How—"

"It is possible that he was murdered."

"Murdered? But what about his suicide note?"

"That's a puzzle."

"Oh my God. I knew it all along. My Leifur was never depressed. I told you that over and over."

Birkir said, "Did your son have a habit of goose hunting?"

This startled Sólveig. "Is there some connection with those murders down south?"

"We don't know yet," Birkir replied. "It's under investigation."

"Well, yes, he loved hunting. I told the police last year that his hunting gear had disappeared from the storeroom here."

Kristján nodded in agreement.

"Could he possibly have been on a hunt when he disappeared?" Birkir asked.

"That's what I initially thought," Sólveig said. "It's what I told the police when I reported him missing."

Kristján said, "That was what we assumed in the beginning. And at the time, we directed our search accordingly. That's why we didn't find the car immediately."

"Did he go hunting often?" Birkir asked Sólveig.

"Yes. Whenever he could."

"Where did he go?"

"Just here around Eyjafjördur. He went wherever he expected to find birds and could get a hunting license. He used to sell his kill to restaurants."

"Did he go on his own?"

"No, he usually went with a friend of his."

"But he was alone when he disappeared?"

"Yes. His friend was visiting some people down south."

"Was there anything unusual about this particular hunting trip?"

"I don't know. I didn't even know he'd gone."

"Was that typical?"

"Yes. Leifur hardly ever told me when he was going hunting. He was a grown man and lived his own life, even though he still had his room here. I never assumed he would be here for meals unless we had prearranged it. I usually eat at the hospital, myself. Sometimes I didn't see him for days. He always had his cell phone, though. I knew I could call him if I needed to."

"Did you not get anything from the phone log?" Birkir asked Kristján.

"No. The last signal came from here in Akureyri. The phone was off after that."

Birkir turned back to Sólveig. "Did you notice any changes in your son in the days before he disappeared?"

"Not really. He was maybe a little restless. His best friend was moving away, and a girlfriend of his was also about to go abroad to study—not a romantic girlfriend or anything, she was just a friend. I couldn't completely dismiss the conclusion made by the police that he had killed himself, but I found it very unlikely. Besides, there was no body. I always wondered if maybe he was still alive; that's what I always hoped deep down inside. I told myself that perhaps he'd gone abroad."

She turned to Kristján. "Are you absolutely sure this person you found is Leifur?"

Kristján nodded. "His wallet was in his pocket."

"May I see him? Maybe it's not him."

"That would be fruitless. I'm very sorry, but you wouldn't recognize him," Kristján said. "We'll check his dental records and do a DNA test. We will keep testing until we are completely certain."

Birkir asked Sólveig, "Who are these friends of Leifur's that you mentioned?"

Sólveig stood up and left the room, returning shortly with a large, framed color photograph, which she handed to him. It showed three young people, two men and one woman, all tanned and smiling, on some tropical beach. The men were incredibly alike—both brown-eyed, their dark hair styled similarly.

Sólveig said, "Leifur is on the right, and the one on the left is Jóhann. They'd been friends since elementary school. People used to call them 'the twins,' but they weren't at all related."

Birkir peered at the faces and was astonished to see that the Jóhann in the picture was without a doubt the same Jóhann who had been involved in the shooting down near Selfoss the previous year.

Sólveig continued. "Jóhann was also in an accident last year. He lost an eye."

Birkir reflected. What on earth was going on? Jóhann had been in a shooting about the same time Leifur had disappeared. Birkir looked through his notebook to verify the dates: Leifur's mother had reported him missing to the police in Akureyri two days after Jóhann had presented with facial wounds at the hospital in Selfoss. Could the incidents be linked? It seemed possible, even very likely. But were they connected with the three killings that had just occurred, an entire year later? That was the bigger question.

He continued to examine the picture, now directing his attention to the young woman. He had definitely seen her before—no question—but where? She was similar in height to her male companions, both of whom were tall, Birkir knew. He suddenly made the connection. The young woman in the picture was the very same one he'd bumped into on the stairs when he went to visit Fridrik Fridriksson's widow. It had seemed at the time like she lived in the building.

"What is the girl's name?" he asked.

"Hjördís. She was a friend, not a girlfriend. For quite a few years the three of them were nearly always together."

"Do you know where she's living now?"

"She went abroad to study last fall. I heard that she came back to spend the summer in Reykjavik, but that's all I know."

15:30

It took Gunnar a while to get a cell phone from the office, buy a SIM card for it, and find Emil Edilon again. He then had to educate Emil in the device's high-tech wizardry. As soon as the old writer learned how to make a call, answer a call, and hang up, he set about locating his panel of experts.

Gunnar thought it unlikely that an Icelandic writer would name one of his characters Solitaire, but if that were the case, he felt certain Emil's buddies would quickly locate the source. He, meanwhile, went off to the National Library to conduct his own search of its English literature shelves. It was slow going. The first book he looked at was *The Hitchhiker's Guide to the Galaxy* by Douglas Adams. He turned quickly to the last page and then returned the book to the shelf. Next was *Dark Laughter* by Sherwood Anderson, then *The Caves of Steel* by Isaac Asimov. By ten to five he had arrived at *The Remorseful Day* by Colin Dexter. Then, at last, Emil called. The other patrons in the library shot Gunnar unfriendly glances as he fished his cell out of a jacket pocket.

"Gunnar speaking."

"It's Edilon."

"What have you got for me?"

"*Live and Let Die* by Ian Fleming. James Bond."

"Who got it?"

"The Ginger Journalist. He's obsessed with Bond."

"Did you tell him it was me looking for it?"

"No."

"Thanks," Gunnar said and hung up.

He moved swiftly over to the *F* shelf, dialing Dóra's number as he went—she would be waiting at her computer. He spotted the book at the moment she replied.

"Wait, don't hang up," he said, taking the volume down from the shelf. With trembling fingers he flipped to the last page. There it was—some broad called Solitaire looking up and asking what about her back. He spelled out the book's title for Dóra.

22:00

There was still no reply from the Gander. Dóra sat at her computer, staring at the box where new mail would appear. There was no sign of life.

"He's not likely to be sitting glued to a computer," Gunnar said. He was hoping their adversary was getting fed up with this game. Then maybe they'd have time for some proper detective work.

Once Birkir had returned to Reykjavik, the team—Birkir, Gunnar, Magnús, and Anna—had gathered at headquarters for a meeting. On the table before them was the file on Leifur Rúnarsson's suicide. Anna chain-smoked while riffling through the papers.

"I'm absolutely certain Leifur wrote this," she said firmly, pointing at a photocopy of the suicide note. "I had really good material to compare it with." She picked up a copy of a postcard with a Spanish stamp. "His mother gave us this card, which he'd sent her earlier that summer. It even uses the same phrases: 'My dearest Mom.' 'Your son, Leifur Albert.'"

Magnús was not convinced. "Are you quite sure?" he asked.

"Yes. All the characteristics match. The same slant to the letters, the same shapes, the same distance between them, the same proportions. There are other fine details we look for in such testing, but none raise any question of doubt."

Birkir asked, "Can you tell anything else from the handwriting? Could he have been forced to write this farewell letter?"

Anna sucked on her cigarette and regarded the photocopy. "No. There are no signs of stress. I actually commented on that in last year's report. It seemed odd to me how effortless the writing was. This is exactly like the card from Spain. Almost casual."

Magnús said, "We need to talk more with these young people, that's clear."

"Jóhann is on duty tonight," Birkir said. "I called him, and he's willing to talk to me during his eleven o'clock break."

He produced a sheet of paper. "Hjördís, the girl who spent so much time with these two guys, is also on the list Fridrik's widow put together for us. She's listed as a neighbor and a prayer recipient."

"What's that mean?" Magnús asked.

"The family prays for people—unasked."

"That's kind."

Birkir shrugged and said, "Depends on how you look at it."

Gunnar changed the subject. "Are we going to assume, just like that, that there's a link between these cases? I mean this killing and the Gander murders?"

Birkir shook his head. "We can't assume anything. It's actually very unlikely. There doesn't seem to be any obvious connection."

Símon entered carrying a stack of papers. "The pictures from the Hvalfjördur tunnel tell us nothing," he said. "I've located all the drivers and gotten their stories, and confirmed them with third parties. Their journeys through the tunnel on those mornings were perfectly legitimate."

"What about the motorcycle?" Gunnar asked.

"That's still a puzzle. I've requested the pictures for between four and six every morning that week; they'll show us whether he's on the move every day. The Akranes police are putting a car there tonight to see if he turns up."

"We have a question!" Dóra yelled from her computer.

Gunnar jumped to his feet and hurried over to her. He read aloud from the screen:

"Question three: They give a man the taste for death. Who is the man? You have ten hours."

Dóra typed the sentence into Google. Six thousand hits. She quickly began scrolling through the results.

"Well, this one's easy," said Gunnar. "It's a poem by someone called A. E. Housman. We'll send the answer in the morning."

23:10

Birkir found Jóhann Markússon in the security company's cafeteria drinking coffee from a thermos and eating a thick sandwich.

Jóhann glanced at his watch. "We have thirty minutes," he said. "What do you want?"

"The body of your friend Leifur was found this morning."

Jóhann's good eye looked quickly at Birkir.

"In the river?"

"I can't tell you that now. But tell me about your friendship."

The good eye looked back at the sandwich. "How do you know we were friends?"

"I saw a photograph of you together. How did you know each other?"

Jóhann took a large bite out of the sandwich and chewed as he thought. At last he said, "Leifur and I were best friends starting in elementary school. We were always together. Almost right up to when he disappeared."

"How come you got along so well?"

"We always had the same interests. It was soccer and skiing when we were little. By the time we were older, it was traveling, body building, and cars. Finally, when we were old enough, it was guns and hunting. We both left school at seventeen and started working. Sometimes together, sometimes separately. Preferably somewhere we could make good money quickly. We just raked in dough for a few months and worked out in the evenings. Then we took time off to have fun. We'd go skiing abroad, or to a tropical beach somewhere. We liked to just do whatever crazy thing came into our heads, and keep at it until the money was gone."

He stopped, and took another bite of his sandwich.

"Why did you part ways?" Birkir asked.

"What do you mean?"

"You weren't living in the north when Leifur disappeared."

"Just a coincidence. I wanted to spend a few months in the south. We hadn't talked much about it, but I was assuming Leifur would come south, too, to work. Nothing seemed to have changed. I assumed we'd be hanging out together again soon. Then there were a few weeks when I didn't actually hear much from him, but I was busy, and it didn't occur to me to see how he was doing. Then came his disappearance and the appeal for information. I would have gone up north immediately, of course, but I was in the hospital because of my eye, and I wasn't allowed to move. The cops in the north called me, and I explained where our usual hunting grounds were. Naturally, I was stunned when they contacted me to say he'd killed himself. Still can't believe it, actually."

"So it came as a surprise to you that he took his own life?"

"It wouldn't have surprised me if he'd gotten killed in an accident. He was totally daring, and sometimes reckless. But, as I told you, I found the news of the suicide hard to believe."

"What did he do that was dangerous?"

"He was into extremes. He'd go rock climbing without a rope or a harness. He'd snowboard or ski on slopes that were almost vertical. He'd do anything: dive into the sea from steep rocks, fly a hang glider, parachute off a cliff. He didn't know what vertigo was. And he drove like a maniac."

"What about you? Didn't you take part in this?"

"Yeah, sure. But he always took bigger risks. There are certain safety precautions that I always took, but he didn't worry about that at all."

"Did you have any enemies?" Birkir asked.

"Enemies? Nah, we didn't bother anybody."

"How did you meet Hjördís?"

"Hjördís? Why do you ask?"

"I'm trying to get a perspective on Leifur's situation. That means finding out a few things about his other friends."

Jóhann looked cautiously at Birkir. Finally he said, "Oh, all right. I'll tell you about Hjördís. She's a bit special."

He smiled momentarily. "Leifur and I had long since left school when Hjördís moved to Akureyri and started high school. Her dad was a doctor, and had come to work at the hospital. They'd lived in America before. Leifur and I were always at the gym, and that's where we got to know Hjördís. She worked out whenever she wasn't at school. We became friends. The high school gang was not her sort of crowd. She wanted action—working out, rock climbing, clay-pigeon shooting. Even though Hjördís is great with a shotgun, she never came hunting with us. It wasn't for her—she couldn't stand dead animals. She went to Spain with us three times. We had a ball. We hit the beach during the day for water-skiing, jet-skiing, diving—that kind of thing. Then we'd work out at the gym before dinner. At night we'd go out clubbing."

"Was there no romance between you?" Birkir asked.

Jóhann grinned. "We weren't really into that, but in the end I found out that Hjördís is one of us boys, if you know what I mean."

"She's gay?"

"Yeah. She only likes girls, but we didn't know that at the time. Leifur and I both tried to get it on with her in the beginning, of course, because she's a fucking classy chick. But she just said that she loved both of us and couldn't choose between us. That's how it was during those four years we spent together. Leifur and I were always picking up girls, but Hjördís was never with a guy and we just didn't think about it. Leifur and I would have dropped her if she'd gone out with someone else—it would have been too weird. I think she liked being with us because we could save her from the guys who tried to hit on her. If anybody was making conversation with her and she didn't dig it, she'd give us a sign and we'd be there like a shot. You should have seen the look on the guys' faces when we showed up and both put our arms around her. They just froze in the middle of trying to pick her up and backed off immediately. I thought we'd continue to be friends after Leifur disappeared, and wondered if perhaps something more might develop. But then she showed up with a girlfriend and I finally understood how things were. Should, of course, have picked up on that earlier."

"Do you know where she lives?"

"She was renting an apartment someplace on Kleppsvegur this summer. I can't remember the building number."

"Do you know where she works?"

"She works from home. I think she's got projects she needs to complete before going back to college in New York."

"Did you and Leifur have any other friends?"

"Friends? Maybe not particularly close friends, but plenty of buddies from the various sports we did."

"Can you make a list of them? Also, relatives, neighbors, colleagues, and anybody else you've had contact with."

Jóhann sighed. "I'll try to jot down a few names. Is it okay if I give them to you tomorrow? My break's over."

"Yeah, tomorrow will do." Birkir stood up, but Jóhann remained seated.

"Listen," he said. "There's something I'd like you to know."

Some moments passed before he continued. "Leifur was the best friend a man could possibly have. I haven't really found my feet since he disappeared. Life is not fun like it was before, if you know what I mean. Sometimes I find myself on the brink of calling his cell number to tell him something I've been thinking about. His disappearance left a big empty space inside me."

"I'm sorry for your loss," Birkir said. Jóhann seemed to be tearing up.

23:15

Gunnar was thirsty after the evening meeting. He bought himself two hot dogs in the Hlemmur kiosk and then walked to the bar on Smidjustígur. On his way, he called home.

"Mother, I'll be home late tonight," he said in German, then hung up.

It had been a miserable day. Dealing with stupid riddles from a total nutcase of a killer was not his thing at all. He was beginning to regret that he hadn't insisted on going to Akureyri with Birkir. At least there was a trail to follow there; time would tell whether there was any connection with the Gander.

The bar was quiet except for a few regulars. There was some kind of meeting in the upper room. He rapped twice on the bar, and shortly afterward the bartender set his usual Holsten and Jägermeister before him and said "You're welcome" in bad German.

Gunnar replied with a "Thanks, jerk," took the glasses, and sat down at a table opposite Emil Edilon, who was playing chess against himself. Then he looked cautiously around.

"You can relax," Emil said without looking up. "The Ginger Journalist's gone north to Thingey. He's going to take a look at the hole where they found that body."

Gunnar downed the bitters in one shot and grimaced.

"Right, so it was on the news tonight?" he asked. "I didn't know there'd already been a press conference."

"No, it wasn't on the news. The Blue Baron's brother sometimes drives the hearse up there. He called the Ginger One and told him all about it. He'll probably get paid for the information."

"Ah. But now you've got something you can use for your thriller. You just need to change it a bit. Guys digging for an electrical pole out in the wilderness, or some such thing, find a body in the ground." Gunnar took a sip from his beer.

Emil looked at him with contempt. "Do you really think that a chance occurrence like that is material for a crime novel? There's no way you can use complete coincidences in a plot line, never mind something as fantastical as this body's discovery."

"But it actually happened. Surely that means it should work in a crime novel."

Emil Edilon shook his head. "A novel should not be about things that may happen, but things that are likely to happen. I hope you're a better policeman than you are a writer. Did you get any more riddles?"

"Yeah. We finally got an easy one. 'They give a man a taste for death. Who is the man?' It's from a poem. The answer is A. E. Housman. That's the guy who wrote it."

"No, no, no!" Emil gasped. "It's a trap! It's from a crime novel."

"What do you mean?" asked Gunnar suspiciously.

Instead of replying, Emil took out the cell phone Gunnar had lent him; he seemed to have fully gotten the hang of speed dialing, and he quickly got through to somebody.

"What's the name of the murderer in P. D. James's book *A Taste for Death*?" he asked the person on the other end of the line. Then, impatiently, "No, I need to know right away."

Turning to Gunnar, he said, "I'm talking to the Blue Baron. He sits at his computer all day and he's lightning fast at Internet searches."

"Are you quite sure?" said Gunnar.

Emil didn't look up. He was listening intently, the cell phone pressed to his ear, pencil at the ready.

"Yes, yes, that figures," he said, scribbling something on his napkin. "No, it's none of your business why I'm asking. Thanks and bye."

He looked at Gunnar. "Who is the man? Dominic Swayne is the man."

Gunnar took a sip of his beer and thought about this.

"Okay. We'll go with that," he said and then downed his beer in one gulp. "Let's have a game of speed chess."

"Loser buys the next round," Emil said, and began to line up pieces.

"Agreed," Gunnar said.

A mere ten minutes later, he went to the bar to buy fresh drinks for the two of them.

"Well, look, if it isn't the fat cop," he heard someone next to him say. "Still chasing kids and old folks?" He looked to his right and saw Kolbrún Gudjónsdóttir.

"So the lass from Dalasýsla is in town?" he said warily.

She smiled faintly. "I'll leave you in peace," she said. "You're not happy." She turned her back to him.

"Dead right," he said, and ordered another round.

CHAPTER 6

07:40

Gunnar arrived in good time at the squad room to give the reply to question three. He typed Dominic Swayne is the man, double-checked what he'd written, and clicked Send. He sat by the computer and waited.

Dóra arrived at eight o'clock. "Morning," she said. "Message from the Akranes police. They called this morning. They waited by the Hvalfjördur tunnel all night for the motorcyclist. He arrived at four thirty precisely."

Gunnar looked up, interested. "And?"

"A young fellow. Lives in Kjalarnes and works as a farmhand north of Akranes. He has to be there early for the morning milking."

"No shotgun?"

"No, no shotgun." She looked at the computer screen. "Have we got a new question?"

"No, but I got a better answer to question three from Emil yesterday." Gunnar showed her the reply that he had sent.

"Do you think that's correct?"

"Emil was very emphatic. Said it was a trick question. It's a line from a poem, sure, but it's also the title of a crime novel in which this Dominic Swayne is the killer. Cross your fingers and hope we got it right."

Dóra was silent, thoughtful. Gunnar opened a new browser window and began to read the news pages. "Is there any coffee?" he asked.

Dóra didn't respond to the question. "Who do you think is playing these games with us?" she asked. "Do you think it's someone we've spoken with?"

Gunnar shook his head. "I doubt it."

"What about Tómas, the lawyer who's sleeping with Helga? Do we know anything about him?"

"He had plenty of books in his house," Gunnar said. "He hasn't got an alibi for the first two murders. He was with Helga when the third was committed."

"There's something weird about the third murder. I think that may be the reason for this quiz game. The Gander wants to delay us."

Gunnar nodded in agreement. "Good thinking."

Birkir entered. "What's on the agenda?" he asked.

Dóra replied, "I got a list of every valid firearm license in the whole country; it's a few thousand names. Magnús wants me to compare them with the lists of names we got from the victims' relatives."

Birkir looked at her with sympathy. "I would help you, but I have to talk to this young woman named Hjördís, who was friends with the two guys from Akureyri. I'm going to try to catch her around noon."

"I'll be okay," Dóra said. "I'll do it on the computer."

"I found fingerprints." This news came from Elías as he entered the room.

"Where?" Gunnar asked.

"The plastic wrapped around that body in the north had prints on it."

"Do we know who they belong to?"

"No, but they'll be good for comparison when we find our suspect. I think we've got all the fingers on both hands. Whoever wrapped the body wasn't wearing gloves."

"Bravo," said Gunnar.

"Are the prints all from the same person?" Birkir asked.

Elías nodded. "Yeah, we think so."

Gunnar said, "And now for the big question: Was the Gander at work up there in the north as well?"

"Why don't we just ask him?" Dóra suggested.

"We can try," Gunnar said. He typed, "How many people have you killed?" and sent it. They waited for several minutes, but nothing happened. Birkir was the first to lose patience and leave the room. Then Elías. Dóra turned to her task and began to flip through lists of names. Gunnar got himself a cup of coffee and sat down at his computer to resume looking at the news, and scrolled to a sports page.

Half an hour later the computer signaled new mail. The subject line was: Question Four.

Gunnar opened the e-mail and read it aloud.

"Hurrah! A good reply to question number three deserves an answer from me to one of your questions. I have killed three so far, and will kill another if you cannot solve question four: Who died? SSIEHITDSOABTEHHGTIPSUAEHKCAUTS"

"He says he's killed three," Gunnar said. "That means he didn't do the one up north, or that's what he wants us to think. We're going to have to treat it as an unconnected case."

He peered at the screen and reread the message. "But I can't make any sense of this question at all," he said, and checked his watch. "We've got until four o'clock."

"Is it German?" Dóra said.

"No, not German. Can you try googling it?" Gunnar stood up. He knew Dóra was much more adept at computer tasks than he. She sat down and copied the string of letters into the search window. No results.

Gunnar looked at the clock. "It's probably too soon to call Emil. He'll get grouchy if I wake him up this early. I'll give him another hour."

12:15

Birkir got to the apartment building on Kleppsvegur at noon. He saw Hjördís's name and apartment number on the directory and was about to press her buzzer but abruptly changed his mind and instead buzzed the number for Fridrik Fridriksson's family.

The widow answered the intercom and Birkir introduced himself. A short while later he was standing in the apartment. He had interrupted their lunch: the children were seated around the dining table eating rice and sausages. At the head of the table sat the preacher, a napkin around his neck. In front of him sat a bowl of rice and an open Bible.

"Bon appétit," Birkir said. He showed the widow the picture of Hjördís and her friends. "Do you know this woman?"

The widow nodded, "Yes. She lives in this building."

"Her name was on your list as…a prayer recipient," Birkir said. "Whatever that means. Have you or your husband had any dealings with her?"

The widow looked at the preacher. He stood, removed his napkin, and placed it on the table. He then took up the Bible, crossed the room to where they stood, and contemplated the photo Birkir held.

"This woman lives here. That is correct," he said.

Birkir looked alternately at the widow and the preacher. "Do you have you a shotgun?" he suddenly asked.

"Me?" said the preacher.

"Yes. Have you got a shotgun?"

"No."

"Where were you last Friday morning?"

"You mean when Fridrik was murdered?"

"Yes."

"May God forgive you for asking such a question."

"Where were you?"

"I was at home."

"Can anybody corroborate that?"

"No, actually. I am not married, and I live alone."

"I see," Birkir said. He turned his gaze back to the picture. "Has the family gotten along well with this woman?" he asked.

The preacher replied quietly, "I would not say they have gotten on badly, but this young woman is on the wrong path in her life. Instead of following the teachings of the Lord, she lives in sin and lust. She shares a bed with another woman and has carnal relations with her."

"How does that affect this particular household?" Birkir asked, looking at the widow.

The widow remained silent as the preacher continued to provide the answers. "The woman has fondled her companion physically in front of everybody, children as well as adults."

"In what way?"

"They embrace each other and kiss."

"Is there something wrong with that?"

"They kiss with the lips...and the tongue. It is a sin and a blasphemy."

"I see. Who observed these...kisses?"

"Fridrik and the children. The worst part was that the children had to witness it."

"Couldn't their father explain to them that it's just what grown-up people do when they're fond of each other?"

"This is not normal fondness. It is the filthy lust of homosexuals. Fridrik bade me convert the woman."

"Did that work?"

"The woman refused to accept the word and blessing of the Lord. She cursed my offer and uttered blasphemy."

Silence fell, and Birkir waited for further explanation. None was offered, so he asked, "Did this result in any conflict between her and Fridrik?"

"No. As far as I know, they had no further conversation. I have visited here a few times in recent weeks, and we have, on these occasions, called upon God in front of the woman's closed door and asked Our Father to grant her guidance. These children here have joined us in these moments of prayer, in order that they may gain understanding of the difference between good and evil in people's lives."

It took Birkir a moment to grasp what the preacher had said.

"Are you telling me that you've stood outside Hjördís's apartment and prayed?"

"Yes."

"With the children?"

"Yes."

"Isn't that taking things a bit far?"

"One can never go too far when the soul is at stake. God's will is quite clear on that in the Good Book."

The preacher opened the Bible at one of many bookmarks and read, "Epistle of Saint Paul to the Romans, chapter one, verse twenty-six: 'For even their women did change the natural use into that which is against nature: And likewise also the men, leaving the natural use of the woman, burned in their lust one toward another; men with men working that which is unseemly, and receiving in themselves that recompense of their error which was meet.'"

He turned to another page and read, "The First Epistle of Saint Paul to the Corinthians, chapter six, verse nine: 'Know ye not that the unrighteous shall not inherit the kingdom of God? Be not deceived: neither fornicators, nor idolaters, nor adulterers, nor effeminate, nor abusers of themselves with mankind, nor thieves, nor covetous, nor drunkards, nor revilers, nor extortioners, shall inherit the kingdom of God. And such were some of you: but ye are washed, but ye are sanctified, but ye are justified in the name of the Lord Jesus, and by the Spirit of our God.'"

Closing the book, he said, "These words evince how God Almighty looks upon any kind of homosexuality and lust."

"Right," Birkir said.

"Are you a Christian in your heart?" the preacher asked.

"I was baptized and confirmed," Birkir said.

"But do you possess living faith?"

"I try to treat others the way I would like them to treat me. I try to be kind to people, rather than treat them badly. I belong to Iceland's national church, and I usually celebrate Christmas in some way. That is my living faith."

The preacher put his hand on Birkir's shoulder. "Do you think that this is enough to inherit God's kingdom, if there is no prayer? Heaven is costly. It demands sacrifice. Man must reach out for God."

Birkir loosened the man's grip from his shoulder. "I think that God doesn't mind whether or not we talk to him. There is no doubt, on the other hand, that he would like us to be kinder to one another. That we show tolerance in matters that harm no one. Beyond that, I think that God is only part of the physics of infinity."

It was obvious that the preacher had no clue what Birkir meant by this last sentence, and indeed Birkir himself didn't understand it. It had just popped out of his mouth all of a sudden.

"You need help to understand the word of the Lord," said the preacher. "With my guidance, you can gain living faith. If you attend our assembly you will see the light."

"Thank you for that. I think I would rather light a candle," Birkir said.

13:30

Hjördís's apartment was close by, just two floors up. Birkir rang the doorbell. He didn't have to wait long before the door was half opened and Hjördís appeared. She was dressed in faded jeans and a white sleeveless T-shirt, her bare feet clad in gray sandals. Birkir remembered her being tall but was still caught by surprise at the sight of her looming in the doorway.

"Yes?" Hjördís looked questioningly down at Birkir. He took a step back.

He introduced himself and showed the ID pinned to his shirt.

"I'm from the detective division. You were a friend of Leifur Albert Rúnarsson, and we're investigating his death."

"Still? He disappeared last year."

She opened the door further and stepped aside. "Please come in."

She led the way into the living room and offered Birkir a seat on a small white sofa. She sat down cross-legged on the floor with her back against the wall, ignoring the chairs in the room.

Birkir sat and observed the young woman. Her face was pretty, but would probably have seemed masculine without the makeup she wore. Nevertheless, she possessed a kind of elegance and even an enigmatic sex appeal. She had a well-defined jaw and high cheekbones, and her mouth was small but full lipped. Her blonde hair was cropped short and had some striking red and black stripes on one side. Freckles peppered her straight nose, and her blue eyes were sharp.

"The Akureyri police talked to me last year," Hjördís said when the silence had become awkward. "I'm not sure if I can tell you anything new."

Birkir said nothing and looked around the room. On a high worktable stood two computers, one with a large flat-screen monitor that displayed a slide show of photographs featuring special effects—sometimes they shattered like glass, sometimes they dissolved and dripped fluidly down the screen, sometimes they turned into white snow that blew away. Then a new picture emerged. There was a large printer on the floor, and various examples of graphic art were piled up on the floor or stuck on the wall. Fixed up along one side of the room was a prominent display of the alphabet; the large black letters appeared in order from A to Z. Each letter had its own page with uppercase and lowercase side by side. This was not a living room; it was a studio.

Hjördís continued. "I could not explain Leifur's disappearance last year, nor can I now. He was not an unhappy man. On the contrary."

"How did you and Leifur meet? Why did you become friends?"

"Do you think that story will help you explain his death?"

"Any information we get helps us create a more detailed picture of him. I don't know whether that will lead to some sort of breakthrough."

"Well, okay. Since you're here, I'll try to help you."

After a pause, she began. "I'll have to tell you a bit about my personal circumstances to explain our friendship. It began when my family moved to Akureyri from Boston when I was sixteen. My dad had done graduate studies in medicine in New England and had worked there for a few years after. Then he got a job as a consultant in one of the departments of the district hospital in Akureyri. This was a terrible upheaval for me at a difficult age. I was born in Iceland, and my family often came back to visit while we were living abroad. We also always spoke Icelandic at home, so the language was not a problem. But to move from a big American city to a tiny Icelandic town like Akureyri was a bit of a culture shock. I went to a really big high school in Boston, and anything you can think of was on offer in terms of classes, sports, and the arts. There was always something going on, and I had loads of friends."

Abruptly, she stood, got a bottle of water from the worktable, and took a sip from it. Still standing, she spoke again. "It wasn't just that I lost my friends when we moved to Iceland. There was something else that made my life more difficult to deal with."

She hesitated. "I'd started to have serious doubts about my sexual orientation. During my adolescence in America, it hadn't bothered me that I was never attracted to the guys like my girlfriends were. I just thought that it would happen later for me. In Akureyri, being interested in boys was even further from my mind. Compared with my classmates in Boston, the Icelandic boys rated really badly for manners; they were clumsy and sometimes just plain rude. Their posturing just didn't appeal to me, but they were always trying to get my attention."

She shook her head and smiled faintly. "Oh, yes, they tried. You could easily describe most of their behavior as sexual harassment, but that's another story."

She took another sip of water. "After a while, I met and became friends with a girl who was very much into all types of sports in Akureyri—team handball, soccer, and swimming, to name just a few. She was a glamorous, athletic girl, a year older than me and almost as tall. I suddenly realized I had a crush on her, and, my God, what a shock that was. I completely stopped seeing her and shut that part of myself off. My parents were very worried about me for a few months, but finally, my courage began to come back. I avoided girls, though, because I found any hint of those unwelcome romantic feelings very uncomfortable. I had a good relationship with my parents, but I didn't dream of discussing this with them, nor with anyone else.

"Then I met the 'twins,' as they were called: Leifur and his best friend, Jóhann. Back in Boston I'd done gymnastics in high school—they had fantastic facilities. I did very well, but being so tall held me back. It's not an asset in that sport, and I knew I was never going to reach the top ranks. Everyone wanted me to take up basketball because of my height, but I could never learn to hit the basket."

The memory brought a smile to Hjördís's face. "When I came to Akureyri, I gave up gymnastics and got into working out. I could do it on my own and didn't need help in the gym. I already knew many of the strengthening exercises and stretches from gymnastics, and I liked improvising, too. I enjoyed losing myself in a workout when I was feeling really low; the exertion relaxed me and brought a feeling of well-being that I experienced all too rarely. The guys, the 'twins,' were always in the gym as well, and we began to get to know each other. They were, of course, just as dumb as the other guys in town, but they were always together and that made them easy to handle—neither tolerated any harassment or lack of respect toward me from the other. We began to work out together and then became friends outside of the gym. I didn't need to worry about other guys, because Leifur and Jóhann kept them away from me."

She took another sip from the water bottle and put it aside. She looked intently at Birkir. "I assume that you're heterosexual. You can try to put yourself in my place by imagining that you can't go out on the town without most of the men constantly hitting on you. That felt just as abhorrent to me as it would to you. I just shrink from the idea of touching a man in a sexual way. I had no heterosexual experience, and I didn't want to contemplate a situation where it might be forced on me. Leifur and Jóhann ensured I didn't need to fear anything like that. I could have fun with any interesting guy, but if he became too fresh, all I had to do was to give my friends the sign and they were there. Then he'd leave me in peace."

Hjördís fell silent as she recalled this and then said, "Other girls found my two friends very attractive, and, little by little, I learned to enjoy the company of beautiful girls without blushing in embarrassment. But it never occurred to me to take things any further in that direction. That didn't happen until last fall, when I moved to New York to go to design school, where I met a woman and ended up in love and in a relationship."

"Where is she now?" Birkir asked.

Reaching across to one of the computers, Hjördís hit a key to stop the slide show and selected a file with the mouse. A photo of a muscular black sprinter appeared. Hjördís said, "This is Rose. She's in New York right now training. She's a heptathlete."

Soon the picture disappeared and the slide show started up again. Many of the images were Hjördís's family photos. Birkir saw her whole life on show: baby pictures, toddler birthdays, everything up to the present. Each picture stayed on the screen for a few seconds.

"I don't have picture albums and I don't hang photos on the wall," Hjördís said. "I just have them as a screen saver, so I can always see them. That way, they're with me wherever I go and wherever I'm living."

"How many are there?" Birkir asked.

"There are about a thousand on this loop. It shows ten a minute, so it takes a hundred minutes to go around. I've got more sets."

In one of the photos that came up, Birkir recognized Jóhann standing next to a young man who looked a lot like him.

"Leifur and Jóhann. Tell me more about them," Birkir said.

Hjördís had spotted the picture, too, and froze it on the screen with a keystroke. She was silent for a bit and then said, "Although they were quite unrelated, they looked incredibly alike. Like twins, actually. And not just in appearance, their mannerisms were almost the same."

She restarted the slide show.

"What do you mean, *almost* the same?" Birkir asked.

"Leifur was just a bit more of everything. He was usually more proactive in their escapades, and he always went just that bit further. He was more of a leader. But it wasn't obvious, and I didn't realize it until I'd known them for a long time."

"Tell me more about them."

"Well, they both left school early, but they weren't stupid—far from it. Perhaps just a bit immature in some ways. It was obvious that their main interests lay outside of school. They read all kinds of literature but they weren't interested in lesson plans. They were into philosophy and history books and they read novels. They even listened to New Age music—at Jóhann's instigation, I remember. They practiced all kinds of extreme sports and spent all their money going on trips abroad. They turned everything into a competition. Sometimes they would spend days playing computer games—not PlayStation-type stuff, but serious games on the Internet that had participants from all over the world. The same game would sometimes go on for days and they'd take on a huge number of competitors. They'd take turns playing their opponents, working in shifts. I was never involved in this particular hobby; I found other things to do."

"How do you spend your time? Apart from the gym?"

"Graphic design," Hjördís replied quickly. "I've always been good at drawing, but I wanted to improve. I was forever reading design magazines and stuff like that. I'm really into typography—at the moment I'm designing a new headline font for an American architectural magazine. It's a very interesting and demanding project."

Hjördís pointed at the pictures on the walls.

"Is it something you're studying?" Birkir asked.

"Yes. I enrolled in a very interesting school last fall. I got lucky, because at first they placed me on the waiting list. Then someone dropped out and they offered me the spot. That's why

I went to New York so suddenly last year. I couldn't even attend Leifur's memorial service."

"Your friends, did they have any enemies?"

"What do you mean?"

"Do you know of anyone that might have wanted to do them harm?"

"No."

"When was the last time you saw Leifur?"

"The three of us were together in Spain last August, but I flew home before they did to check out study options for the coming winter. I'd applied to several schools and had to follow up. We didn't see each other at all during these weeks before I went to New York. That chapter of my life was over, and I didn't need them anymore. I felt terrible, though, when Leifur disappeared."

"What about Jóhann?"

"He came to New York last fall, but we didn't spend much time together. He was a bit funny, of course, when I introduced him to my girlfriend. I'd never explained my leanings to him and Leifur, or to anyone, for that matter. I was completely in the closet during the years I was friends with them."

Birkir mulled things over. Then he said, "I understand that Fridrik, your neighbor, poked his nose into your private affairs—that is to say, your sexual orientation."

"The guy who was murdered?"

"Yes."

"Do we have to talk about that?"

"He harassed you, didn't he?"

"Yeah, he did. What about it?"

"That must have been unpleasant?"

She shook her head. "No. It doesn't disturb me having people standing out in the hallway mumbling prayers. They're entitled to their opinions, as far as I'm concerned. I don't need their consent to live my own life. It's much worse when people hide their prejudices and pretend to be well-meaning but then are offensive behind your back."

"What was it that bothered Fridrik?"

"Rose, my girlfriend, stayed with me for two weeks this summer. I said goodbye to her on the sidewalk when she took a taxi to the airport. We kissed goodbye. Just at that moment, Fridrik came out with the children; he muttered something unpleasant, but I didn't give it any thought until that weird preacher of theirs suddenly appeared on my doorstep. It wasn't hard to get rid of him, but then I began to hear murmuring out in the hallway. At first it made me lose concentration when I was trying to work— that was bad, as I'm already a bit behind on all the projects I've committed to. But I got used to it."

Birkir took from his notebook a photograph of Ólafur Jónsson and handed it to Hjördís.

"Do you know this man?"

She examined the picture. "I feel as if I've seen this face. I might have met him at one of the Icelandic parties in New York last winter. Is that possible?"

"Maybe. What about this one?" he asked, showing her a photo of Vilhjálmur Arason.

"No. My grandmother might know him."

Birkir pretended not to notice the irony in her tone.

"Who are these guys?" she asked.

"Victims of the recent murders. Then there is Fridrik, your neighbor."

Hjördís seemed surprised. "You think that this is linked to me in some way?"

"If there's a connection between these killings and the attacks on Leifur and Jóhann, then yes, that is a possibility. You would be the only person who has had dealings with two parties in the case, so far as we know."

"The attack on Leifur? Are you saying he was murdered?"

"He was shot. Yes."

"Oh my God, I didn't know that." Her right hand flew to her cheek. "I was told he'd committed suicide."

"Can you tell me what you were doing in the early mornings of last Thursday, Friday, and Sunday?"

"Why not Saturday?"

"Nobody was murdered then."

"Do you really think that I know something about these deaths?"

"We need to exclude everyone with the slightest connection to these events."

"Well, all right. Early morning, you said? Tuesday I went up north to visit Mom and Dad, returning around midday Thursday. Friday I was definitely asleep here at home. I usually work into the wee hours and wake up late. Saturday night I went out on the town, and I slept somewhere else that night. I stayed there until noon Sunday."

"At what address?"

"I'm not telling you that. I met a woman and we were together. I'm not particularly proud of this fling, but Rose and I have an open relationship, and sometimes we don't see each other for ages."

Birkir had been keeping one eye on the slide show, and now a picture appeared that caught his full attention: a young woman, not yet twenty, carrying Hjördís on her back. She had long, dark, flowing hair, a cheerful face, and crooked front teeth.

"Who is that?" Birkir asked quickly, pointing at the screen.

By the time Hjördís had turned her head to look, a new photo was showing on the screen.

"This one?" she asked.

"No, the one before."

She turned to the computer, hit a key to interrupt the slide show, and flipped back to the previous picture.

"That one," said Birkir.

"Her name is Kolbrún. She was our au pair when I was ten or eleven."

"Is she from Dalasýsla?"

"Yeah." Hjördís smiled. "She was very provincial when she came to Boston."

"Have you met her since then?"

"Yeah, just recently. She works in a seafood store I sometimes go to. They've got really good, cheap fish dishes that you can just heat up in the oven or stick in the microwave. I went there the first time this summer and recognized her immediately. And she recognized me."

"Have you kept in touch since?"

"No. We sometimes gossip in the store if it's not busy. She's told me how life's treated her since she was with us. Why are you asking about her?"

"We encountered her during our investigations."

"In what way?"

"One of the victims was shot near the farm where her father lives."

"Oh. I didn't know that. Poor thing."

"So you've had no more than this casual contact?"

"Nope."

Birkir was not convinced she was telling the truth.

15:45

Gunnar, Magnús, and Dóra were gathered around the computer when Birkir got back to the office. Gunnar held a phone to his ear. "We're not getting anywhere with this," he said.

"With what?" Birkir asked.

"We need the answer to the latest riddle," Gunnar replied. "We're running out of time, and Emil's helpers still haven't found the answer."

"What's the question?"

Dóra pointed at the computer screen: Who died? SSIEHITD-SOABTEHHGTIPSUAEHKCAUTS

Gunnar said, "The search engine can't find it, nor can anyone else."

"Let me see," said Birkir, and he leaned over the screen.

"It's some kind of anagram," he said. "Have you tried putting it into a different order?"

"Yes, both backward and forward," Gunnar replied.

There was a brief silence as Birkir studied the text. Then he said, "Try every other letter, backward."

Dóra did as he said.

S U C H A S I G H T A S T H I S appeared on the screen.

Dóra read, "Such a sight as this?"

"And now the rest of the line, also backward," Birkir said.

T A K E U P T H E B O D I E S.

"Now google it," Birkir said, straightening up.

Dóra did so, and after a few clicks of the mouse they found themselves looking at:

Take up the bodies: such a sight as this
Becomes the field, but here shows much amiss.
Go bid the soldiers shoot.

It was the end of Fortinbras's monologue, the final words in *Hamlet*.

"Hamlet. How the hell did you do that?" Gunnar asked.

"When I was in grade school there was a craze for writing messages in various kinds of code. I got good at cracking them."

Gunnar looked at the clock. "We've got ten minutes until the deadline."

Birkir said, "The goddamn Gander is playing with us. This stupid distraction is making us focus all our attention on solving bizarre riddles instead of continuing to search for him."

"What can we do?" Magnús asked. "Stop responding?"

Birkir shrugged. "He'll surely get bored with this in the end, and then it's anybody's guess what he'll do next."

Dóra typed the answer in an e-mail—Hamlet died—and clicked Send.

Two minutes later the reply came: Heavens above! You are geniuses. I applaud you.

They all waited, staring at the screen, for the follow-up.

"We're playing it totally his way. Just standing here like zombies," Birkir said. "What's the next thing on the agenda, Magnús?"

"Next?" Magnús glanced at the clipboard in his hand. "We don't yet have the list of Leifur and Jóhann's friends. You were going to get it."

"Here's something," Dóra said. She opened the mail and they all peered at the screen.

Question five: In one of his books the crime writer Ed McBain used a famous play in the plot. Which book? Three hours.

Dóra typed "Ed McBain" into the search engine and selected one of the pages that came up.

"Pseudonym of Evan Hunter," Gunnar read. "Any of you read anything by him?"

"Yes," said Birkir. "They're great crime novels."

Magnús also nodded. "I know them, too."

Dóra continued searching. She got a listing of all of McBain's books and counted them. "There are at least fifty books in his 87th Precinct series. How are we supposed to solve this one?"

She tried "Ed McBain famous play" but waded through a mass of hits without finding anything helpful.

Gunnar grabbed the phone and dialed. "Emil," he said. "Listen, I've got another riddle for you."

17:00

Birkir called Jóhann Markússon's cell. Jóhann answered immediately.

"I need that list of your and Leifur's friends," Birkir said.

"I'm just leaving the gym and I'll be home in ten minutes. Meet me there. I jotted them down this morning. The note's ready on the kitchen table."

He gave his address, and Birkir noted it down before hanging up.

Jóhann lived in an apartment building in Lower Breidholt. The parking lot was empty when Birkir arrived. He waited a minute or two, and then a sporty black BMW glided into the spot next to him.

"That's a cool car," Birkir said as Jóhann got out.

"It's a lot older than it looks. I bought it this spring," Jóhann said as he locked it with the remote. "It's been very well looked after, but I think I'll be selling it. I'd rather be driving an SUV in the winter."

They walked together into the building. Jóhann said, "We'll have to be quick. I need to get to work. I'm still on night shift."

He opened the door to an apartment on the second floor. The interior was hot and airless, and Birkir immediately noticed an unpleasant odor.

"The renter before me had badly trained cats. I haven't been able to get rid of the smell," Jóhann said as he opened the door to the balcony.

Birkir looked around. The furniture was mismatched and in poor condition. The sofa's covering was torn, and there was a large scorch mark on the table in front of it. Two shotguns hung from nails on the wall; on the floor were three open boxes of books. Some large, framed photographs of Leifur and Jóhann were leaning against one wall and showed the friends rock climbing, posing on the beach, skiing, and shooting.

"This is not a home for the future," Jóhann said. "I rented it furnished and don't plan to stay here long."

He pointed at the pictures. "Hjördís took those. She's a great photographer. I really like them. I'm thinking about whether it's worth putting them up on the wall."

Birkir looked into one of the boxes and examined the uppermost book.

"Ed McBain. Are you interested in crime novels?" he asked.

"Yeah, some of them. I've got almost all the McBain books, I think. The ones about Precinct 87. I think there must be more than forty in that box."

"Why do you like this author so much?"

"I love good crime stories. And you learn a lot of English reading them. I'm also thinking maybe I'll apply to get into the police."

"Do you really think you learn something from these books?"

"Yeah, I think so. McBain knew completely what he was writing about. But I don't know if you'd have me in the police, because of my eye."

"You probably wouldn't be the worst on a team," Birkir said. "But I've just had a thought. Can you answer a question for me? In one of his books, McBain used a famous play in the plot. Do you know which book that was?"

Jóhann seemed surprised. "Why do you ask?"

"I heard someone mention it recently."

"It's a very easy question," Jóhann said. "It's called *Ten Plus One*. In the book, he uses a play by Eugene O'Neill, *The Long Voyage Home*. The book came out in 1963."

"Why is it an easy question?"

"It's the only one of McBain's books that's been published in Icelandic. It's called *The Sniper* in the translation. One of my favorite books."

"Why?"

"I found an error in it. That's what I like best when I'm reading. Finding errors."

"What error?"

"In one place the murderer is asked to come outside for a cigarette, but says that he doesn't smoke. But a few pages later he lights up. I know I'm not the only one who enjoys looking for mistakes like that in fiction. There are even websites that catalog lots of these sorts of things. Stephen King makes a lot of errors."

"What's the McBain book about?"

"*Ten Plus One* is about a serial killer who kills most of the people who took part in a particular performance of the play. That's all—the actual plot of the play doesn't feature in the book."

Birkir took out his cell and called Gunnar.

"I've got the answer to question five," he said.

After a brief conversation, he turned back to Jóhann.

"Do you have that list of names for me?"

"Yeah." Jóhann fetched a piece of paper from the kitchen and handed it to Birkir.

"Sorry it's handwritten. My printer's broken."

Birkir glanced at the paper. The handwriting was not stylish, but it was quite legible.

"Can you read it okay?" Jóhann asked.

"Yes, I think so," Birkir replied.

"I hardly ever write anything by hand. When the three of us were in Spain, it was Hjördís who wrote the postcards for Leifur and me. She could imitate our handwriting better than we could write ourselves. She's so good at drawing."

"Right."

Jóhann pointed to the list of names. "It's all there," he said. "Skiing companions, hunting companions, traveling companions, old girlfriends, and family. I wrote it up for both Leifur and me, as well as I could."

"Do you and Hjördís sometimes meet?"

"No, not anymore."

"Why not?"

"Something happened between us. Something I don't want to talk about."

"Did you fall out?"

"Yeah, you could say that."

"Did that happen after Leifur disappeared?"

"No, before."

"Are you sure you don't want to explain it?"

"Off the record?"

"The police don't operate like that. I'm not a psychologist, not a doctor, not a priest, and not a journalist."

"Then I can't say anything."

"So be it," Birkir said. "I'm not going to force you to say something you don't want to say. But sometimes it can be good to talk about what's on your mind."

Birkir wasn't expecting these words to bring any result, but they nevertheless stirred something within Jóhann. He was silent, thinking things over, patently uncomfortable. Finally he said, "I'll tell you something that I'll never say again, and I'll never admit to having said it. You haven't got a tape recorder on you, have you?"

He came over and patted Birkir's jacket pocket.

"No. I'm not carrying a recorder," Birkir said.

"Switch your cell off," Jóhann said.

Birkir took his cell phone out, turned it off, and showed it to Jóhann.

"You wanted to know why Leifur and I fell out with Hjördís," Jóhann said.

"Yes," Birkir said quietly.

"Okay. We went to Spain in August last year. It was our third trip in as many years, and everything was just as usual. It was the three of us together in an apartment for two weeks of non-stop fun. One night during the second week, we drank more than usual and somehow all ended up in the double bed at our apartment. We were just playing and fooling around, but then Leifur and I got just a bit too excited. We began to peel the clothes off Hjördís, and we didn't hear—or we didn't listen—when she told us to stop. One thing led to another, and it ended by us...basically...simply raping her. It just started somehow, and before we knew it we were both done. It had just seemed like banter and silliness to start with—we were too drunk to realize what we were doing. It had happened a few times before that we both screwed the same girl, and they weren't always pleased about it, either. It didn't dawn on us until the following morning what we'd done to Hjördís. During the night she'd packed her things and split. She flew home on the first available flight. We didn't see her again until we were back in Akureyri, and she ignored us completely. It has been hanging over me like a nightmare I can't forget for the past year. I can't forgive myself for having been a part of it. It was bad enough losing a best friend, without the feeling of guilt over what we did."

Jóhann looked as if he had a toothache; but then he tried to smile.

"I'm now using you as a psychologist. You probably don't think much of me."

Birkir had no answer to this. He saw no cause to grant absolution for the despicable crime Jóhann had just confessed to. More than anything, he wanted to do his duty as a cop and charge the guy. But Jóhann would deny having said anything, and Birkir's evidence would be of limited value unless he could persuade Hjördís to bring charges—surely there was no doctor's certificate or any physical proof, and the crime had been committed abroad.

This was not, however, at the top of his mind at this moment.

"Does Hjördís also read Ed McBain?"

The question seemed to take Jóhann by surprise. "She does, actually. She was the one who brought most of these books from America. She gave them to me later, after she'd read them all."

Birkir thought very carefully, and framed his next question as clearly as he could. "Do you think it's at all possible that Hjördís tried to take revenge on you and Leifur for what you did to her?"

"How..."

"By shooting at you."

"Do you really think that she—"

"Is it possible?"

"I don't know. My God, I don't know."

He had started to cry.

18:30

The whole investigative team reconvened at the station.

Gunnar sat at the computer and waited until the last minute before sending the latest answer: *Ten Plus One*. Or *The Sniper* if you're using the Icelandic translation. He had popped over to the City Library to double-check the answer; it was just as Jóhann had explained it to Birkir. Gunnar was grateful. Emil and his team had looked through the McBain books they had on hand, but hadn't been able to solve the riddle. Instead, the answers seemed to be falling into their laps from the most unlikely sources. Perhaps their luck was turning.

Soon, another question arrived by e-mail.

Question six: this question is about a crime novel. Euphemism for death and bloodless hands. How does chapter 28 begin? Six hours.

Gunnar copied the clue into a Google search, which yielded many hits, none linking to a book. He tried changing the word order and shortening the clue, but to no avail. "Bloodless" by itself referenced a song but not a book title.

His only option was to call Emil Edilon yet again to ask for help. First he read the whole question to him, and then he had to spell out *euphemism* so Emil could write down the question. "This seems complicated," Emil said. "I'll be in touch."

Gunnar hung up. "Now what?" he asked.

"We've got to look at this from different angles," Birkir said.

"The question?" Gunnar asked.

Birkir shook his head. "No. The homicides we're investigating. Remember those?"

Gunnar grinned apologetically and nodded.

Birkir stood up, turned to the others, and asked them to listen. He gave them a blow-by-blow account of his conversations with Hjördís and Jóhann. "In conclusion," he said, "it seems that there was considerable tension between Leifur and Jóhann on the one hand, and Hjördís on the other. I think we need to take a very close look at her."

"Could she be the Gander?" Magnús asked.

"I don't think so. She says she has an alibi for two mornings out of three. We'll get that verified if need be. We have to consider the possibility that these are separate cases."

Gunnar said, "We began to take that view when the Gander claimed responsibility for only three murders, not four. But of course we won't let him dictate our methodology."

Magnús agreed that they needed to investigate the trio—Leifur, Jóhann, and Hjördís—much more thoroughly. Tasks were allocated: Birkir was to undertake a comprehensive examination of Hjördís's circumstances; Gunnar and Dóra were to continue looking for answers to the Gander's latest riddle; and Símon was to visit the schoolteacher, Ragnar Jónsson, and pick up the list of names of the family and friends of his father-in-law, Vilhjálmur Arason. Símon planned to take a photo of Hjördís with him to show to Ragnar and his wife, Bára. If they knew her, it might be a major clue.

20:10

Símon didn't think Ragnar Jónsson was looking very well. He had dark rings under his eyes and he had messed up on his shaving that morning—there was prominent black stubble on his upper lip, and he had a Band-Aid on his right cheek.

"I've been having trouble sleeping," he said. "I need to arrange my father-in-law's funeral, and I am trying to write an obituary. My dear Bára has also been very miserable. She was so fond of her father. Recently he gave us money toward a larger car that would be easier for her to sit in. It's so difficult for her to get into our little one."

Símon examined the piece of paper on which Ragnar had catalogued Vilhjálmur's friends, family, and other connections in tidy, clear handwriting. There were in all only fourteen names and Hjördís was not among them.

"Are you sure this is all?" Símon asked.

Ragnar nodded. "I've looked at the names over and over," he said.

Símon showed him the picture of Hjördís. "Have you ever seen this woman?"

Ragnar took the photograph and scrutinized it. "Is she in some way linked to these murders?" he asked.

"It's possible."

"What's her name?"

"Hjördís."

Ragnar mulled this over for a long time. Finally he said, "There was an incident a couple of weeks ago."

He thought some more. "My father-in-law has a small apartment he rents out. The tenant had moved out a while ago, and he'd advertised it for rent. He and I arranged to meet at the building, because he wanted to paint the walls, and I was going to help him that evening. You know how these renters treat premises."

Símon nodded, and Ragnar continued. "When I got to the building, my father-in-law was arguing with some woman. She went off in a huff when I arrived, and my father-in-law said she was someone he knew slightly—the daughter of one of his acquaintances, or something. I think he said her name was Hjördís. Apparently she wanted to rent the apartment for peanuts because she was a sort of family friend, and she completely lost it when my father-in-law wouldn't agree. That's what they were arguing about. I'm just wondering if it's possible she was the woman in the picture. I think it's quite possible, actually."

"Are you sure?"

"Yes, almost. Do you think it could have been her who shot my father-in-law?"

"You saw the killer. What do you think?"

"Well, I didn't see whether it was a man or a woman. But come to think of it, I remember that the person had rather broad hips."

"Did you see the face?"

"No. It was too far away."

"What about the hair?"

Ragnar looked back at the picture. "It might well have been short and blonde."

"Did Vilhjálmur say anything else about this woman?"

"He said that she was like…insane."

"Did he know if she was a lesbian?"

"Yes, he mentioned that, too."

20:30

Detective Superintendent Magnús Magnússon was married. In most people's judgment, he had married well—his wife, Vilhelmína, was partner in a law firm with two other attorneys and a number of associates, and they had some very upscale clients. These types needed constant legal advice and were sufficiently well-off to pay large bills on the due date, frequently.

Vilhelmína didn't bother with the housekeeping. She knew some women put up with tasks like cleaning and washing, but she preferred to hire help and avoid being involved in such drudgery. Magnús was in charge of these arrangements, and he drew up the list of tasks for the help and made sure everything was tidy and in order.

At lunch Vilhelmína usually ate with clients, and in the evening she just had a piece of fruit or something light in front of the television. A shopping list stuck to the fridge told the help what to buy. Magnús ate his lunch in the police station cafeteria and, at home after work, often dined on *skyr* and rye bread, sometimes with smoked lamb, sometimes with raw herring. He loved traditional Icelandic food, especially the yogurt-like *skyr*. He and his wife hardly ever ate together unless Vilhelmína had put it on her calendar; when they did eat at home, it was Magnús who cooked. They had separate bedrooms and only spent nights together by prior appointment. Lately, Magnús had started taking Viagra when these encounters were forthcoming, so he could be confident that nothing would go wrong.

This household system suited the two of them very well, and there was little danger they would get bored with each other—they simply didn't spend enough time together for that. They led their separate lives and mostly did what they wanted. The only condition was mutual fidelity in their conjugal life, and it didn't occur to either of them to test that particular rule. Their only son lived with his wife and child in Washington DC and worked for the International Monetary Fund; they followed a prearranged schedule of twice-yearly family get-togethers.

When Magnús arrived home, tired after what had been a long day, his wife was sitting in front of the television with her laptop on her knees, talking on the phone. He went into the kitchen, spooned some *skyr* into a bowl, and sat down at the table to scan the daily newspapers. The killings had attracted the biggest head-lines; he glanced through the various reports and saw they merely repeated the information the police had given out in the press conferences. Nothing of significance had leaked out yet. One of the papers had taken the trouble to send a photographer to Litla-Fell after the police had left. The picture had evidently been taken in the farmyard through the side window of a car, because the rear-view mirror could be seen at the bottom of the picture. In the foreground were two snarling dogs.

Magnús made coffee and took his wife a cup. She glanced up from her phone and computer to give him a smile and then turned back to the television; she was watching CNN with the sound turned off while she talked on the phone.

With that, his domestic duties for that evening were complete, and he took his coffee into his den. The room was a trout fisherman's temple. On the walls hung stuffed fish, pictures of rivers and anglers, and framed fishing flies in carefully arranged rows, each fly identi-fied on a white label. The bookshelves held many volumes on trout fishing, and above the worktable was a transparent plastic organizer with many small drawers containing the various raw materials needed to make trout fishing flies—feathers, hair tufts, and the like.

He sat at his worktable, turned on the radio, and resumed knotting a fly he had started making the night before; secured to a small clip beneath a large magnifying glass and work light, its main feature was tiny green and blue feathers.

This was Magnús's favorite pastime—making flies, and fishing for trout in the summer. His job really just occupied the time in between. He didn't particularly need the salary, but it covered the purchase of fishing licenses and replacing the SUV every other year. Any surplus went to investments; Vilhelmína paid the household expenses.

The police work had, until now, been a convenient diversion. He was usually pretty astute when picking his colleagues and had created a department that more or less ran itself, which effectively put him in the role of administrative supervisor. Now, however, the office was in chaos, with four unsolved homicides and a probable serial killer at large. Maybe it was time to retire.

He pondered the first message the murderer had sent.

You ask why. Will that change anything? It is done and cannot be undone. What is that urge that drives the hunter a far distance into the predawn cold to bag a few geese he will hardly bother to eat? Or the urge that prompts some people to go fishing and then release their catch in the hope that the fish will either live and breed or be caught again?

I am a killer by nature. I hunt men and I never let go.

Was this directed at him? He caught trout, sometimes salmon, and he often released his catch, usually, to be honest, because he couldn't be bothered to gut the fish and dress them for storage. He only liked freshwater fish smoked and generally didn't really care to eat what he caught. He was not a "killer by nature." The killing was an unpleasant part of the process, necessary in his view only when the fish swallowed the bait and you couldn't extract it without injuring them. Magnús's hunting instinct consisted in laying bait for the fish, and landing the catch after it had taken the bait.

The telephone on his desk began to ring, but the answering machine picked up the call instantly, its mechanical voice reading out the phone number and prompting a message. Somebody began to speak; Magnús recognized the voice of the minister of justice and reluctantly pushed the speakerphone button to reply.

"Magnús speaking," he said loudly.

"Any news?" came the voice from the speaker.

"No, nothing significant, but we're looking at a number of leads."

Magnús continued tying the fly as the minister droned on, giving him the benefit of some good advice—things he'd probably seen in police dramas on television—and said that the ministry would help them in any possible way. Magnús had started on a new fly when the minister asked whether it might not be a good idea to bring in foreign specialists to help with the investigation.

Magnús made a face. "I don't think that's appropriate just yet," he said, and blew on a tiny drop of glue he had placed on the end of the line to bind the feathers to the hook. "But I'll check what possibilities we've got as far as that goes," he added to prevent the minister from getting involved himself. The conversation ended, and Magnús soon lost himself in daydreams of trout fishing by a still brook, in calm weather with just a hint of drizzle.

21:00

After speaking with Ragnar, Símon was able to go straight home to his wife. He was not needed back at the station. Dóra was on sole duty that evening, monitoring the computer and the phone; the others were to gather strength, as Magnús had put it, and have a good night's sleep. There was to be a meeting the following morning, and Símon was looking forward to seeing the looks on their faces when he delivered his report—this was brand-new information on the case, and it was he who had brought it to light. He had asked the right questions at the right time. Maybe now the others would treat him as part of the team and give him meatier tasks.

Símon had been in the detective division for just under a year, having been in crime prevention the previous two years. He had started young as a traffic cop, when he'd also been playing soccer for some of the top teams in Southwest Iceland. Then he had moved to Norway to play semiprofessional soccer for a second-division team in Oslo. While there, he had enrolled in the Norwegian Police Academy to study planning and crime prevention. Part of the reason he got in was that the police commissioners of Reykjavik and Oslo had met at a Scandinavian police conference and decided to set up a student exchange program between the two countries' police academies. Símon had been the first from Iceland to take part in the exchange—since he was in Oslo anyway playing soccer he'd been the obvious choice. Naturally, a Norwegian student had also gone to Iceland; but the guy had given up after two weeks, convinced he would never get the hang of the strange language spoken by Icelanders. Símon graduated from the academy after struggling mightily with the course work; he never stopped to wonder if they'd passed him only because it would have seemed rude to fail the police commissioner's exchange student. Nobody seemed surprised when this first exchange turned out to be both the beginning and the end of the student program.

When Símon started having trouble getting positions on soccer teams in Norway, he returned to Iceland and took up his old job as a traffic cop. Then the position of head of the crime prevention unit became vacant, and as Símon could show that he had graduated in that specialty in Norway, it was impossible to pass him over when he applied. It soon became apparent that he was completely unsuited for the work; but it took his superiors two years to find a solution to the problem, which was to redeploy him to the detective division's violent-crime unit with the promise of a swift promotion depending on his success in the job. The promotion wasn't happening fast enough, in Símon's opinion, and it irritated him no end that he was always assigned to work the most trivial crimes. If someone got a smack in the face downtown, it was Símon who had to chase witnesses, write reports, and try to make sense of the endless lies spun by the respective petty criminals and psychopaths. But when more serious cases came along, he got pushed aside. This time he was going to show them he could solve real homicides.

These daydreams absorbed his whole mind and, by the time he got home, had become so exaggerated that he had solved the case all by himself and was explaining to his open-mouthed colleagues how it all hung together. He was on such a high that he knew he'd want to tell his wife, Ingirídur, all about it.

They had been married five years, and, to tell the truth, Ingirídur was not particularly enthusiastic about her husband's profession. The hours were irregular and the salary was shamefully low.

It had, in fact, always irritated Ingirídur how poorly her husband provided for them. His professional soccer career had come to nothing, and in his present job he evidently wasn't a favorite. It seemed like the boss never told him anything. Over and over she read about major crimes in the papers, and Símon knew no more about them than she did. He was, after all, supposed to be a member of the detective division.

Now at last he had something to say. In one short interview, he had managed to connect the most likely suspect with more than one murder. He explained Hjördís's association with Leifur and Jóhann; the relationship with Fridrik in the Kleppsvegur house; and finally how he himself had found the link to another victim. And to top it all, she was a lesbian.

Símon ate a reheated fish stew as he related his story, and afterward took his cup of coffee into the living room and lay down on the sofa to catch the ten o'clock news.

After supper, Ingirídur cleaned up in the kitchen and thought about this deviant lesbian's unfortunate neighbors in the apartment building on Kleppsvegur. Her view was that the public needed to be told about dangerous, immoral characters at large in the community. If she broadcasted the news, she thought, she might even save a life. She seized the telephone and dialed a number she had often seen advertised in the newspaper.

23:00

Gunnar met Emil in the bar.

"Any answers yet?" he asked.

Emil shook his head. "No. I asked everyone. Nobody has called back so far with an answer."

"Fuck. Time's running out," Gunnar said.

Emil looked at the handwritten note that lay on the table. "I wonder if it's possible to find a list of euphemisms for death, and then check if anything reminiscent of a book title crops up."

Gunnar called Dóra.

"Can you google something for me? 'Euphemism for death, examples.' Call me when you've got something."

He stood up to get a couple of beers and a Jägermeister for himself. When he got back to the table, his cell rang; Dóra was ready with a list. As Gunnar listened, he repeated the words to Emil, who listened with concentration. "At room temperature, be no more, became a root inspector, bite the dust, ceased to be, crossed over, flatline, go into the fertilizer business, liquidated, mortified, passed away, permanently out of print, six feet under, swan song, terminated, the big nap, turned their toes up—"

"Hold it, hold it," Emil said. "What did you say, the big…"

"The big nap."

"*The Big Sleep*," Emil said. "That might be the book title. Try looking for 'The Big Sleep, bloodless hands.'"

Gunnar relayed this to Dóra.

"I found something," she said. "Great Paragraphs: *The Big Sleep* by Raymond Chandler." He listened intently as she read a substantial chunk of text until at last the sought-after words came up.

"That's it! Bloodless hands!" said Gunnar. "Now we need the beginning of chapter twenty-eight. Can you find it?"

Time passed, and Gunnar had nearly finished his beer by the time Dóra spoke again. "No. I can't find the complete text anywhere on the net."

Gunnar turned to Emil. "Do you have this book?"

Emil shook his head. "You'll have to go to the library."

"It's closed. How am I going to get in?" Gunnar looked at his watch. "We've got barely an hour to answer this."

Emil shrugged. "Maybe you'll have to break in."

As Gunnar pondered this problem, he noticed a familiar face by the counter and instantly got an idea. He finished his beer, stood up, and strode to the bar.

"Kolbrún," he said.

Kolbrún Gudjónsdóttir looked up at Gunnar in surprise, then nodded and said, "Well, if it isn't the fat cop himself. What in the hell do you want?"

She wore a thick, black leather jacket, jeans, and sturdy leather boots.

Gunnar took her arm. "You told me you were a cleaner for the City Library in the evenings. Have you finished cleaning for tonight?"

"Yeah, I was down there just now," she said, shaking off Gunnar's grip.

"I need to borrow a book."

"Oh yeah?"

"Can you let me in?"

"Now?"

"Yeah."

"Are you out of your mind?"

"It's really important. Do you have keys?"

"Yeah, but I wouldn't dream of letting you in. I'd be fired. Besides, I have no intention of waiting on you—I've been working since eight o'clock this morning."

"I'll make it worth your while."

"What do you think you can do for me?"

"Maybe something to do with your father's farm. I could talk to the executor and try to get him to sell the farm to you."

"Can you do that?"

"I can try talking to him. I can be very convincing sometimes."

Kolbrún thought it over. "Just one book?"

"Yes."

"Got a car?"

"No, but we can walk. It's not far."

"We'll take my bike. It's just outside."

He followed her out of the bar. A big old Harley-Davidson was parked up against the sidewalk, a white helmet strapped to its saddle.

"I haven't got a spare helmet," she said as she put it on. "But you've got a thick skull."

She mounted the motorcycle and kick-started it. The engine roared into encouragingly lusty life.

Gunnar got on behind Kolbrún and put his arms around her hips, the bike almost sinking to the ground under his weight. She gunned the accelerator, and Gunnar had to hold on tight as they rode off. In little more than a minute the powerful machine took them to the library, where Kolbrún stopped on the sidewalk in front of the main entrance and they dismounted. She opened the outer door with her key, they entered, and she tapped in a security code to open the inner doors. There was enough light for them to see their way around, and they made for the foreign fiction section on the second floor; the novels were arranged in alphabetical order of authors, and between Cervantes and Theresa Charles were two titles by Chandler—one of them was *The Big Sleep*.

Gunnar took down the book and moved to where there was better light before paging to chapter twenty-eight.

He phoned Dóra and began carefully to dictate the words of the first sentence.

"What kind of ritual is this, for fuck's sake?" Kolbrún asked when the reading was over and Gunnar had hung up.

"I'll tell you another time," said Gunnar, and he returned the book to its place on the shelf.

"Do I get a lift back to the bar?" he asked when they were outside the library once more.

"No. I'm going home," she said. "Remember what you promised."

Gunnar nodded. "Oh, one more thing," he said. "Do you know Hjördís..." He couldn't remember her last name. "Her father's a doctor. They lived in Boston."

Kolbrún seemed to be of two minds as to how she should answer. Finally she said, "Yeah, I do know a girl called Hjördís, actually. I looked after her in Boston when she was little. I worked as an au pair for the family."

"Are you in contact now?"

Kolbrún nodded hesitantly and said, "We sometimes gossip at the fish store. She also borrows my bike sometimes; she contributes to its maintenance in return. Why are you asking about her?"

"I'll tell you later," Gunnar replied.

Kolbrún's expression indicated that she was not happy with this answer. Without a word she put on her helmet and was gone, leaving Gunnar standing there, wondering whether to return to the bar for another beer or go straight home. He decided to go for the beer. He deserved it.

CHAPTER 7

WEDNESDAY, SEPTEMBER 27

09:00

W hen Dóra got to work and turned on her computer, there was a new e-mail in the inbox:

Question seven: What is Jake Martin's other name? Reply by three o'clock, please.

A search offered three hundred sixty thousand web pages for this name.

Soon after, Gunnar arrived; on reading the e-mail he called Emil, waking him up. He read the question to him.

"Jake Martin. Is it spelled J-A-K-E?" Emil asked irritably.

"Yes."

"Before three o'clock?"

"Yes."

"I'll give it a try, but this is starting to bore me."

"It'll be over soon," said Gunnar. "I can sense it."

But his senses hadn't at all prepared him for what happened next.

Magnús came storming into the conference room brandishing a newspaper.

GOOSE HUNTER MURDERS: POLICE TRAIL YOUNG LESBIAN was the banner across the front page. Beneath it a badly lit picture showed the apartment house where Hjördís lived.

"Who leaked this?" Magnús thundered at his subordinates.

The members of the team looked at one another in silence. They all shook their heads in unison.

"This means that we'll have to pick up the woman right away and talk to her. We will also need a warrant to search her apartment," Magnús said.

10:30

"Are you nuts?" Hjördís said to Birkir when he announced that she was under arrest and was to accompany him to the police station. Gunnar, Dóra, and Símon were also present. Hjördís was wearing a thick tracksuit and a fleece jacket.

"Were you on your way out?" Birkir asked.

"No. I went for a short walk. I just got back."

"We'll wait if you want to change your clothes," Birkir said. "Our female colleague will watch you."

"I'm drowning in work and well behind schedule. What in hell do you want with me?"

"We'll explain that at the station. We also have a warrant to search the apartment. Our colleagues will do that while we talk to you." Birkir indicated Dóra and Símon.

Hjördís looked in disbelief at the paper Birkir held in front of her.

"Do I have to put up with this bullshit?"

Birkir nodded. "I'm afraid so," he said.

"All right. Let's get it over with." Hjördís turned to Dóra. "I want all my work stuff to be the way I left it when I return," she said.

"We will also need to have your computer checked," Birkir said.

Hjördís shook her head. "This is persecution. Are we in a police state now, or what?"

"We need you to explain some things. It won't take long," Birkir said unconvincingly.

"Fucking bullshit," Hjördís said and disappeared into the bedroom followed by Dóra. Ten minutes later they reappeared and went into the bathroom. Another ten minutes passed before Hjördís came out and said she was ready. Birkir indicated that she should follow him, which she did, having grabbed a coat and put on shoes. Gunnar followed.

"I want an attorney," she said once they were in the car.

"Do you have anyone particular in mind?" Birkir asked.

"No. I just want a female one. I've had enough of men."

Gunnar called Magnús on his cell. They had to respond positively to this request. As a result, they had to wait for two hours in the interrogation room until the attorney got there. They used the time to take Hjördís's fingerprints—with her consent but after some discussion.

"I don't know what you think you've got on me," she said, "but these fingerprints can only prove my innocence. I hope."

Finally the attorney arrived. "Urdur Jónsdóttir," the small, gray-haired woman in her sixties greeted Hjördís. "We can begin."

She threw onto the table the newspaper with the scoop on Hjördís.

"We'll begin by discussing this."

Hjördís reached out for the newspaper and read the headline.

"My God," she said, throwing her hands up. "Is this a nightmare?"

Urdur said, "I don't know what sort of game you police think you're playing, but your business with this young woman had better be based on something solid. Let's hear it."

Gunnar spoke. "In our investigation into four murders, your name, Hjördís, has been mentioned three times. You have admitted that there has been conflict between you and your neighbor, Fridrik Fridriksson."

Hjördís interrupted Gunnar. "Listen, pal. There was no 'conflict.' That was one-sided harassment that I did my best to ignore."

"All right, maybe so," Gunnar said, "but since then a witness has stated that you knew the late Vilhjálmur Arason. That contradicts what you said in an interview with my colleague." Gunnar nodded toward Birkir.

"You mean the old guy?"

"Yes."

Hjördís looked at Birkir. "I've only ever seen him in the picture you showed me. What bullshit is this, for heaven's sake?

Urdur asked, "Did this witness point at Hjördís in a lineup?"

Gunnar shook his head. "No. He recognized her from a photo."

"Then that doesn't prove a thing," the attorney said.

Gunnar continued. "You know Kolbrún Gudjónsdóttir?"

"Yes."

"What is your relationship with her?"

"She looked after me when I was little."

"And now, at the present time?"

"I buy fish from her."

"And you borrow her motorcycle. Right?"

Hjördís leaned toward Urdur and spoke briefly to her, too softly for the others to hear. Urdur nodded and Hjördís said, "Yes, I have borrowed her bike."

"Why didn't you tell this to my colleague when you were discussing Kolbrún yesterday?"

"Because I've only got an American motorcycle license. I don't know if it's valid for Iceland, and I was afraid of getting into trouble."

Gunnar glanced quickly at Birkir. "Details have emerged to suggest that you quarreled with Leifur and Jóhann."

Hjördís was astonished. "That's not true at all. We were all very good friends."

"Something happened between you in Spain just over a year ago."

"No." Hjördís shook her head. "Nothing happened."

"You left your hotel in the middle of the night and went back to Iceland ahead of the two of them."

"I went back to Iceland ahead of them. That was the plan all along. I was preparing for my studies. And I didn't leave in the middle of the night. It was an evening flight."

Gunnar glanced again at Birkir, who shrugged his shoulders indecisively. Gunnar turned back to Hjördís and said, "We have testimony that says Jóhann and Leifur raped you on the last night you spent together."

"Raped me?" Hjördís sprang to her feet. "That's not true. Who says such fucking horseshit?"

She looked questioningly at the policemen, but when they didn't answer she sat back down. "Has Jóhann been arrested?" she asked.

"No, not yet. He won't be arrested unless you bring charges."

"I won't bring any charges. There was no rape. This is a lie. Who the hell told you this?"

"Did you have consensual intercourse?"

"No, of course not. We never slept together. I always slept in the living room, and they slept in the bedroom, unless they had girls with them."

Gunnar looked at Birkir in bewilderment but turned back to Hjördís and pushed a photocopy of a postcard toward her.

"Did you write this postcard on Leifur's behalf?" he asked.

Hjördís looked at it in surprise. "No, of course not. That is not my handwriting."

"You do not admit to having copied his handwriting?"

"No. Why would I have done that?"

Urdur put up her hand to stop her and said to Gunnar, "Where are you going with this? There are no links between my client and these deaths. Your line of questioning seems to rely on nothing but hearsay, and has not the slightest connection with the murders. Please get to the point if you've got anything on my client, or shall we just walk out of here now?"

Elías poked his head into the room. He said nothing; he merely shook his head. Hjördís's fingerprints had not matched the prints on the plastic wrapped around Leifur's corpse.

"Do you read crime novels?" Gunnar asked.

"No, no, don't answer that," Urdur said. "Enough is enough. Hjördís and I are walking out. Now."

Birkir and Gunnar had nothing to say. Then, when Birkir was just about to open his mouth to speak, the door opened again. It was Símon. With a look on his face as if he had just had an orgasm, he placed on the table a clear plastic bag containing two pieces of camouflage material.

"We found this in the trash," he said breathlessly.

"In what trash?" Urdur asked.

"The trash in the basement of Hjördís's apartment building," Símon said, looking knowingly at the young woman.

Urdur said, "What does this trash have to do with my client in particular? Please enlighten me."

Gunnar turned to Hjördís and said, "Have you seen this before?"

Hjördís picked up the plastic bag and examined the scraps of material. She leaned toward Urdur and they conferred quietly for a moment. Finally Urdur nodded and Hjördís said, "When I got back from my walk this morning, I emptied my mailbox. There were just some fliers and an unmarked white envelope containing this stuff. I assumed it was something some kids had been playing with, so I chucked it along with all the other bits of paper into the garbage chute on my way upstairs. That's all I know. What are these things?"

"These pieces of fabric may be linked to two of the murders," Gunnar said.

Urdur took up the newspaper and held it up in front of them. "You have advertised this young woman's address thoroughly enough to give the murderer an excellent opportunity to plant this so-called evidence in her mailbox this morning. Was there anything else?"

Gunnar and Birkir glanced at one another. Birkir shrugged.

"No," Gunnar said.

"Then, we'll leave." Urdur said and stood up. She indicated that Hjördís should follow her. "I'll drive my client home. I'll be sending you my invoice," she added.

The three detectives watched as the women walked out of the room.

"Does she get to leave—just like that?" Símon asked, now looking as if somebody had squeezed his testicles.

"Yes," Birkir said. "The whole thing is one big fucking mess."

14:35

Anna took the camouflage specimens to her lab.

Birkir and Gunnar sat and waited. There didn't seem anything else to do. Finally Gunnar's cell rang. It was Emil Edilon. "We have a hypothesis regarding this 'Jake Martin' question. It was the Crippled Critic's suggestion. Want to hear it?"

"You bet." Gunnar grabbed a pen.

"In 1973, a film based on a crime story by the Swedish couple Maj Sjöwall and Per Wahlöö was produced in the States. The original was called *Den skrattande polisen* in Swedish, and it was one of ten books in a series about a detective named Martin Beck. Are you with me?"

"Yeah, I know about those books. Go on."

"The story is about a massacre on a bus."

"Another mass murder?"

"Yeah."

"Okay."

"So, in America the movie was called *The Laughing Policeman*, and it was an adaptation set in San Francisco instead of Stockholm. Walter Matthau played the Martin Beck character but they changed his name in this version to Jake Martin. Do you get it?"

"You mean that the answer to the question 'What is Jake Martin's other name?' is 'Martin Beck'?"

"Yes."

"We'll have to give it a try. We haven't got anything else."

Gunnar hung up and looked at the clock. "The deadline's in fifteen minutes. If it really is Hjördís who's been playing with us, she'll have to get to a computer somewhere to reply. We've still got her two."

Birkir replied, "I don't know what her role is in this drama, but I'm worried she'll tear Jóhann to pieces because of the story he told me. Maybe I should warn him."

He tried Jóhann's cell number but only got voice mail. He left a message: "Please call Birkir at the detective division."

Gunnar posted the answer to question seven before joining the others in the incident room for a briefing from Anna.

"First, the camouflage pieces. These are definitely the missing halves of the bits taken from Ólafur's and Fridrik's clothing. We have a blank white envelope in which the pieces were found, but the only fingerprints on it belong to Hjördís."

"I knew it!" said Símon.

"That's not remarkable," Birkir replied. "She told us she took the envelope out of her mailbox and opened it."

Anna continued. "Over the last couple of days we've mainly been concentrating on the shotgun pellets. Our findings are interesting."

She lit a cigarette and took out a large board with two cross-section pictures of shotgun shells.

"This display shows a cardboard shell," she said, pointing to one of the pictures with her cigarette. "We can forget that type, as we now know that all the shots in question were from plastic shells." She indicated the other picture and went on, pointing out the relevant details as she spoke. "The primer, which ignites the powder when the gun is fired, is at the bottom. Between the powder and the pellets is the wadding. It's made of plastic. Its lowest part, the cushion, is a kind of shock absorber that mitigates the impact on the lead pellets when the powder burns, minimizing the deformation or shattering of the pellets caused by the shock of the explosion. The top part of the wadding, the shot cup, acts as a kind of shield around the pellets, protecting them and the interior of the gun's barrel as it's fired. There are slits in the sides of the shot cup so that as the shot emerges from the barrel the cup peels open and disintegrates. Once it has served its purpose, the pellets are free to spread. These plastic cups, particularly the cushion component, vary in design according to the type of shot employed. The fragments from the shot cups fall to the ground between ten and thirty meters from the marksman.

"We found a number of spent shells left by the Gander in Dalasýsla, and two at Rangárvellir. We've established that they're all of the same type, Federal Premium, and that they were all fired from the same weapon. In the Mýrar killing the murderer fired one shot but we couldn't find a shell. We do, however, have the pellets and the fragments of the wadding and shot cup that we found in the wound on the body. The range was too short for any significant spread of the shot to have taken place, but long enough for the shot to only partially penetrate the body. We have been trying to put these fragments together to figure out what the make is. Our conclusion is that the shots that hit Ólafur and Fridrik are of the same type—they're common goose-hunting rounds. The shot that hit Vilhjálmur is also a common goose-hunting round, but of a different make, Hlad Original. This type is produced here in Iceland, and the wadding is easily recognized. Another point of interest is that these shells are the same type as what the witness had in his gun. It's not possible to verify that the shot that killed the victim came from that weapon, but the only spent shell we found at the scene was from the gun the witness used."

The detectives looked at each other.

"So you think Ragnar murdered his father-in-law?" Magnús asked.

"I do not draw conclusions," Anna said, taking a drag on her cigarette. "I report facts. You draw conclusions and work on them. Another thing worth reminding you of is the fact that no patch was cut from Vilhjálmur's jacket, as happened with the other victims. The business of the patches was not mentioned in the media, so the copycat did not know about it. If, that is to say, it wasn't the Gander that killed Vilhjálmur."

Magnús raised his hand and said, "If this theory is correct, how come Ragnar recognized Hjördís from a picture—knew her name and that she's a lesbian?"

Everyone looked at Símon.

"I don't know," Símon said. "He was quite sure about it."

Birkir said, "Hjördís has, on the other hand, flatly denied having known Vilhjálmur. It is also very unlikely that she would have been looking for an apartment just now, since she has a very decent home and she's planning to go to New York soon."

"Any other problematic points?" Magnús asked.

Gunnar replied, "Ragnar didn't mention that he had fired a shot at the scene until I had checked his gun and brought it up in questioning. The Gander would surely have reloaded if he'd been shot at, and then there'd probably be spent shells on the ground."

"Anything else?" Magnús asked.

Birkir replied, "This solution would explain why we didn't find any suspicious person in the area after the murder despite extensive searches. That didn't figure."

Magnús nodded. "Right. Let's take this bit by bit. Motive, intent, opportunity."

Gunnar said, "The opportunity is obvious. The intent is surprising. Motive?"

"Money," Birkir replied.

"How so?" Magnús asked.

"Ragnar and his wife are Vilhjálmur's sole heirs. Maybe Ragnar didn't want to wait decades to get their inheritance. Vilhjálmur seems to have been healthy and still active," Birkir said.

Magnús said, "If it turns out that this death is not the Gander's responsibility, then we'll have to change the whole pattern of our search for connections. We'll need to reexamine everything we've got."

"Do we go pick Ragnar up right away and question him again?" Gunnar asked.

Magnús nodded. "If he is guilty, we'll need to get a confession from him. The evidence we have is not sufficient to convict him. You've got to be clever."

Magnús's phone rang. He picked it up and listened. When he hung up he said, "It was the computer guy. We have information on the Hotmail address at last. It was set up on one of the computers that are for public use at the City Library."

Birkir asked, "Are there logs of who uses them?"

"They're going to check on that for us."

16:45

Birkir and Gunnar arrived at the house in Fossvogur to find Ragnar outside raking leaves. He was clad in blue work pants, a gray fleece jacket, yellow gardening gloves, and high black rubber boots. He had heaped three small piles of brown leaves on the grass and was working on a fourth. He didn't look up as they approached, but continued to rake with slow, mechanical movements.

The detectives stood next to him and Gunnar said, "Good afternoon, Ragnar."

"I'm nearly finished," Ragnar said, still not looking at them.

"We need to ask you to accompany us to the police station," Gunnar said.

"I just need to put the leaves into a bag so they won't blow away. It won't take me long."

Gunnar looked at Birkir, who nodded.

A black plastic trash bag lay by one of the leaf piles, which Ragnar began to transfer into the bag.

"Let me help you," Birkir said. Bending down, he took the bag and held it open while Ragnar scooped the leaves into it with his hands. With that pile cleared, they went on to the next one, which went the same way. In the end, Birkir had to pack the leaves down into the bag to make room for the last pile. They did all this without saying a word, watched by Gunnar. When the work was done, Ragnar picked up the bag and looked sadly around the garden. "Fall has arrived," he said.

"Do you want to change your clothes before we go?" Birkir asked.

It seemed to take time for this to register, but eventually Ragnar shook his head. "No. My dear Bára's fallen asleep in her chair. She'll wake up if I go in. Better go with you just as I am. This won't take long, will it?"

"Hopefully not," Birkir replied.

"It would be good to get back before she wakes up," Ragnar said.

He closed the bag with a knot and took it to the garbage area. Birkir followed him with the rake.

"We can go now," Ragnar said.

Gunnar opened the rear door of their sedan and indicated for Ragnar to get in. He closed the door, went around to the other side of the car, and got in the back next to Ragnar. Birkir drove.

"This is a beautiful house," Ragnar said, looking out the rear window as they exited the parking lot. "We've lived here for twelve years."

No more was said on the way to the police station. Birkir parked the car in the detective division's space, and they went into the building through the rear entrance. Ragnar took his boots off in the lobby and stood them against the wall. Then he followed them along the corridor in his stocking feet.

Dóra met them.

"We've received another question," she said.

Birkir showed Ragnar into an interview room and waited by the open door.

"Let's hear it," Gunnar said.

"Who was Buffalo Bill? We've got until ten o'clock tonight."

"An American buffalo hunter and circus artist of the nineteenth century," Birkir said.

"No," replied Gunnar said. "It'll be a trick question. That much we've learned."

He thought for a moment and then asked Dóra, "Did you look on the Internet?"

"Yeah, there were five hundred thousand pages."

"We'll need help with this," Gunnar said. He jotted a phone number on a piece of paper and handed it to Dóra. "Call this number and speak to Emil Edilon. Say hi from me and tell him the question. Tell him I'll get in touch later. Don't worry if he starts saying bizarre stuff. Just ignore him."

Dóra made herself scarce, and Gunnar followed Birkir into the interview room. It was sparse—just a table and four uncomfortable chairs, with a two-way mirror on the wall that was visible from the next room. On the table there was a tape recorder and a brown document box marked "Vilhjálmur Arason."

Gunnar pulled out a chair and motioned for Ragnar to take a seat. Birkir took the chair opposite Ragnar and switched on the recorder. "Ragnar Jónsson, school teacher, is here for questioning and is hereby informed that his legal status is that of a suspect in the investigation of the death of Vilhjálmur Arason on September twenty-fourth last. Present are detectives Birkir Hinriksson and Gunnar Maríuson. Do you understand what it means to have the legal status of a suspect?"

Ragnar nodded.

"Can you please say it out loud?" Birkir pointed at the recorder.

"Yes, I understand," Ragnar replied.

"You may refuse to answer our questions, and you may request that an attorney be present."

"I know," Ragnar said.

"Would you like an attorney to be present?" Birkir asked.

"No. That's unnecessary trouble."

Gunnar took out his notebook and began. "Our inquiries have revealed that your father-in-law's murder differed in significant detail from the other goose-hunter homicides we have been investigating. Can you explain that?"

Ragnar shrugged.

"Out loud, please." Birkir pointed at the recorder.

"No. I can't explain that."

"Please describe for us the killer you saw," Gunnar said.

"She was wearing camouflage hunting gear and had blonde hair, I think."

"What fucking bullshit is this?" Gunnar bellowed. "When I first talked to you, you said it was a guy."

"That's what I thought I saw."

"So why do you say now that it was a woman?" Gunnar rasped.

Ragnar hesitated before saying, "The policeman that spoke to me yesterday said the murderer was a woman. He was very kind."

"And you recognized her from a picture?" Gunnar asked.

"Um…yes."

"What's her name?"

"I can't remember. Something ending with 'dís.'"

"But you remembered it when the policeman spoke to you yesterday, didn't you?"

"No, not to begin with. He told me, and then I remembered it."

"Herdís," Birkir said.

"Yes, that's it. Herdís."

"Or Hjördís," said Gunnar.

"Was her name Hjördís?" Ragnar asked.

"You haven't a clue who this woman is, and you've never seen her," Gunnar said. "But let's talk about the actual shooting. You fired one shot at the gunman. Why?"

"To frighten him. So he wouldn't come after me."

"Was he likely to do that?"

"Yes. He came running and aimed his gun at me—I mean, she did."

"This is not the description you gave me on Sunday."

"No, but I can remember it now."

Gunnar threw his hands up in the air. "We'll be here all day if this bullshit goes on."

Ragnar said quietly, "I can't stay here long. Bára will be waking up soon. She can't be left alone."

Birkir said, "We will be quick if you tell us the truth now."

Ragnar looked at Gunnar and then back at Birkir. "I'd like him to leave. He makes me nervous. I can't think when people yell at me."

Gunnar got up and sighed. "I'll take a break. You want some coffee, Birkir?"

"Yes, please," Birkir replied. "Ragnar, would you like some coffee, too?"

"Yes, thank you. With a little milk, if it isn't too much trouble."

Gunnar made a face and went out, slamming the door behind him.

Birkir said, "Gunnar Maríuson leaves the room. Interview is suspended."

He turned off the recorder and leaned across the table.

"This is just between the two of us," he said. "We need to find a way to make this easier for all of us."

He opened the box on the table and took out an empty shotgun shell in a plastic bag.

"This is the shell my colleague retrieved from your gun," he said. "Our forensic people have collected every single fragment of the round that killed your father-in-law: the shot, the wadding, and the shot cup. The range was so short that it all entered Vilhjálmur's body; most of it stuck there, and what was left went through him and was found on the ground just in front of him. Our forensic team is piecing it all together now under a microscope. Once they've done that, we can prove that the shot came from this shell. Then we shall have no further conversation with you, and the case will be sent to the prosecutor. You will be charged with murder. If, on the other hand, you decide to be open with us, we might be able to help you out. Maybe we could establish it was an accident. Involuntary manslaughter. Like in a car crash."

Ragnar sank down in the chair. "I can't tell my Bára that I did it."

Birkir held his breath. This was an unexpected surrender, but it wasn't enough. Ragnar had to keep talking.

"I'll tell her it was an accidental shot," Birkir said, "if you tell me the whole story now."

He restarted the recorder.

There was a long silence, and then Ragnar spoke quietly. "I have always dreamed of having a small single-family home with a sheltered yard where I can make all the gardening decisions for myself—about the flower beds, the rose bushes, and the trees."

Ragnar raised his voice. "Where I live now, I always have to go to the other renters in the building to ask permission to do my planting and gardening. Some of the young parents are not pleased; they think my interest in keeping things tidy prevents their children from playing in the yard. I don't know why they complain. It's in the building rules that nobody can play soccer on the lawn."

Ragnar looked seriously at Birkir as if to emphasize the importance of this homeowners' association regulation.

"I see," Birkir said.

Ragnar continued. "I think I'd better go back a bit. Bára and I met at the elementary school where I teach. At that time she was working in the children's cafeteria. I have to admit that I wasn't particularly taken with her to begin with, but her father owned this fishing company. He was a widower and Bára was his only child. I had decided early on in life that I would marry a woman who was well-off in order to secure a reasonable financial future, and I knew that Bára was due to receive a generous inheritance. So I began to spend time chatting with her in the school kitchen. We then started dating, and subsequently got married. I rather assumed that Vilhjálmur would help us in our times of want, and that bit by bit we would be able to save up enough for somewhere nice to live.

"You see, Vilhjálmur was very well-off, financially, and also owned a trawler. Neither Bára nor I earned high salaries, and then she had to give up working when she put on all the weight. Her legs couldn't take all the standing. She has become more or less an invalid, but she has refused to apply for disability pension. It's a sensitive issue for her. So we've had to live off my teacher's salary, which is not great. Vilhjálmur knew this and yet he never helped us in any significant way. Then, when he was sixty, he retired and sold his company—the boat, his fishing quota, the whole business. He said he was going to use the money as his pension. He gave us a miserly sum toward buying a bigger car, as Bára couldn't get into our old Golf anymore. I knew that was all we would be getting from him."

He fell silent.

"Tell me what happened last Sunday," Birkir said.

"That morning, when we were on our way to the hunting ground, Vilhjálmur was talking about how happy he was that I looked after Bára so well. He said that I was such a good and considerate husband and son-in-law, and that he felt relief that he didn't have to worry about his daughter. He said he was looking forward to traveling all over the world and leading a comfortable life for the rest of his days. He had worked out how much he would be able to spend each year until he reached eighty. Then he hoped to find a place in a nursing home, unless, of course, Bára and I wanted to offer to have him. He was blathering on about it the whole trip, and I realized that Bára and I would never have our own house—he was going to fritter away all the money. Then we arrived at our destination, and it occurred to me as I walked behind my father-in-law, away from the car, that it would be incredibly convenient if the killer were to pick him.

"Then I just sort of held the gun up and kind of aimed it at him thinking that it wouldn't take much, and then it just accidentally went off and he fell like a log. And I didn't mean to do it." Ragnar had begun to weep.

For a while there was no sound apart from his sobbing; then Gunnar appeared bearing three cups of coffee.

Birkir said, "Detective Gunnar Maríuson enters the room."

Gunnar put the cups on the table.

"There's one more thing," Birkir said. "Why did you try to put the blame on this young woman whom you didn't know at all?"

The question seemed to surprise Ragnar. "Well," he said. "Hadn't she already committed several murders? Would one more have made a difference?"

"Maybe not," Birkir said. "We will have to impound your weapon and your ammunition. Will you consent to that or would you prefer for us to get a warrant?"

Ragnar fished a key ring from his pocket. "You can go get the gun. It's in the storeroom at home."

He pointed at the keys. "This blue one is the front door key and the yellow one is the storeroom key. It's labeled two-one. The two stands for second floor and the one stands for apartment number one. I labeled the storerooms myself."

Birkir looked at Gunnar.

"Do you want to go?"

"I've got to go talk to Emil Edilon about finding an answer to the new riddle. I called him already. His helpers are passing it around."

"Okay," Birkir said. "I'll go. You can finish up this report."

Gunnar nodded.

Birkir said to Ragnar, "You will tell my colleague this story again in full detail. Together you will write a statement, which you will then sign to confirm it is correct. Gunnar, my partner, will not get angry again, so you don't need to worry. Is that all right?"

Trying to be reassuring, Gunnar gave a big gap-toothed grin. Ragnar looked at him a little warily, but nodded.

18:30

Birkir, Elías, and Dóra went to bring in the gun. Two was the usual number for such an errand, but Dóra went along to undertake the task of talking with Ragnar's wife, Bára. Using the blue key, Birkir let them in the front door, and they climbed the stairs to the second floor. At first nobody answered when they rang the doorbell, but at the second attempt they heard a voice from within the apartment say, "Come in."

Birkir opened the door and indicated for Dóra to go in.

"You know what to say," he said. "You'll have to play the rest by ear."

Dóra nodded. She was used to tasks like this one. They might end up having to call a doctor.

Birkir and Elías went back down to the basement. Birkir opened the storeroom marked 2/1 with the yellow key, and Elías entered. The shotgun was in a bag hanging on the wall, and there were some boxes of ammunition on one of the shelves.

Birkir looked at the lock on the storeroom door. It was not a substantial fastening; a good kick would be sufficient to break in here. This was unsuitable storage for a firearm, but that was not their problem just now. Elías took a few photographs and then left with the gun and the ammunition.

Birkir remained behind to check the storeroom. One of the shelves contained gardening tools and a bag of fertilizer; on another were a number of books on plants and gardening, which looked well-used, some of them dog-eared and dirty. Apart from that the room seemed to be more or less full of the usual sort of junk that piles up in such places when families live in the same building for a long time: old clothes, shoes, folders of paperwork, old vinyl records, cans of paint and worn-out brushes, two boxes of Christmas decorations, a sleeping bag, a tent, and an old pair of cross-country skis.

He sifted through it all to make sure there were no more firearms or ammunition. Finally he got down on his hands and knees to look under the bottom shelf. There was nothing there save a single shotgun shell that must have rolled off one of the shelves above. Birkir gazed at the little cylinder awhile, reflecting that a shell just like this one, maybe even from the same pack, had killed a man and would change the lives of two other individuals very much for the worse. He stretched under the shelf to retrieve the shell and, standing up again, put it into his jacket pocket. Then he went upstairs to the apartment.

Dóra had indeed been forced to call a doctor for Bára; the doctor had assessed the situation and called for an ambulance. The woman was unable to get up from her chair without assistance and her blood pressure was way too high. They could not leave her helpless in the apartment.

Dóra was not sure how much Bára had understood of what she had told her about her father's death and her husband's part in it. The woman seemed like she was in shock and did not respond to questions when asked—she just moaned and breathed erratically. The doctor feared her heart would fail if she was subjected to much more stress. It took four ambulance attendants to carry her out to the emergency vehicle.

20:30

Jóhann finally called when Birkir got back to headquarters. It was a poor connection.

Birkir asked him if Hjördís had been in contact with him.

"No. Why?" Jóhann seemed surprised.

"We spoke to her and I asked her about the incident in Spain you told me about."

"What incident?"

"The rape."

"You asked about the rape? Are you crazy? I told you that in confidence."

"No, it wasn't in confidence. I told you that everything you told me was on the table. But Hjördís flatly denied that it had happened."

"That's good. Then it didn't happen."

"What do you mean?"

"She says it didn't happen, then it didn't happen."

"She was very upset," said Birkir.

"That I can believe."

"You're sure she hasn't called you?"

"Yes."

"All right." Birkir was about to hang up.

"Listen," Jóhann said.

"Yes?"

There was a short silence before Jóhann continued. "I'm at the Bláfjöll skiing area, visiting a friend of mine from Akureyri. He's an attendant in one of the lodges here. He knows Hjördís, too. They went to school together in Akureyri. He told me she came here on Monday and asked if she could park her skis in the storeroom."

"And?"

"My friend is kinda nosy and he had a look in her ski bag."

"Yes?"

"There were no skis in the bag. Just a couple of shotguns."

"Shotguns?"

"Yeah. It seemed weird to me. It's probably of no consequence."

"Did she tell him there were skis in the bag?"

"Hang on, I'll ask."

Birkir heard voices but was unable to make out the words. He turned on the phone recorder.

Jóhann said, "No. She didn't mention what was in it. She just asked if she could put a ski bag in the storeroom."

Birkir said, "I wouldn't mind having a look at these guns. Will your friend agree to letting the police take a look at the contents of the bag? He can give consent since he's in charge of the storage room."

"Hang on a minute."

Again Birkir heard indistinct voices, and then Jóhann returned to the phone. "He says that's okay."

Birkir looked at the clock. He had some things to deal with first. "How long are you going to be there?"

"Until well after midnight. We're painting a couple of rooms."

Gunnar was still working on the statement with Ragnar when Birkir stopped by the interview room. Birkir beckoned him out into the corridor and told him about the shotguns.

"I'll go check it out in a little while," Birkir said.

Gunnar nodded. "I'm about to call it a day with Ragnar. Then it's just getting the answer to 'Buffalo Bill' and a jug of beer."

"Have we got the answer?"

Gunnar nodded. "We think so. Dóra kept on googling. She noticed how some of the later riddles have seemed to involve serial killers, so she searched for 'Buffalo Bill' and 'serial killer' together. She got *Silence of the Lambs.* You know, the book and the film—remember?"

Birkir nodded. "Hannibal Lecter."

"Yeah, but Buffalo Bill was the serial killer the lady cop wanted to get Hannibal to help her to find. The one who was stitching a 'woman suit' out of his victims' skin."

"Sounds right."

"Símon is on computer duty tonight. He is to send the answer at five to ten. He'll then tell us if there's a new question."

Birkir shook his head. "Hasn't the time come to stop this game? At some point we won't be able to find the answer and what happens then?"

"That remains to be seen. But if the Gander behaves himself while we play with him then it's worth it. We'll just have to see how things pan out."

22:15

Símon stared at the computer screen and moaned. "Fuck, fuck, fucking fuck."

He'd had Gunnar's reply ready on a piece of paper and was waiting at the computer for the right moment. He was going to send the answer at exactly five to ten, but then he got sidetracked looking at a cool porno page that someone had bookmarked. When he remembered where he was, it was only one minute before ten, but then he couldn't find the note with the details for the Hotmail account. After ten minutes of frantic rummaging he finally discovered the note stuck to the bottom of the coffee cup he'd been shoving to and fro around the desk. With trembling fingers he punched in the address and password. The page opened to reveal a new e-mail with the subject line: Too late. Tonight I am going to catch a cop.

A shiver crept down Símon's spine.

"Fuck, fuck, fucking fuck," he said over and over.

He opened the e-mail but it contained no text. Just the subject line. On the spur of the moment and without giving it any further thought, Símon tagged the post and pressed Delete. The message disappeared from the screen. Then he sent an e-mail with Gunnar's answer. He sat there in a cold sweat, thinking about his next move. If luck was with him nobody would notice that the answer had been posted too late. But which cop was the Gander planning to catch? What should he do?

He got up and wandered out into the corridor. In the interview room he found Gunnar and Ragnar eating a pizza—actually, it was Gunnar who was eating while Ragnar watched him in amazement. The small man didn't seem to have any appetite.

Gunnar saw Símon and glanced at his watch. "Do we have a new riddle?"

"No." Símon shook his head.

"Keep an eye on it."

"Yeah."

"Great. And then can you take our friend here into custody?" Gunnar pointed at Ragnar.

"Yeah," Símon said. "Do you think it's possible that we in the force are in danger?" he added.

"How do you mean?"

"Do you think that the Gander will try to get at us?"

"Us?"

"Yeah."

"No. No more than anyone else. You want some pizza?"

Símon shook his head. He didn't feel like pizza but he felt a bit better; he somehow felt that Gunnar had cut the noose around his neck. Hopefully the Gander was just joking.

22:20

When Dóra had completed all her day's tasks, she went to work out. She was glad she'd found a gym that stayed open until after midnight; she hardly ever went before ten o'clock at night. She didn't mind exercising late. When her mind was exhausted, it was great to get going on the weights and finish her body off, too. She slept better after a workout.

She had written up her conversation with Bára Vilhjálms-dóttir—actually, it had not been a conversation at all, because the poor woman had not uttered one intelligible word. The fate of the family was quite tragic. Dóra couldn't see how Bára gained anything from having her father's murder solved. It would probably have been better for her to continue having her husband at home to look after her. Maybe that would have been punishment enough for him. Now, she would probably be insti-tutionalized.

Dóra did special exercises to strengthen her thigh muscles. She had not fully recovered from the fracture yet, and the circum-ference of her right thigh was noticeably smaller than that of the left. She still had appointments with a physical therapist every three weeks to work on it. She was hoping to recover fully enough to go skiing in February. She had booked a trip to Italy with a girl-friend—an old schoolmate from Ísafjördur—and she was looking forward to it. Her friend was a champion skier who had competed at the highest level all over Europe. After she'd given up competing, she'd started inviting Dóra along on her annual winter ski trip, and they always ignored the regular trails, teaming up with other winter sports fanatics and taking a helicopter up to virgin slopes. She would need all her muscles to be working at full strength for that.

There were not many others in the gym at this time of night. All the equipment was available, and it didn't take her long to work through her program. Her iPod pumped rhythmic music into her headphones, and she was fully absorbed in her efforts. After she was done, when she was doing her stretches, she noticed a man in a black leather jacket standing by the front desk, looking at her. Being somewhat nearsighted, Dóra had to squint to recognize him. It was Tómas, the lawyer. When he saw that she had spotted him he turned and left.

She went into the dressing room, which was empty apart from a fit young woman standing in her underwear in front of a mirror blow-drying her hair. Dóra nodded to her but saw no sign the woman had noticed her. She seemed to be in her own world. This was another advantage of being here so late in the day. During busy hours the room was full of women and everything was a mess; Dóra found that hard to tolerate. She wanted to have the peace to do her final stretching exercises in a good, long, hot shower.

23:20

Birkir was quite happy to go for a drive. It gave him space to think. He took off from the police station and headed out of the city. What were these guns that Hjördís had wanted to put away in storage—or rather, it seemed, hide in storage? She couldn't have been involved in Ólafur's or Fridrik's murders herself; her story about the trip to Akureyri had been confirmed. So why did she need to hide guns? Was there an accomplice? All this occupied his mind during the twenty minutes it took to reach the turnoff to Bláfjöll.

As he approached the ski slopes, he slowed down and observed the area. The sky was clear and the moon poured a cold light onto the bare trails. Although one could see occasional white snowdrifts in the gullies, everywhere else was black; it would be some time before skiing would be possible here. The tall towers of the ski lifts stood like mechanical trolls forming straight lines from the foot of the mountain to its summit. The cables and the chairs were barely visible, except where silhouetted against the dark-blue sky.

There was no sign of life at the first ski lodge, and no cars parked outside. Birkir drove on to where there were more buildings dotted around. Outside one of the lodges he saw Jóhann's car, and next to it an old motorcycle. There was a light on in one of the lodge windows.

He parked his car and stepped out. It felt about five to ten degrees below freezing, but the evening was calm and not uncomfortably cold. He was perfectly warm in the down-filled parka he'd pulled on over his suit, and he took a few moments to inhale the fresh air, gaze at the sky, and listen to the silence.

23:30

Gunnar finally finished writing up the events surrounding Vilhjálmur's death. All things considered, it was not actually a long story, but it had still taken some time to detail the full account, which covered all of the evidence Ragnar had given from the beginning, including all the things he had deliberately lied about.

Having waited patiently, Ragnar read through the statement—correcting several spelling mistakes—and then neatly signed his name.

"Do you know if it's possible to get some gardening work at the Litla Hraun prison in the summer?" he asked. Gunnar didn't reply, but the question struck him as the last straw, and gave him good reason to visit the bar. Símon was to take the prisoner into custody. His workday was over.

There was nobody in the bar on Smidjustígur that Gunnar knew or cared to know, so he just stood at the counter with his bitters and beer. This time he decided to drink half the beer before tasting the bitters. He sometimes did this when he was thirsty, and concluding the case of Ragnar and Vilhjálmur had made him very thirsty indeed.

"Hello, fat cop," a voice behind him said. "Are you buying?"

Gunnar signaled to the bartender by pointing to his beer glass and raising one finger, and then turned. "Hello Kolbrún. Good to see you."

"Do you need to get to the library at all tonight?"

"No, not especially. Have you got your bike?"

"Not tonight. I lent it to someone. I felt like having a drink. I don't have to be at work at the fish store until around noon tomorrow so I'm hanging loose. You do remember what you promised me, don't you?"

"Yeah, I'll talk with the executor. I just need to find out who it is. Then I'll try to work out a good price for the farm."

"I don't have much money. I'll need to get a loan."

"I'll look into that with you, too. Then we should start a rumor that the farm is haunted. Maybe that'll make other buyers less interested. Know any good ghost stories?"

"Yeah, I like the sound of that," Kolbrún said.

The beer arrived, and they chatted about farming at Litla-Fell and what scary ghost stories might work. When they'd had another beer, Kolbrún looked at her watch.

"Look," she said. "It's too expensive to drink here. I've got a six-pack of beer at home. You can come, too, if you want."

23:50

On her way out of the gym, Dóra said good night to the young man at the front desk, who was engrossed in a motocross program on some foreign TV channel. He wore a black shirt open to the waist, showing off his bare, darkly tanned chest and muscular stomach in a way that was not exactly modest.

"Good night and thank you for coming," he replied in a high-pitched voice, not looking at Dóra. She was probably several years too old to spark his interest. He, on the other hand, had aroused hers, and as she made her way out to the parking lot she tried to pinpoint what was unusual about him; it wasn't until she had climbed into her old Escort that she realized what it was. He'd shaved off all his upper-body hair. Perhaps the rest, too—the parts she couldn't see.

When she arrived home, she poured a glass of orange juice and turned on her computer. She was just going to check her inbox and then go to bed. There were three unread e-mails. She thought the one from jestertoyou@hotmail.com must be junk mail, because she didn't recognize the sender's address. She was about to delete it when she spotted the subject line: Ford Escort at 23:52. She immediately realized this was the time she had headed home in her Escort. Had somebody been following her?

Four JPEG files were attached. So there were pictures. The text read: I see you decided to take a bath, as I suggested. I'll give you a chance to apologize suitably for your conduct. Otherwise I'll send these pictures to every single police e-mail address tonight. I'll be waiting at home. You know what I want to do.

Dóra downloaded all of the pictures onto her computer and opened the first one. It had been taken in the shower room at the gym and showed her naked, washing her hair. The other three images were similar. All were well lit and sharply focused—evidently the work of a professional.

Dóra tried to remember the situation in the changing room.

So that's how it was. The woman with the hair dryer had been doing Tómas's dirty work. Dóra wrinkled her nose. You could get people to do anything if you had the right connections.

"It's just typical for me to end up in shit like this," Dóra said aloud as she examined the photos. There wasn't really anything to criticize apart from her short legs. Other than that, she was slim and graceful. Pretty good abs, too.

Dóra was not prudish about her own body, but she certainly didn't want these pictures to be distributed among her colleagues. There was already enough distracting them from their work. She considered how to respond. What a piece of work the guy was, trying to coerce her into sex like this.

After a short deliberation, she looked up the police group e-mail list and composed an e-mail with the subject line Virus warning! READ IMMEDIATELY and the text: Warning: Mail from jestertoyou@yahoo.com contains a dangerous computer virus that will wipe all data on the hard drive if opened. Delete the mail immediately without opening it. If there was anything that her colleagues in the force were frightened of, it was computer viruses. Most of them had half-finished reports somewhere on the network, and the backup system was not infallible. As long as Tómas used the *jestertoyou* address, it was almost certain all his e-mails would be destroyed. If not—well, que sera, sera.

Lastly, Dóra replied to Tómas's e-mail: Coming as soon as I can. Put the white wine on ice.

She hoped this would keep the asshole awake well into the night. She could do no more for the time being, but tomorrow she would have a quiet word with Gunnar. He had ways of sorting out difficult situations.

She turned off the computer and her cell before crawling into the comfort of her bed. She fell asleep the moment her eyes closed.

CHAPTER 8

00:10

Birkir knocked on the door of the lodge and walked in. "Hello," he shouted. "Jóhann, are you there?" The hallway was dark, and he hesitated before going farther.

"Hello," he repeated. "Is anybody here?"

"Come on in," he heard Jóhann call from inside a dimly lit room.

Birkir entered and tried to work out the layout of the place. In the center of the room, which was otherwise bare, stood a small table flanked by two chairs. In the feeble glimmer of the light bulb that hung over the table, Birkir could see a solitary white plate with what appeared to be a small pebble on it. He walked over to take a closer look, and felt a jolt as he met the uncanny, almost human, stare of a glass eye. Suddenly all the lights in the room came on and it was so dazzling that Birkir had to close his eyes momentarily. Then he looked up warily.

"Welcome to the game," he heard a voice say behind him. He spun around and saw it was Jóhann dressed in dark camouflage pants and a green sweater, his face painted in full camouflage. He wore a dark-green patch over his left eye socket. Then there was the shotgun he was holding.

"Welcome to the game," he repeated, and then he switched off the lights so Birkir saw nothing but darkness.

"What do you mean?"

"You are now a player in Shotgun. That is to say, an active player. Until now you have been merely a pawn. But now you will have a major role."

"Are you feeling okay?"

"I've never been better," Jóhann said. "Sit down."

He emerged from the shadows and pointed at the chair with his weapon.

Birkir did as he was told.

"Put your cell on the floor," Jóhann said, "and push it away from you. Hard."

Birkir took his cell from the pocket of his parka and slid it across the floor. A shot rang out and the phone, still moving, disintegrated. Swift as lightning Jóhann pumped a fresh round into the barrel and the spent shell flew out onto the floor.

"That was just to make it clear that the gun is loaded and that I still know how to shoot," Jóhann said. He moved closer until he was standing directly across from Birkir, with only the table between them.

"Take your parka off," he said. "Otherwise you'll get too hot."

Birkir took off his parka and laid it on the table.

Jóhann picked it up and searched the pockets. "I know you're not usually armed," he said. "But I'm taking no risks. Stand up and pat all your pockets."

Birkir obeyed.

"Unbutton your jacket and open it."

Birkir did as he was told.

"Put your feet up on the chair and show me your calves."

Birkir put his right foot on the chair and pulled his pant leg up. Then he did the same with the other leg.

"Thanks. As I expected. Now I will explain the game to you. First I have to tell you what's already happened. You do know some of it, of course, but not everything. And none of the most important things. Aren't you excited?"

Birkir shrugged nervously. He was, basically, too shocked to be able to speak. He didn't trust himself and preferred to be silent rather than reply with a tremble in his voice. That would not be good as things stood now.

"Sit down," Jóhann said, and he sat in the chair opposite Birkir. "I can tell you everything now—it doesn't matter, since only one of us will survive this night. If I win the game, you will die, and everything you're about to hear will die with you—disappear, vanish into thin air. If, on the other hand, you win—and rest assured you will get your opportunity—I will die and the game will be over. Then it will be really important for you to explain the game to others, because it's an amazing game. It's meticulously designed. Do you understand?"

"Yes." Birkir nodded. When he was sure that his voice wouldn't let him down, he asked, "Is Hjördís here?"

Jóhann grinned. "Yeah, she came earlier."

"Is she all right?"

Jóhann laughed. "No. She's rather miserable."

"Is she hurt?"

"No. Just a bit confused. Maybe airsick."

"Where is she?"

Jóhann pointed out the window with his gun. "Can you see the big ski lift out there? The one with the gondolas?"

"Yes." Birkir nodded.

"She's in the gondola that's hanging between the two top towers."

"Did you send her up there?"

"Yeah, I worked on a ski lift in Italy once. I know how to operate this stuff."

"She'll freeze to death."

"Maybe."

"This is evil."

"She's got warm gear on. If she managed to come up here on the motorcycle in this cold, she can swing in a closed cable car for a few hours. Meantime, she'll leave us in peace."

"What about your buddy, the ski lodge attendant?"

"You are so incredibly naive. There never was a buddy. I have the key to this place because the company I work for looks after the security. Nobody's coming here tonight. I just had to con you into coming. To join the game. Get it?"

Birkir shook his head. "Why are you doing this?"

Jóhann smiled. "That's exactly what I'm going to tell you now. Explain everything."

"Go on, then."

Jóhann laughed. "This whole thing began in Spain last summer. There was some history building up to it, but on one day in particular I felt I'd reached a turning point. That day was when the game was first truly created. You see, Leifur and I were sunbathing on the beach and we were watching Hjördís in the sea—topless, of course. She was by far the best-looking chick around, as usual. You know, tall and fit. Incredibly muscular, well defined. Great breasts, full and pert. Deeply tanned with blonde hair, twinkling blue eyes, gleaming white teeth, and a smile that was always so seductive. Every guy on the beach was watching her and her only, but she didn't even seem to notice. Honestly, I think every guy there could hardly contain himself. It was true of us, too. The whole thing was beginning to become unbearable for me and Leifur. Hjördís had, for a long time, been the only real woman for both of us, but she always said she loved each of us too much to choose one over the other. We tried many times to push her into choosing, but it was obvious she found the situation uncomfortable, and she began to distance herself from us. Then we eased up and stopped talking about any kind of relationship or attraction, and she came back to us. At any rate, she decided to visit Spain with us. But the agonies my friend and I suffered didn't stop."

He grinned, took his right hand from the gun, and rubbed his crotch provocatively.

"We were lying there on the beach, devouring her with our eyes, the two of us. We were both thinking the same thing, but Leifur was the first to say that he couldn't bear the thought of any other guy besides himself being with Hjördís. Not me, not anybody else. I said I felt exactly the same, and that's how our idea came into being. We talked about whether we should compete for her in some way; it seemed right that whichever of us lost would have to disappear—move abroad or something—and let the other have a clear run at her. We were totally confident that one of us would get her if the other were out of the picture. She hadn't shown interest in anybody else the entire time we'd known her. We were her best friends."

Jóhann's voice cracked as he uttered these last words. He looked out the window and contemplated the silhouette of the ski lift against the sky. It was as if he was mourning something that had been important to him. When he continued, his voice was quieter and the words came slowly. "We discussed all the different kinds of challenges we could undertake—shooting, aerobics, swimming, running, or a combination of them all. The conclusion was always the same. Neither of us could even contemplate losing and having to endure Hjördís being in a relationship with the other, living with him, marrying, even having children. And then this amazing idea came up. I don't know which one of us said it first, but we'd probably both begun to think the same thing before one of us mentioned it. At any rate, we both jumped at the idea simultaneously. We were going to fight a duel to the death. There was to be no compromise. The solution was simple and absolute. Only one of us would remain."

With this last sentence, Jóhann leaned forward and banged both fists on the table. Then he paused, watching for Birkir's reaction. But Birkir remained inscrutable, and Jóhann resumed his story.

"We began to plan the thing, and it was fantastic. We devised absolutely watertight rules—we each had exactly the same chance, and the one who lost would be out of the game completely. He'd be dead. We were going to make it look like suicide so that there would definitely not be any trouble for the one that survived. We called the game Shotgun."

"What about the rape?" Birkir suddenly asked. "How on earth were you going to get Hjördís to accept you after that brutality?"

Jóhann laughed loudly. "The rape never happened. I just made it up. It was a great story, don't you think? It misled you all and, of course, tormented Hjördís. I directed your attention to her to make her sweat a bit. She deserved it after treating us, her best friends, like idiots for so long. Saying she loved us both and then turning out to be a cheap dyke. One of us ended up dead as a result of that deception. Maybe I'll let her have a go at the game after you've finished your round."

"But what about the postcard you said Hjördís had written, and the suicide note?"

"She never wrote any postcards. Leifur himself wrote to his mom once. But we joked one time that whoever lost at bowling should write ten cards for each of the others. Hjördís lost, but no cards were ever written."

"What about the patches from the parkas?"

"I'd warmed you up good, and then this report about her appeared in the paper. I knew you'd move in on her then."

"Was it you who told the journalist about Hjördís?"

"No, but that's not important. I put the patches in an unmarked envelope and snuck it in her mailbox this morning. I assumed you'd be searching her home and would find them. Either inside her apartment or in the garbage. Which was it?"

"In the garbage," Birkir said. "So you shot those guys?"

"Yeah, but we'll come to that later."

"What about the riddles?"

"They were just a kind of interlude to confuse you some more. I'd already sent you the pieces of camo and set up the Hotmail account when I heard you'd stopped by the security company office last Sunday and asked about me. I wanted to distract you from thinking about me for a few days, and it was so fucking hilarious when you turned up at my place and asked about the McBain story. That was just over the top. But that game is over now. I brought my laptop up here with me, and I checked the inbox at ten o'clock. The answer to the eighth question didn't arrive by the deadline, so the cease-fire officially ended. You will pay for it now."

Jóhann grinned. "But first I'm going to tell you about the Shotgun duel. Leifur and I had identical guns: three-shot pump-actions. They were to be our weapons in the game and all the ammo was exactly the same—just ordinary goose shot. There was nothing suspicious about buying a few packs of those. If we'd bought bigger shot, then someone would have started to wonder what sort of hunting trip we were planning. Dimmuborgir, near Lake Mývatn, was the playground, and the game was to take place in the middle of the night."

Jóhann paused his story and blinked his good eye several times; then he lifted the patch from the empty eye socket and tilted his head to one side. Birkir saw that clear liquid trickled from the hole. Jóhann immediately brandished his gun menacingly—which was unnecessary, because Birkir sat there as if paralyzed. Jóhann straightened himself again, repositioned the eye patch, and then gave a big smile and continued as if nothing had happened.

"The date was fixed for last fall, October first—or rather the night before October second. We drew lots to determine which of us would leave Akureyri to put distance between us during the last weeks before the duel. We thought that would make the story about the suicide more credible. I lost the draw and left for Reykjavik at the beginning of September. I pretended to be looking for work, but I spent all my time practicing shooting. I was pretty good at hitting clay pigeons and live birds, but I knew this would be utterly different. I found good training grounds in some of the lava fields around Reykjavik. I would go at night and set up various targets, and practice shooting in the dark, running around and climbing on the lava, shooting as I moved. And I ordered a very dark camouflage outfit for our nighttime battle. You can get them in America."

He stood up and showed off his pants to Birkir like a proud little boy. "See? They're invisible in the dark. Unfortunately, the parka got messed up," he explained. "The night before October first, I headed north according to plan. I had a very good SUV, and drove north across the central desert on the Sprengisandur route. There was very little snow and the road was still reasonably passable—the only problem was that since the conditions were below freezing, the route was iced over, making it impossible to drive fast."

Jóhann stroked the top of the table with his index finger. Then he looked at Birkir as if expecting a question. Birkir remained silent, however, and eventually Jóhann continued. "Late that morning I found a mountain refuge hut, where I rested most of the day. When I woke up, I continued on my way up to Bárdardalur and then headed east toward Mývatn. I refueled at the Reykjahlíd gas station and had a bite to eat. Then I drove up the east side of Jökulsá River to Dettifoss, where Leifur and I met up in the parking lot at six o'clock in the evening, exactly as planned. We were totally alone there; there are never any tourists around at that time of year. Nobody was going to disturb us. We went over the plan once again and agreed on everything. We left my SUV there and took Leifur's car over to Mývatn. On our way we made a small detour onto the western Dettifoss road, where we dug a hole big and deep enough to take a body. One of us would stop by there after the game was over, and it was a slightly weird feeling to stand there, by that grave. Leifur had brought some plastic bags, tape, and a spade in his car, so that the survivor would have no problem with the burial."

Jóhann paused a long time, staring despondently into space.

Finally he seemed to come around, and asked, "Where was I?"

"You dug the grave," Birkir replied.

"Yeah, we did," Jóhann said. "And after that we made for Dimmuborgir. At that point, I remember, it was getting dark. We'd brought a picnic and we had a good meal. We were both in a great mood and were shaking with excitement. We were already on an adrenaline rush. We had our suicide letters ready—we'd drafted them in advance and each of us had handwritten his own copy. The one who survived was to take the other's body, dump it in the hole, and shovel some earth over it. He was then to drive to the parking lot at Dettifoss and leave the dead man's car there with the letter on the front seat. Everything was preplanned. It was set up to look as if the loser had jumped over the falls. It's happened before and the bodies are hardly ever found. It was a foolproof plan."

"Why couldn't you throw the body into the falls?" Birkir asked.

"We couldn't exclude the possibility that it might be found in the river. A gunshot wound would have raised suspicion," Jóhann replied. He looked at Birkir as if expecting some sort of acknowledgment, but Birkir merely stared back, expressionless. He didn't want to show any reaction, but when the silence became uncomfortable he finally nodded.

Jóhann continued. "We waited until two in the morning. Nobody lives near Dimmuborgir, but we wanted to be sure there'd be no interruption. I was wearing my new camouflage outfit but Leifur was in his old one, which is lighter in color. So I already had a bit of an advantage. We helped each other to paint our faces in dark camouflage colors, even the lips. Now we were ready to start. After a short ways, the footpath from the parking lot splits in two to go in a circular route around the whole area. There are two or three different circles signposted, in fact. Have you ever been there?"

"No," Birkir lied.

"It's like a jungle of enormous rock pillars and boulders, hillocks, and caves. There's birch shrubbery all over. A perfect place for our game. A complete labyrinth. The game consisted of heading off in opposite directions around a particular circle: the path is pretty narrow so we knew we couldn't miss each other. According to the rules of the game, we were supposed to touch all the stakes that line the path every few meters either with a foot or with the gun. That would ensure that we'd keep to the path and force us within range of each other sooner or later."

"Wouldn't it have been easy to cheat?"

Jóhann shook his head. "I didn't need to cheat," he said. "It would have ruined the game for me. Remember that it wasn't just a contest with Hjördís as the prize. The contest itself was the most phenomenal experience of our lives. It had to be absolutely honest."

"I see," Birkir said unconvincingly.

Jóhann continued. "It was time to part. We tossed a coin for which direction each should go in. I was to head north and Leifur south. It was our last moment together as friends and it was emotional for both of us. We embraced, kissed, and wished each other good luck. You'll probably think it's strange, but I had never been fonder of Leifur than at that moment. We both felt we were about to embark upon the best night we had ever experienced together. This was the game we had always been looking for. A fight to the death with a worthy opponent. We backed away from each other, and the last I saw of Leifur was when he smiled and waved. Then he took off quickly along the path."

Jóhann stood up and backed into the shadows, reappearing soon with two cans of Coke. He sat down again, opened one can, and pushed the other toward Birkir. "It was overcast and very dark. We had identical flashlights and were free to use them whenever we wanted; the catch was that the light made you an easy target. I'd switched mine on when I started walking, but turned it off after five minutes. At that point, I couldn't see anything at all because my eyes weren't used to the dark. I stood still for several minutes until my night vision improved. I also became aware of the silence. It was completely still, and there were no natural sounds—no birds or anything like that. The only thing I could hear was the sound of my own breathing, and automatically, I tried to breathe silently. Then I started inching along. Suddenly one fact became clear to me. Leifur had, of course, trained for the contest just as I had, but he had very probably done it in this exact place and at night. This had become his home ground. That was why he had run off so quickly and confidently when we parted. And he had smiled, too. I almost panicked in the darkness when I realized this. It occurred to me to turn around and flee. The keys were in the car and I knew I could get to Akureyri before he realized I was even gone. But then I began to see a bit better in the dark, and the competitive spirit returned."

He reached for his Coke, took a swig, and belched loudly.

"The path is very clearly marked, so it was relatively easy to follow despite the darkness. But I knew that soon I would have to abandon it and take to the rough ground, or I would be an easy target. The game was really about being the first one to sight one's opponent. So I cut off to the left of the path and felt my way over the lava. I went very slowly, because every step had to be carefully thought out. Not only was I in danger of stepping into a hole or a cave, but I also had to be careful not to be too conspicuous or make a noise. And at the same time I had to concentrate on watching for Leifur."

Jóhann looked slowly to the right and to the left as if searching for something. Then he said in a rush, "Suddenly I saw a glimmer of light ahead. I stopped dead and aimed the gun."

He fell silent briefly, before continuing his story at a normal speed. "The light was at a distance of about fifty meters but then it went out. Leifur was evidently there. I had arrived at the field of battle, which was good to know. I was surrounded by tall lava pillars and could hardly see a thing. I got down on my stomach and edged toward where the light had been, listening. There was complete silence and I hardly dared breathe. Meter by meter I eased myself closer to uncertainty. Adrenaline was flooding through my body and I knew I had to keep moving forward. I felt that if I stopped, my nerves would betray me. The tension was unbearable and I imagined that in slowing down, I'd start to panic; once that happened, I knew I wouldn't be able to shoot when the moment arrived. The light came on again briefly and then went out. I couldn't understand what Leifur was up to. At a range of about thirty meters, I lost my patience. I got up on one knee and fired three times in the direction of the light."

Jóhann paused a beat. "But then the shot suddenly came. Wham!"

He banged the table with the palm of his hand on the last word, and fell back as if hit. "That was the one that hit my face and almost took me out. But it hadn't come from the direction of the light; it was from the side of the path."

He pointed to the right as if an invisible opponent were hiding there.

"Immediately, there were two more shots, but by then I had gotten down, and I heard them whistle past over my head. A slight rise in the ground between us meant Leifur couldn't get a clear shot at me, whereas I now knew precisely where he was.

I reloaded while I reviewed the situation. I knew I was hurt but didn't know how badly. But it was obvious I couldn't let the battle drag on—one eye was completely numb and all I could see with it was a blurry mist. My forehead was bleeding, too, and I had to be careful to prevent blood from trickling into the other eye. I only thought about this briefly, and then I quickly crawled back a few meters and stood up. Behind me was a jet-black lava pillar, so I must have been as good as invisible in the darkness. Then I ran, my gun raised, directly toward Leifur's position. Halfway there I fired two shots and threw myself sideways onto the ground."

Jóhann lowered his voice. "I heard a half-stifled scream, followed by total silence. I lay still with my face to the ground, waiting for return fire, but nothing happened. I thought to myself that Leifur would now be able to locate me and would soon direct some shots in my direction. I reloaded carefully and waited for about ten minutes. Then I lifted my weapon and crept on my front toward his hiding place. Wormlike, I inched my way, gun aimed the entire time. In front of me was a lava plinth that I knew he must have sheltered behind. I crawled to one end of it and peered around the corner. There was nobody there, but I glimpsed something lying in the grass. As I came nearer I saw it was Leifur's shotgun. I switched on my flashlight and saw two severed fingers lying next to the gun. By some incredible luck I had made a direct hit on the lock, destroying the trigger housing and taking off his index finger and thumb."

As he spoke, Jóhann pointed with his left hand at the fingers of his right hand, clutching the trigger of his weapon. "When he was hit, Leifur must have been resting the gun on top of the lava plinth, while sheltering his head behind it. Now that the gun was useless, he had made a run for it. I beamed the flashlight around. Right away, I found what I was looking for: a small pool of blood that trailed off into the darkness. The track was a cinch to follow, and once I'd reloaded I was on my way, almost at a run, squinting at the flashlight beam with my good eye. Leifur was waiting for me at a distance of about a hundred meters. The flashlight must have made it easy for him to follow my approach, but I didn't think about that at all.

"Though unarmed, he still had a perfectly good pair of legs, and he used them. Suddenly I felt a massive kick to the chest, and it flung me backward. The shot that came out of my gun was purely accidental and could have landed anywhere. But for the second time that night I was incredibly lucky and Leifur was incredibly unlucky. The shot hit him directly in the groin as he prepared to jump on me. You could see the sky through the hole. He collapsed, and I got up and took two steps toward him. The duel was over, and we both knew it. The worst thing was that he spoke to me. Just two words, but they were words I didn't want to hear."

There was a long silence. Then Birkir asked, "What did he say?"

Jóhann replied quietly, "He said…'Don't shoot.'"

"So what did you do then?"

"I shot him in the head, of course."

There was another long silence. Then Jóhann continued. "I sat down and didn't move for at least twenty minutes. I was breathing as if I'd been sprinting. My chest was sore as hell after the kick and my face was weirdly numb. I felt almost dead in a way. But in the end, I forced myself to my feet. I had to tidy the place up. I went back to get Leifur's gun, and chucked it down a deep crevice in the lava. Then I found his flashlight, which I'd smashed to pieces with my first shot. That was disappointment number two. Not only had he visited the location before to explore the lay of the land, he'd set up a trap for me. He'd made a box for the flashlight with a peg and a coil that pressed the flashlight's switch. He'd placed the box next to the path, and with a length of string attached to the coil was able to switch the light on and off from a distance of twenty meters. This way he could make me think he had the flashlight in his hand, and as soon as I fired a shot at this device he could know exactly where I was. This was a clear breach of the game's rules. We were not supposed to use any kind of equipment unless it had been agreed upon beforehand and was available to us both. My best friend had tried to cheat me at the most important moment of our friendship."

Jóhann shook his head and Birkir thought he could see tears.

"I threw the box and flashlight down the same crevice as the gun. Now I had to deal with Leifur. I managed to lift him onto my shoulders and headed back. I also had to carry my gun and light my way. It was incredibly hard. The bleeding from my face had mostly stopped, but the fight had drained all my stamina and strength. Step by step I stumbled onward, and when I was near the parking lot, I put my load down next to the path. I got the plastic bags from the car and wrapped him up before putting him into the car. As luck would have it, Leifur had brought a large roll of bags, so there was plenty of material to cover the seats and floor, and wherever my blood-covered outfit might come into contact. I put on gloves that I had in my pocket, and drove off. I was very careful to only hold the steering wheel in one place so I wouldn't wipe off Leifur's fingerprints. First I drove to the grave we'd dug by the western track to Dettifoss, and chucked the body into it. It didn't take long to shovel the earth over him and smooth the surface. He should never have been found there. You can just imagine how flabbergasted I was when that guy happened to pick that very spot for his excavation. The odds were so infinitesimally small in all that vastness."

He shook his head as if he still couldn't believe it. "I drove back to Route 1 and then up to Dettifoss by the eastern route. I parked up in the lot there and cleaned the car. I took all the odd scraps of plastic and put them in my car, also the remnants of our picnic, and anything else connected with the game. All that remained was Leifur's car, with the keys in the ignition and his letter on the passenger seat."

Jóhann paused; he seemed to be thinking back. "By the time I'd done everything it was seven in the morning and reasonably light. I knew I needed medical attention for my face, but I couldn't do that in the north. This was something we had forgotten to plan for—that the survivor might be wounded. I decided to drive back the same way, over Sprengisandur, and seek help in the south. On the way, I made up the story about the accidental shooting in the Landsveit area. When I reached civilization, I ditched my jacket and the rest of the stuff in a Dumpster by the road. The jacket was drenched in blood and completely ruined. I really miss it. Then I went to the Selfoss hospital. The doctor picked most of the pellets from my face—and called the cops. I gave a statement on the spot, and then they sent me to Reykjavik by ambulance, because of my eye. You know the rest of that story."

Birkir nodded and Jóhann continued. "I was in the hospital while they tried to save my eye, and so I didn't need to invent any more stories while the cops were looking for Leifur in the north. It seemed to take them an incredibly long time to find the car—it wasn't until some tourist visiting Dettifoss came across it that they solved that issue. The Akureyri police called me to ask if Leifur had been depressed and stuff. I told them I hadn't talked to him for several weeks before he disappeared. Apart from that

I couldn't be of much help to them. Despite there not being a body, he was declared dead and they held a memorial service in Akureyri. I went north and was going to look up Hjördís. I imagined we would comfort one another and the relationship would develop from there. But she didn't show up at the service, and I discovered that she'd gone to New York to study graphic design. I couldn't believe it. Hjördís had, it's true, talked about going back to school. We knew she'd been in touch with some colleges; but she'd always found it difficult to make up her mind. And then she picked the exact worst time to make her decision and leave. Just when I needed her most."

He sprang to his feet and paced back and forth several times before sitting again. "So, the only thing for me to do now was to follow her to New York. I called her a few times and we exchanged e-mails. We talked mostly about Leifur, trying to find a reason for the suicide. I wanted us to write an obituary together, but that never got further than a draft. Then I told her that I wanted to come and visit. I sold my car and knew I had enough money to support myself for a few weeks; I figured after that I'd find some way to work under the table. I flew to New York and arrived in Manhattan, where Hjördís lived, late in the evening. She was sharing a tiny apartment with two other Icelandic chicks and they didn't have room for visitors. It was just a kitchen, bathroom, and a large living room where they all slept together. They let me stay on the floor that night, but then I had to find a cheap hotel room. Initially, Hjördís was really pleased to see me, as always, and we met every day that first week. She showed me the city and we went together to museums and stuff. I started saying that we should rent an apartment together and that I could get myself a job. But she only smiled, as if I wasn't being serious. We had no place where we could be alone, so I was never able to approach her. Sometimes I put my arm around her or we walked hand in hand, but that was exactly what we'd done so often before, when Leifur was alive. I never succeeded in taking the next step. Then came days when she wasn't able to see me. Projects for college and other stuff seemed to be more important. I didn't know anybody else in New York, so all I could do was wait for our next date. On the phone, I pretended I was meeting up with other people and had plenty to do. Then, one time when I called her she told me to come over for a visit. For once, she was alone at home, and I imagined that my big opportunity had arrived. But then she said she needed to explain something to me. She told me that she was gay and that she had a girlfriend."

He seemed to find it difficult to continue his story. Finally in a shaky voice he said, "It was as if I'd been hit on the head with a sledgehammer. I tried to tell her that she wasn't a lesbian at all and that we should be together as a couple. I tried to put my arms around her, but she only pushed me aside as if I was some disgusting freak. Then I told her that Leifur had died because of her. 'How because of me?' I remember her asking. But I was neither willing nor able to explain it. And then this so-called girlfriend arrived, and on top of everything else, she was black. Hjördís asked me to leave, and we didn't meet again in New York."

Jóhann shook his head and clenched his fists. "Afterward, I was very depressed. I'd killed my best friend for this woman and sacrificed an eye. There was nothing left to live for."

02:20

Jóhann was silent and stared into space for a long time. Birkir also sat motionless—he was determined to force his opponent to take the initiative in their dialogue. At least twenty minutes passed. Then, all of a sudden, Jóhann picked up as if nothing had happened. "I returned home to Iceland and drifted about Reykjavik for a few weeks. Then I got this job with the security company. After everything that had happened, I didn't feel like living in Akureyri; there were too many memories.

"I started weight training like I'd done before, and sometimes I practiced shooting. I felt at my best when I had the gun. The duel with Leifur had, in spite of everything, been an amazing experience. I can remember every second as if it had happened today, and I only had to think about it for the adrenaline to start flowing. It was an incredibly powerful feeling, and eventually I realized it was something I wanted to experience again."

He stood up and straightened himself.

"That's when I had the idea of repeating the game," he said. "Find a worthy opponent and take him on. I had nothing to lose. The only thing was how to go about it. Goose-hunting season had started, and there were guys around with guns. I only had to get one of them. A real hunter, who wouldn't let himself get killed without a *fight*."

He punctuated this last word by raising his gun and firing a single shot over Birkir's head. Dust arose from the hole that the pellets punched in the wall panel. It scared the hell out of Birkir. He had ducked the instant the shot was fired but now calmly sat up again, rubbing the back of his neck where his sudden reaction had put a crick in it.

Jóhann kept speaking as if nothing had happened. "A real man, who was tough enough to be in the line of fire without pissing and shitting himself. Somebody who would fire back if attacked," he said, brandishing the gun and firing another shot into the wall.

"Three o'clock last Thursday morning, I went to Ártúnshöfdi and waited," he said. "I knew hunters would show up soon. I'd seen them there before, buying gas and provisions, when I was security-checking the place. What I was looking for was a guy, wearing camouflage, alone in a car. He would be my opponent. My mark arrived at four o'clock on the dot in a big SUV, and bought gas and a sandwich. Just as if we'd arranged it beforehand. When he drove on up the Ring Road, I followed him and tried to be inconspicuous. I guessed he was making for somewhere near Borgarfjördur, but of course it could have been anywhere. All around Kjalarnes it was pitch-dark, but I turned off my lights and drove almost blind, following the yellow marker posts about a kilometer behind him. It was a bit difficult, because the guy drove really fast. But my car is quite powerful, so I can put my foot on the gas when I need to. If anybody came from the other direction I turned the lights on in good time while we passed one another, but turned them off again after."

"Did you follow him through the Hvalfjördur tunnel?" Birkir suddenly asked.

"Actually, no," Jóhann replied. "The guy stopped at a turnout just before the tunnel, probably to take a phone call. I didn't see it until I was right on top of him, so I couldn't hang back. I just went ahead of him and parked off the road farther on, beyond the tunnel."

"Ah," said Birkir, biting his lip. He was thinking about the surveillance cameras. Nobody had thought of checking the cars that had gone *before* Ólafur, only the ones that went *after*. A bit more thought, and they might have solved the case then.

Jóhann looked intently at Birkir. "I held back as we continued north, to increase the distance between us. I'm not familiar with the countryside around there, but I knew the highway well because I've driven between Akureyri and Reykjavik so often. I guessed he'd make for Borgarfjördur. The next time I saw him he was crossing the bridge over the fjord, and I turned off my lights like before. He didn't seem to have realized anyone was following him, because he continued driving at exactly the same speed. He was probably on cruise control. I thought I'd lost him when he turned west toward Dalasýsla, but then I saw his headlights up on the ascent and went after him. By then I couldn't play hide-and-seek anymore—I had to stay close to him to see where he was going. It didn't seem to bother him that I was following about three hundred meters behind, and we carried on like this for twenty or thirty kilometers. Then he turned off the highway and headed along this gravel road. I made sure he was completely out of sight before I turned as well. I turned off my lights and drove a few hundred meters until I found a place where I could come off the road and leave the car.

"I got my gun ready and strapped on a belt holding goose shot. We'd be on equal footing when the battle began. I'd dressed in my new camouflage gear and painted my face before leaving home. I took off walking, and before long found his abandoned SUV. But the hunter was nowhere to be seen. I crept along the track until I caught sight of the decoys in a potato patch below an old ruined wall. I realized he had to be hidden behind the wall. I got nearer and saw I had a choice of hiding places—a ditch between the ruin and the track, or, a little farther up the hillside, in a group of large boulders within range of the ruin. It was still too dark to see the guy, but I knew exactly where he was. I just had to get him going and offer him some serious hunting. I took plenty of time checking the lay of the land and planning my attack. I could leave nothing to chance.

"I was just about to get back down into the ditch when the first flight of geese arrived. They shied off, of course, because I was so conspicuous on the edge of the ditch. I got my first glimpse of him when he peered over the wall to see what had startled the birds. I took aim at one of his decoys and fired. I knocked it over, even at a range of sixty meters. Then the guy began to shout, so I fired a shot into the ground in front of him. He ducked straight back behind the wall, but soon after he stuck the barrel of his gun up in the air with his cap on the end of it. He was obviously testing the waters, and I clarified the situation by shooting at the cap.

"Then the goddamn dog appeared. I hadn't expected him to have a dog with him, and it scared the hell out of me when this black thing came running at me. I didn't want to do it but I had no choice—I had to shoot the animal. The good news was, though, that now my opponent knew exactly what the game was about. This was a shootout, man to man.

"A short while later he fired the emergency flares, though, and I had to change my plan. Maybe somebody would see the flares and come to check what was going on. Time had become an issue. So I ran uphill from the ruin and shot at the guy from there to force him to shift his position. The range wasn't close so I didn't really wound him, but I did get him going, and he began to shoot back. That was when I felt the same special feeling I'd had when Leifur and I were fighting. The thrill of the chase. Adrenaline flooded through me and all my senses were on high alert. I moved back to the ditch so the guy was just about within range again; we exchanged fire, but I still needed to get closer. Then the unexpected happened. I'd crouched down to reload, and suddenly shot rattled against my back and the back of my head. It penetrated my gear and lashed my skin, but nothing worse than that. Still, it was damn painful, like being flogged with a whip. My back was bleeding, too, but I didn't know that until much later. Everything happened in that split second—the shot hailed down on me, I got up to shoot, and suddenly the guy was almost on top of me. I fired and the shot hit him in the thigh and took his leg off. He fell on his face and dropped his gun. He was finished. If he'd waited a moment longer before firing his shot I would have lost the game and my life. This guy had proven a most worthy and clever opponent, but I had outwitted him, or perhaps was just luckier—luck is important, too.

"The aftermath was a holy moment. One shot into the head to extinguish his life, game over. Then I cut a patch from his jacket. The badge of the champion. Finally, I made my escape as quickly as possible. I took his gun with me. I'll let you use it later; then we'll see what you're made of."

03:30

Again Jóhann seemed to get lost in thought and forget where he was. He sat for a few minutes staring at the table. Birkir copied him. Remaining absolutely motionless but perfectly alert seemed like the best thing to do, given the situation.

He wondered if he might get an opportunity to snatch the initiative from his opponent. But then, suddenly, it was as if Jóhann woke up. He grabbed the can of Coke and gulped down its contents; stood up and paced a circuit of the room; and finally sat down again, ready to continue his story. "I found my Friday adversary in a different way. By accident, really. It was unexpected. Pure luck, yet again. The thing is, now and then I visit

Hjördís. Not in the conventional way as you'd probably call it—I visit her in spirit. When I can't sleep, I sometimes go for a drive around town, ending up at Hjördís's home.

"I park outside her house and look up at her bedroom window. Sometimes the light is on, sometimes not. Sometimes the window is open, sometimes not. I think about what we would be doing if she hadn't betrayed me. What we do depends on how I'm feeling. Sometimes we need to talk; sometimes we just sleep and then make love. That's the best part and it's so real. You probably think that I'm a bit cracked, that this is something unnatural. Okay, so be it. I don't need to justify it to anybody. Nobody knows what my reality looks like."

Jóhann paused and looked at Birkir as if expecting a reaction. Birkir decided to remain silent, but reached out for the untouched Coke in front of him, opened the can, and took a swig.

Jóhann continued. "When I got back to town after last Thursday's combat, I was still totally consumed by the thrill of it. The game had been a complete success and I was ecstatic. I couldn't stay still to save my life. I just paced around the apartment reliving the game second by second. Every single moment between me and my opponent was so clear in my memory. I knew by then that I'd injured my back, but I didn't feel a thing, thanks to the endorphins buzzing around in my system. That night there was no way I was going to be able to get to sleep, so I went to visit Hjördís. It was one thirty when I got there, and our bedroom was dark. The window was open so there was plenty of fresh air in the room. Here I finally calmed down, and probably fell asleep in the car. I woke at four o'clock when a man came out of the house and the front door slammed shut. He was dressed in camouflage gear and had a shotgun bag. He also had some decoys in a small duffel bag. It was obvious that this was a goose hunter on his way to catch the morning flight. Suddenly I was wide-awake and rested, even though I was freezing cold. My back also hurt, but not too bad. It was, actually, almost a good feeling, because it reminded me of the fight with the previous night's opponent. The guy loaded his stuff into a car and drove off. I drove after him, thinking everything through. All my gear from the previous day was still in the trunk—I'd stopped on the way home to take off my camouflage gear and stow it, since the back had been badly torn by the shot that had hit me. I couldn't let anybody see that. But there was no reason I could think of not to trail the guy and repeat the game. See what he was made of. I felt tension begin to build at the thought and I welcomed it. I didn't need to report for work until that evening when I was scheduled for the night shift. If all went well, I could even hit the hay for a few hours in the afternoon and turn up for work fully refreshed—I don't need much sleep. All I had to do was follow the guy and play it by ear.

"He refueled at Ártúnshöfdi like my previous partner had done the night before. But this guy headed east. I was more laid-back in my pursuit this time, and there was a bit more traffic. I'm not familiar with the south of Iceland, apart from the Ring Road and the routes north across Kjölur and Sprengisandur. So I had to keep the guy within sight the whole way; he didn't seem to notice at all. Somewhere east of Selfoss, he turned right. I followed, my headlights off. There was no other traffic. He drove a few kilometers, and then stopped and parked. The area looked like a good hunting spot for the morning flight; it was not long before daybreak. The nearest farm was quite a distance away, which meant peace for both of us—for him to wait for the geese, for me to initiate combat. Despite the darkness, I could track the guy with my binoculars as he walked across the meadows and placed his decoys in a corner where two ditches met. He settled himself there.

"Now I got going. I'd put on the shredded remains of my camouflage jacket, but had no paint to cover my face. Was I maybe getting careless? I don't know—it wasn't really put to the test. I fired the first shot at the guy along the ditch at a range of about sixty meters. I must have hit him, because he squealed like a pig in a slaughterhouse. It wouldn't have been a fatal wound, though, because the range was too great. He had every opportunity to get under cover and retaliate, but what a disappointment—the guy chucked his gun away, climbed up out of the ditch, and ran off screaming as if the devil himself were chasing him. He headed for the nearest house, and I had to give chase, because if he managed to raise the alarm I'd be in trouble. So I ran after him as fast as I could. My back was now painfully tender and bruised after the previous day's injuries, and it ached like crazy when I ran, especially since I was carrying the gun. The nearest farms were, I guess, seven kilometers away, and he managed to run five kilometers before I caught up to him. By then he was completely out of breath and couldn't go any farther. I was in better shape for running than he was. This game was not to my liking and I didn't hang around when I got to him. I just fired two shots into his back and killed him like a wounded animal that has to be put down. I cut the patch from his parka as a hunting trophy and turned back. I was back in my car by eight o'clock and home by ten. There had been no thrill to the game this time; I was just exhausted, hurt, and sore. I went to bed and slept until I was due to start my shift."

Jóhann stood up. "I heard about the copycat killing in the news on Sunday. That really cracked me up. But it trashed the chance of any more shoot-outs, at least for the time being. Then you contacted me—I was thrilled about that. And after I talked to you, I got the idea for the quiz. I've seldom had such fun. Finally, I had the idea to pull Hjördís in and direct your attention to her. I'll never forget when I told you that story about her writing the postcards from Spain. You put on such a poker face, but your toes were twitching with excitement. I'd heard that Leifur's mom had given the cops a postcard from him to help them verify the suicide note. These were all clues like the ones they use in crime thrillers. And then you also took it seriously when I said I wanted to become a cop."

He laughed loudly. Becoming serious once more, he continued. "The plan was to have you arrest Hjördís, which would allow me to play her best friend, and be the only one who believed in her innocence. I planned to give you guys enough evidence to convict her. I imagined I would visit her in jail and show her I was the only person that cared for her. I would meet her upon her release from prison; if she wanted to be a lesbian that was fine by me, but she would have to live with me. It would be enough for me to look at her knowing that I owned her. It didn't need to be anything sexual. But then you released her from custody in no time, and of course she called me right away to ask about the rape story. I swore it hadn't come from me and tried to get her to believe that you cops had made it up. She didn't want to believe me, so I asked her to come up here and talk things over. The idea was to get her here and then to send her back to town. It was meant to look as if you had met and that she had shot you. Then she would have been arrested again. But I couldn't make it work out. She didn't believe my explanations and she refused to leave. So I had to put her on hold. She was quite surprised when I pointed the gun at her and ordered her into a cable car. Then I started the lift and sent her up to the top. She won't be trying to jump down, I can promise you that."

Jóhann went over and peered out the window. Then he crossed the room and fetched a shotgun from one corner. He placed it on the table in front of Birkir.

"This is Ólafur's gun. It is your weapon now. Don't try to tell me that you don't know how to use a gun like this. You'll get the ammunition in a minute. Now stand up and put on your parka."

04:40

The moon lit up the starry sky as Jóhann and Birkir emerged, each carrying a gun. A faint glow from northern lights flickered across the eastern sky and reflected off the frost-covered rocks on the mountain, casting a pale glimmer over the valley.

Birkir found the shotgun remarkably heavy. Or was it just that he was suddenly feeble? He considered throwing the gun at Jóhann and running away. No, that would not save him. He wouldn't be able to get out of range fast enough, and Jóhann would shoot him in the back. His only option was to take part in the game a bit longer.

They walked a short distance along the road before turning off into a raggedy lava field. Birkir went ahead with Jóhann following a few meters behind, barking directions at him, "Straight on here, to the right." They continued thusly until they had clambered a few hundred meters in over the lava—that's when Jóhann gave Birkir the order to stop.

He counted a few shells from his belt and put them on a lava ledge.

"This is where the game starts," he said. "You have a five-shot gun, and here are six rounds at your disposal. That means we're even until you've used all your shells. You better use them sparingly. I've got plenty myself but I know I'll only need two. One to stop you, and the other to finish the game. Don't think you can crawl into a hole and hide. In two hours it'll be light and then I'll find you and kill you. And by then Hjördís will probably have frozen to death. The only hope for the both of you is that you play the game and win it. Which is, actually, extremely unlikely. I know you're a good long-distance runner, but don't try to run away. Your shoes aren't good enough for running in conditions like these, and I'm sure my reaction time is quicker than yours. Don't even try it. This is your one opportunity. Make use of it. Now, turn around and count to a hundred. Yes, like the kids do when they're playing hide-and-seek. Then you can load your weapon. After that the game starts. Understood?"

"Yes." Birkir nodded.

"And you're ready for the game?"

"Yes, I'm ready."

Jóhann smiled approvingly.

"I salute you, opponent. Let the better man win here tonight. Start counting."

Birkir turned to the north. "One, two, three…" As he calmly counted, he focused on how to respond once the count was finished.

"…ninety-seven, ninety-eight, ninety-nine, one hundred."

He turned and saw he was alone. He walked coolly toward the shells and picked them up. He opened the chamber and loaded it with three shots, and then raised the weapon. One more time, he went over his situation in his mind, and then fired one shot into the air. He counted, "One, two, three, four," and then fired again. Again he counted to four, and fired a third shot. Then a pause while he reloaded the gun with the three remaining rounds. Once more he pointed the weapon into the air. Three more shots split the stillness of the night, one after the other, exactly as before.

05:10

Birkir stood motionless in the spot where Jóhann had left the ammunition for him. He breathed deeply and waited for what was to come. The barrel of the shotgun rested against his shoulder, and his right hand clutched the butt tightly, index finger on the trigger. He looked up at the clear sky and gazed at the stars. A long time ago he had known the names of some of the constellations and been able to recognize them, but now they were all one to him. Little dots, some brighter than others, each a sun in another system. And then there was that infinity that nobody understood; the dimensions that nobody had yet discovered. Birkir was almost hypnotized by this vision and he did not look around, not even when he heard Jóhann call out, "Coward! So that's how you are going to play the game? You can be sure that nobody heard you and nobody will come to your aid. But now the game changes. You've used up your chances. Now I'm going to have fun and see how many magnum shells one can fire into a human body before the guy snuffs it. This could be an interesting experiment."

"I'll have to try to deal with that," Birkir said and turned toward Jóhann, who was approaching in the dusk, step by step.

"I see the clown still has guts," said Jóhann, stopping at a distance of forty meters.

"God help us both," Birkir said quietly, swinging the shotgun off his shoulder. The moment the barrel pointed at Jóhann, he fired, at the same time throwing himself down into the moss.

Jóhann turned his back as the shot hailed over him, and staggered three steps back without falling. He doubled over, and then slowly straightened up and turned toward Birkir, brandishing his gun. Birkir rolled away sideways and managed to shelter his head behind a lava spur before the pellets whistled all around him.

"Are you there?" Jóhann shouted. He fired three more shots toward Birkir, who buried his face in the ground.

"Smart move you made there," Jóhann yelled. "I don't know where you got the seventh round but now you definitely don't have any more. And you're cowering there like a worm, waiting for me to blow you to smithereens." Jóhann reloaded and came closer, feeling his way with his feet. Birkir couldn't see what damage his seventh round had done to Jóhann—the round he'd picked up off the floor of Ragnar's storeroom the previous day and put in his pocket without thinking. The seventh round that Jóhann hadn't known about. Again, Jóhann discharged some shots in a wide sweep. One of them pinged against the lava surrounding Birkir, but his cover protected him well.

"He can't see," Birkir thought. "He's not aiming." Ever so slowly and gently Birkir got up on all fours and hurled his shotgun as far off to the right as he possibly could. Then he crawled backward at great speed away from Jóhann, who was still approaching, but swung and fired in the direction of the shotgun as it clattered against the rocks. At that point Birkir got up very carefully, turned, and took off at a run, his head bent low. Jóhann, meanwhile, fired some wild shots in a semicircle in front of him. Birkir felt a few pellets rattle his parka, but the range was too great for them to penetrate. He stumbled, falling to his hands and knees. Careful not to utter a sound, he got back to his feet, crept as fast as he dared away from his opponent, and began once more to run.

"Where are you? Coward!" Jóhann bellowed after him. "Where are you?"

Birkir reached the road and ran back to the houses. The ski lodge where Jóhann had waited for him was still unlocked, and he hurried inside. He switched on the light and after some searching found a telephone.

First he dialed the emergency line. He asked for an ambulance and a police team to arrest an armed man who was probably dangerous...and blind. Also he asked for someone who could operate a ski lift, the reason for which he had to explain. When he was certain that his message had gotten through, he hurried outside and ran over to the lift's control cabin. It was unlocked, but he could make no sense of the buttons and levers, so he decided not to touch anything for fear that he might cause an accident. Instead, he went back outside and ran up the slope beneath the lift. Now and again he stopped and peered up at the cable cars but saw nothing. It was very steep, and he soon had to slow down. In the end he just walked, panting and wheezing. He had almost reached the summit when he became aware of movement inside the topmost gondola hanging from the cable. There was somebody inside, banging hard on the glass. Then the car began to swing to and fro.

"Help is on the way," he shouted as loud as his breathlessness would let him. The car was suspended several meters in the air and there was nothing he could do. He repeated this cry a few times and the banging stopped. Then he turned and walked slowly all the way down to the foot of the mountain.

He returned to the lodge and called the only number he could remember at that moment. After a little while a voice replied, "Gunnar speaking."

"It's me," Birkir said.

"What the hell time is it?"

"I don't know."

"Listen, can it wait? I'm with a woman, and that doesn't happen too often, as you know."

"I found the Gander."

"Do you need help?"

"No. It's all safe now. I just wanted to let you know."

"Great. Who is he—the Gander?"

"The young guy from Akureyri, Jóhann. One of the two friends."

"Ah."

"Yeah...well..."

"Listen," Gunnar said.

"Yeah?"

"This woman I'm with." He had lowered his voice. "I'm going to try to make something of this."

"Something what?"

"A relationship or something. You know."

"Yeah, I see what you mean."

"Yeah."

"Well. Good luck to you. See you later. Bye," Birkir said and hung up.

He went outside and gazed over the lava field. An eerie silence hovered over everything, and yet there was some mysterious tension in the air. Like a sound that wasn't really a sound.

Jóhann was nowhere to be seen. Finding him could prove difficult if he were to wander off. But just as Birkir was thinking this, a single shot rang out in the distance. Then utter silence. The tension vanished and Birkir sensed how all his nerves grew calm and his shoulders relaxed. It was over.

He looked up at the sky and saw it would soon be dawn. He hadn't seen its glimmer creep across the heavens like this for ages, nor had he allowed himself to take time to watch it, really concentrate on it. Somewhere in his memory there was a poem that described this so very well—something that formed the lyrics of a song he had recently heard and then forgotten. He wiped everything else from his exhausted mind and searched desperately for the words. It felt, somehow, as if this was all that mattered now; everything else was futile and vain. It was not until he heard the distant sound of many cars approaching that it finally dripped into his mind, four lines of verse to begin with:

Waking colors, warming now
with the dawn's fire once more burning;
cool the morning kisses you,
crimson life's blood pulses through.

And then four more lines:

First light greeting, full of joy
freed from night's embrace, its dreamings,
sweetly heather scents the day
sundown still so far away.

AUTHOR'S NOTE

As has been our custom with all my books, my friend Adalsteinn Ásberg Sigurdsson wrote the poem "Einsog vonin, einsog lífid" (translated here below) especially for incorporation into this story. Three such poems have been set to music by Eyjólfur Kristjánsson.

Just as hope is, just as life is

In the pale light, absent words,
arcs a lone bird over moorland;
silence reigns: ashimmer here
—just as hope is, just as life is—
scenes of beauty, sharp and clear.

Steepling fell-sides, stony-gray
stories tell of times long over—
heaviest on my heart lie yet
—just as hope is, just as life is—
hurt, remorse, a deep regret.

Just as hope is, just as life is
only slower, rather more,

just as hope is, just as life is
all your senses hunger for.

Waking colors, warming now
with the dawn's fire once more burning;
cool the morning kisses you
—just as hope is, just as life is—
crimson life's blood pulses through.

First light greeting, full of joy
freed from night's embrace, its dreamings,
sweetly heather scents the day
—just as hope is, just as life is—
sundown still so far away.

Just as hope is, just as life is
only slower, rather more,
just as hope is, just as life is
all your senses hunger for.

ABOUT THE AUTHOR

Viktor Arnar Ingolfsson is the author of several books, including *Daybreak*, which was the basis for the 2008 Icelandic television series *Hunting Men*. In 2001, his third novel, *House of Evidence*, was nominated for the Glass Key Award, given by the Crime Writers Association of Scandinavia; his novel *The Flatey Enigma* was nominated for the same prize in 2004. His numerous short stories have appeared in magazines and collections.

ABOUT THE TRANSLATORS

Björg Árnadóttir is Icelandic but has lived most of her life in England; her husband, Andrew Cauthery, is English but fluent in Icelandic. They have worked together for many years, translating both English texts into Icelandic and Icelandic texts into English. They have worked on a wide variety of manuscripts, including books on Icelandic nature and technical topics, as well as literature. Their translation of Viktor Arnar Ingolfsson's *House of Evidence* was published by AmazonCrossing in 2012.